KATH McKAY

Waiting for the Morning

The Women's Press

First published by The Women's Press Limited, 1991
A member of the Namara Group
34 Great Sutton Street, London EC1V, 0DX

British Library Cataloguing in Publication Data
McKay, Kath
  Waiting for the morning.
  I. Title
  823.914 [F]

  ISBN 0-7043-4265-0

Typeset by AKM Associates (UK) Ltd, Southall, London
Printed and bound by
BPCC Hazell Books
Aylesbury, Bucks
Member of BPCC Ltd.

*To my friends and family
and to my children, the future.*

1

Central Liverpool, November 17 1982. Late evening.

The taxi meter ticked on, its green figures changing rapidly.

'The Royal, love?'

Jo Conville nodded.

'Bloody good hospital that, one of the best. It's where my old man passed on.'

Jo laughed.

'You know what I mean, like?'

'Yeah,' Jo grunted.

They drove past a huge hole in the ground, like a tooth with a cavity waiting to be filled. Jo craned her neck to see if she could recognise any buildings but nothing seemed familiar; the streets smaller, narrower, somehow empty. She'd got used to the density of London years before, got used to never going for a walk without there being crowds, rude people who never said sorry but rushed on, heads bent, intent on their destination. It was quiet here, pockets of debris splayed around like sculptures.

'I usually meet that train – I see all sorts coming back,' the driver began in a conversational tone.

'I had one fella . . . !' He leaned forward confidentially.

'Yeah.' Jo's tone was terse. She was in no mood for talking. Let him class her as rude if he wanted, she was too preoccupied with the thought of her mother stuck high in the concrete and glass block that constituted the Royal.

'Suit yourself.'

The taxi driver shrugged his shoulders. Jo held her head in her hands.

'You all right love?'

'Yeah, I'm OK, it was just dead stuffy on the train.' Jo spread her hands and looked vague.

The driver grew silent as he followed signs to the hospital. Even the signposts seemed smaller. If she stepped out, she thought, she might be a giant in a land of dwarves. They drove up to a large oblong building full of windows, shining with artificial light. He turned the meter off, and named a figure which seemed cheap by London standards, but which she instantly forgot. Jo stayed in the taxi, fiddling about in her purse. Really she was preparing herself. Would her mother be conscious, able to speak?

'Are you getting out, or what?' The driver sounded impatient now. He softened when he saw Jo's face.

'Chin up love, don't look so worried, it might not be so bad.'

He accepted Jo's five-pound note without comment, handed her change, and grinned when she passed back a large tip.

'Thanks very much. Are you sure you'll be all right?'

'Yes.'

'Well, OK then love. All the best. Tara.' He circled round and roared off.

Jo stood on the steps, bereft, and contemplated the building. The sense of urgency which had possessed her from that first hurried phone call had gone. Bright security lamps stung her eyes. The remnants of a demo; placards, posters, leaflets, lay tattered like a dragons tail by the entrance.

A wet, ragged, tall, loose-limbed man thrust a leaflet in her face. 'Fight the cuts,' she read. 'Keep Hope Ward open.'

'What's it about?' Jo asked, but she couldn't concentrate on his answers. 'Rationalisation,' she heard, and then was aware he was asking her a question.

'Do you fancy coming the demo on Saturday then?'

'I can't,' said Jo quickly, 'my mum's sick. I've come up from London to see her.'

'Well, you better get in there, then,' said the man, seeming to lose interest.

'She might be dying,' Jo went on, not moving. She didn't want to go in, she preferred to stay out here, amongst the alive and angry.

'I'm sorry for your trouble, love.' The man touched her arm. 'Well, when you're not having such a hard time, maybe you could have a look at our leaflet. With this bloody government, soon there won't be no hospitals left to die in.'

The man walked off, swallowed up by the night.

Jo clenched her jaw, set her teeth and went into the hospital, towards the bare cleanness of Chambers Ward.

The ward boasted high-polished floors, yellow–orange chrysanthemums in chipped glass vases, high-blinded windows, high narrow beds, the smell of Jeyes fluid and damp squishy mops.

The sister, a wide-hipped woman with her uniform tight against her belly, took her into a small room.

'It was a massive stroke,' she said quietly, 'and now she's developed this chest infection. She's still unconscious. We're doing everything possible, of course, but you mustn't hold out false hopes. You look tired, dear, nurse will take you to your mother and bring you a cup of tea.'

A tiny-waisted young nurse escorted Jo along the ward towards her mother.

The ward seemed long and unending; narrow like a tube. Jo's eyes were so tired that shapes grew blurred and fuzzy.

Jesus, she's still breathing. She looks like a corpse already, all blood squeezed out of her yellow-grey face. I can't believe it. It's as if the skin's been stretched and sprung back like an elastic band so that it crumples and wrinkles. Deep ravines are etched into her face and round her eyes. Her mouth is as thin as a matchstick boat in a wide crumpled sea. Tufts of hair sprout from her chin, fine grey curls like hooks. I have them too – I finger my own chin and wonder if its hereditary. I didn't know she'd given me anything. Other kids were passed on photographs, certificates, mementoes. I got a few hairs on my chin.

When I first saw that sunken, cadaverous face I thought I'd come too late, and missed it all. But no, she breathes, in a fashion. Chest rises and falls, if only an inch or two, jaw opens and closes and air wheezes in to mix with the tangled black smoke of years. I was weaned on cigarette smoke you know, that and white bread and endless endless cups of tea. I make a habit now – I eat only brown bread, and drink only the best coffee. I'll spite her yet. I look at her with distaste. No teeth in her jaw – they've taken them out to rattle in a common pile no doubt, lent out on visiting day to all and sundry, or so the rumours say. I watch her jaw – obscene in its pink grey gumminess, like chewing-gum that's been used, spat out. Her cheeks are as deep as caverns. Her hair's all over the place, steel wool that could trap rats behind air holes and stop them gnawing their way out. Her breasts hang out like wrinkled prunes. I pushed them under the bedclothes. She'd be mortified – always so proud, always made up – pats of pancake, a dash of eyeshadow, even for a quick trip out to the shops. The last time I spoke to her she told me, 'I'm a pensioner, you know,' as if it were a secret. 'But I'm one of the young sixty-year-olds, not like those who can hardly look after themselves. I'm lucky, I am.' Lucky. Just look at her now, with her regulation nightgown, hair frizzy from lack of attention.

'Got to make yourself presentable, not let yourself go,' she said to me, last time. 'You should do something with your hair, it looks terrible,' she told me. Always one for plain speaking, never one to mince words.

I cover her up, and sip at cold sweet tea. The heating thermostat clicks somewhere. I shiver. November gloom descends over the city. I can make out the shape of buildings, silent and dark. Streetlights burn a pathway for cars edging outwards. Somewhere down there by the river is where my dad worked, so long ago.

Her hands are as grey as the hands of a dead plaster saint. I see veins sticking out, thick nobbles of blue and green on a pale base, as if an artist has mixed a pigment on a palette. If I touched her hand, would it crumble into dust? Her nails are hospital short, flecked white from lack of calcium, her hands stained yellow and brown from smoking. The smell of nicotine overpowers me suddenly. I must have drunk that smell at the breast. My father's smell was different – sweat, dust, old unwashed clothes, except on Sundays, when he wore a shiny grey suit and his hair became parted, brushed back. He also had a large hooked nose, and hair grew from the nostrils in his proud tight face.

The hospital is white going on grey, like the flat grey city sky we see through the window. I can feel the river in the background, snaking its way out to sea. The docks are silent and empty now – soon they'll dance to a different tune – theme parks, craft fairs, recreations of time past, the ghosts of workers long buried.

Her neck is shrivelled as a rooster's, a lizard on a string. Her eyes are closed, sunken into sockets. She breathes, a little.

I want to plunge my hand towards her, wring her thin, scrawny neck, but, like the cowardly city dweller that I am, I do not. I cannot touch her anyway, her flesh revolts me.

The liquid drips into her arm – thin, sweet-sour, full of useless goodness. Her body's dried up, can't they see? Dried up of water, dried up of oil. She needs less liquid, not more, so that nature can complete the task it's started, and she can crumble into flaky, powdery dust.

'I've never really buried my father.' The words came out of the blue; I surprise myself.

'I've never really buried him,' I say, incongruously, to my mother as she lies in the hospital bed. For once, she cannot answer.

Rosy, April 1961. Kirkby, outside Liverpool.

'Why don't we go out some time?' said Rosy, snuggling down in the bed towards George, her husband.

'We could go dancing down town, or up to that new place they've just opened. Mrs Jenkins could keep an eye on the kids. You could wear your suit, and I've still got that blue dress everybody likes.'

'I'm not old yet,' she whispered under her breath. 'Please God I'm not old.'

George shifted his body away from her and turned over in the bed.

'What for?' he asked crossly, 'What for? And don't be leaving the light on all night, remember. Some of us have got to get up for work in the morning. Goodnight.'

The day Rosy met Sam Greenby she woke to darkness. Six o'clock, said the luminous dials of the bedside clock; cold, but with the merest moth-breath of spring in the air. Afterwards, Rosy always remembered the day as bright, with thin strands of clouds pursuing the sun. But that dark morning, only shadows shifted in the gloom, like outlines in a developing photo.

She gently unwound Eamon, her second child and only son, from round her neck, and crept out of the bedroom. Past the twins, with their bedclothes flung everywhere, past her eldest daughter Jo, an immobile lump, then down to the grey emptiness of the kitchen. Dull light beckoned the promise of another day. She filled the kettle enough for one cup, and pulled out her book. Chapter three – Captain Fogarty had told Sophia he was betrothed to another, but 'fate would bring them together.' Rosy devoured the words, like a lizard devouring flies, and sipped strong sweet tea. At six-fifteen, she reached for her first cigarette of the day. George wasn't due up for another twenty-five minutes. The clock had crept round half an hour when next she surfaced and angry loud movements upstairs soured the taste of the day. Swift as a bird, Rosy prepared George's tea and toast, then pulled out a sandwich tin to begin on his lunch – cheese spread and tomato sandwiches, wrapped in a brown paper bag. Before she'd finished, he strode into the kitchen, angry as a bull.

'Why didn't you wake me?' he yelled. 'I might miss the bus.' Rosy stayed silent. They both knew he wouldn't; he just didn't like the idea of her sitting there alone, enjoying herself.

'I've made your sandwiches already – I'll put them in your gasbag.' Her voice was falsely cheerful. She felt as if her heart might crack in two, like an egg. He grunted.

'Ssh – I wanna listen to this.' An American voice crackled out over the gradually lightening room. The light showed up marks and crevices Rosy preferred not to think about. 'Sources claim the invasion was planned by Cuban patriots trying to liberate their homeland from the despotic rule of Fidel Castro,' the voice said confidently.

George choked and spluttered. 'Propaganda!' he shouted. Blood vessels stood out on his red-purple face. What invasion? Rosy wondered sleepily. She'd heard a man speak of Cuba at a jumble sale the week before. She should try and keep up with events, talk to George. He banged the table. Most of the commentator's words were drowned out, but 'Bay of Pigs', 'Bay of Pigs' boomed out like a chant.

'Everyone knows the CIA and the bloody American government were behind it – who are they trying to kid?' said George, angry. Rosy nodded. She felt more preoccupied with finding the money for Jo's school trip. Jo's class were visiting an old historic house today. She'd have to let her go. Things like that were important to kids, they wanted to be the same as everyone else, although George would never acknowledge it. He'd forgotten what childhood was like; she suspected he'd never had one.

They settled into silence, while an occasional swear word spluttered out from behind the previous night's paper. Rosy glanced across at the top of his head. What had happened to the idealistic young man she'd married such a long time ago? All he ever got worked up about now were news broadcasts from far away places. He'd been a charmer with the 'gift of the gab' when she met him. He'd wooed her with flowers and had a great sense of humour, with a tongue that could turn your head. But now? He sat tight-lipped, tight-shouldered, hunched forward, muscles knotted. His eyes had lost their hope many years before. He was like a shadow of the man he'd been.

As she rinsed breakfast dishes under the tap, mentally she dismissed him, and by the time he'd slung his gasbag over his shoulders and placed his docker's hook deftly through the belt loop of his trousers, he was as far from her mind as usual. At seven-ten, on the dot, he went out, in time to catch the seven-fifteen bus. As the door closed Rosy heaved a sigh of relief. Mistress of herself at last.

Rosy was deep in the arms of Captain Fogarty when a bump, a scream and a small hand scrabbling at the door told her that the day had begun. Chaos reigned for the next three quarters of an hour, while she dressed and fed the twins and bullied Eamon into getting dressed. Jo, as usual, was nowhere to be seen. Fury tingled in Rosy as she ran up the stairs. Jo lay sprawled on the bed, reading.

'If madam would like to come down,' said Rosy acidly, 'there's work to be done.'

Jo's eyes stayed glued to the book. She didn't acknowledge her mother.

'I'll only be a minute, I've nearly finished this chapter, and then I've only got one more.'

'One more bloody chapter indeed, I'll give you one more chapter. Do you know what time it is? Half-past eight! You're supposed to be at school in half an hour. We've had four notes already this term from that teacher of yours. Come on girl, get your bum in gear.' Rosy held her hands rigid against her body. She ached for the relief of hitting this girl.

'You should be helping me with the kids, not lying about like Lady Muck.'

Jo glanced over with cheeky fearless eyes, and rolled off the bed.

'All right, all right. 'I'm up. Satisfied?' Her face begged to be slapped. Rosy turned quickly away. Jo had always been difficult, even as a baby. Eamon and the twins she'd been able to put straight to sleep. Not Jo. Each night as a baby Jo had screamed until she was blue in the face. When you lifted her, her muscles felt rigid with fear; only after minutes of rocking did she relax and calm down. Maybe Jo had sensed even then that she was unwelcome, that Rosy had really wanted a boy. And after Jo came Eamon, the longed-for boy, and then the twins, a novelty. Whatever it was, Jo had always been demanding – a combination of vulnerability and bravura which infuriated Rosy. Just to look at her face aroused Rosy's anger. After Jo the other children had been easy, slipping into her and George's lives as easy as fingers slip into a glove. Jo had always been awkward, Jo had always been trouble. Rosy breathed hard and forced herself downstairs.

'Just hurry up.' A short while later all four children were more or less dressed and fed.

'Take your brother to school,' ordered Rosy.

Jo faced her mother, hard-faced, cool as a cucumber.

'Why should I?'

'That's why.' Rosy lashed out. 'You just do as you're told, see, or you'll get the back of my hand. I don't know, you'd argue with Jesus Christ himself.'

'But it's not fair,' Jo persisted, 'other kids don't have to take their little brothers to school. I always have to. Why don't you take him?'

'Fair, fair, nothing's fair in this life, it's about time you learned that lesson, now get to school the pair of you, I don't want to hear from you again.'

Rosy hustled them out, and bounded up the stairs, a twin under either arm. She locked the bathroom door and sat on the toilet seat, waiting for the rattle of the garden gate. The twins crawled about on the floor. Pat poked Tina in the eye and Tina began to cry. In between separating them, comforting Tina and washing her hands, Rosy listened for the gate. Only when it banged did she sigh in relief and begin to wash the twins. One of these days, she knew, Jo would turn round and defy her, it was only a question of time.

On their outing to the shops later that morning there was a definite freshness, a quickening in the air. The sun warmed Rosy and bunches of daffodils in the greengrocer's made her heart beat faster. Paper bags full of summer bulbs, with small photos of their pink, blue, yellow flowers, gave the promise of a golden summer. Rosy had to restrain herself from buying. After paying for Jo's outing, there was little enough money left. George wouldn't give her extra – he always said school trips were unnecessary.

'What does she want to go to a historic house for anyway? Toffs' history – that's all she'll learn there. Take them down the docks – they'll learn a bit of history there all right; our history, not theirs. Or better still, keep her home, get her to help around the house, do a bit of work for a change.'

But Rosy didn't want that awkward skinny girl under her feet all day, moaning while the rest of her class went off. She'd rather Jo went on the trip with no cause to complain that she was being singled out different. Rosy recalled her own childhood in the orphanage. She'd been marked out as different at school from the start, with her grey worsted socks, stiff with age. Other girls' socks looked soft and hand-tended. They all wore a smock, but hers was rougher to the touch, and creamy, not white. The other kids could pick out the orphanage girls straight away.

'Rosy Sloane, Rosy Sloane,
Your mother's dead, your father's dead
Rosy Sloane,
You wet the bed.'

Rosy had cried quietly each night on her way back to the orphanage. No, it wouldn't be fair to let a kid appear different.

Rosy felt the weight of a pale brown gladiolus bulb. You could almost sense the shoots reaching out from it, spreading upwards towards the summer. With a physical wrench, she placed it back amongst its neighbours. No, George would say, no. He was the gardener of the house anyway, and never bought anything but nurtured and tended plants he'd had for years, dividing, propagating from seed, branch, tuber. He'd accuse her of extravagance if she bought bulbs, say it was unnecessary. There was no way she could sneak them into the garden; he knew every inch of ground. She admired a bunch of pale yellow narcissi with bright orange trumpets in their centre, trumpets which promised fire, passion, soft fragant possibilities. She put them down, full of regret.

'They're nice aren't they?' said a voice behind her.

'Oh, and two pounds of potatoes please, love.' The voice was pleasant, friendly. Rosy turned to see a small pale ginger-haired man, grinning. She recognised him as Sam from the Labour Party committee. He'd been at the jumble sale the week before. Although George hadn't set foot in the Labour Club himself, ever since that affair at the docks, he always encouraged her to help out; secretly, she knew, he liked to be kept informed about his old party colleagues. So Rosy helped at socials and fund-raising, wheeling the twins up in their pram. They liked the noise and all the people. Occasionally she'd have a glass of bitter with some of the women on the committee, but she had never told George about that.

'Yes, they are nice, aren't they?' she agreed, and took delivery of five pounds of potatoes and two pounds of carrots. He stood so close she could smell a faint, not unpleasant scent of fresh sweat and tobacco. They both reached to pick up their shopping. Their hands met briefly; his warm and large, hers cold because of bad circulation.

They spoke little that first time, and afterwards Rosy couldn't remember what they'd touched on, but all the way home that Thursday, with the twins in the pram, Rosy found herself singing, for the first time in ages.

It was a Saturday two days later when they met up again. George was at work in the garden. A dog had jumped over the wall the night before, trampled on the rose bushes and deposited its mess. George, clad in wellingtons and gloves and carrying a shovel and secateurs, was busy cleaning up. Gardening defused his temper, kept him happy. Rosy, in the greengrocer's, with the twins, was trying to decide between cabbage or cauliflower, when a hand tapped her lightly on the shoulder. Sam was in the same position as before, as if rooted, waiting for her to turn up again.

They picked up their conversation like old friends who'd known each other for years, and moved on in tandem to the grocer's. Rosy bought bread, cheese, sausages. He spoke of his wife.

'We're getting divorced,' he informed Rosy.

'She'll keep the kids – it's only right, kids should stay with their mother.' Rosy murmured agreement, as she pushed the twins back and forth in the pram.

'I don't mind that, I'll get to see them, I don't mind paying. I should put towards their keep anyway, that's only fair. It's just, it's just . . .' His voice grew low. Rosy felt a rush of sympathy. She wanted to put her arms round him in comfort, like she would for a child.

'It's just the bitch wants to sting me for everything. Half my wages she wants, every week, for the next few years. I mean, how can I?' Rosy clicked her tongue sympathetically.

'No, it's not bloody fair,' she agreed. 'It's not bloody fair.'

'And she's got this boyfriend.' Sam kicked a lamp-post.

'Loaded, he is. Why does he want it all off me?'

Rosy's heart warmed to Sam, so ready to open to her. 'Unlike George,' said a small voice inside her. She felt sympathy for Sam's predicament. It wasn't right to take everything off a man, it wasn't right. His wife sounded like a bitch. They neared the end of the row of shops. The twins began to wail. Sam pulled a piece of chocolate out of his pocket and split it in two.

'Here you go, girls.' They cooed delighted smiles and smeared it on their faces, their clothes, the pram. Rosy didn't care. They were happy.

'Do you want a cigarette?' he asked. It was a curiously intimate gesture, the way he threw open the packet and leaned over to light it for her, their faces almost touching. As she inhaled deeply and drew herself back, from out of the corner of her eye, Rosy saw something she didn't quite believe – George disappear round the corner of the phone box.

'What the bloody hell are you doing?' she shouted, but he was gone, off into the crowd round the butchers. Unease stole over her. What was George playing at? If he'd wanted to come the shops, why hadn't he said, instead of carrying on like Houdini?

'I better get back now.' She took a few more puffs and stubbed out the cigarette, avoiding Sam's eyes. 'I think maybe George wants his dinner.'

Sam watched her go. Each time she looked back he was still there, waving.

All the long way home, Rosy had the strangest feeling that she was being followed but, when she arrived back, George was nowhere to be seen. She asked Ellen Mack, the neighbour opposite, if she'd seen him.

'Oh, yeah,' said Ellen, all wide-eyed innocence. 'He came out from doing the garden, and asked where you were. I told him Jackie had seen you down the shops talking to Sam Greenby.' Ellen's vixen eyes glinted maliciously.

'Thanks very much.' Rosy stormed away. Ellen was a bitch, always ready to cause trouble. Just because her husband Dennis earned a lot of money on the lorries and they had a washing-machine, a telephone and a fridge, she thought she was better than everyone else.

When George came in later, he was quiet and subdued. He still didn't say anything as they sat together that evening in front of the TV. The large sad eyes and quivery mouth of Bette Davis filled the living-room. The peace lasted ten minutes.

'What were you doing, you dirty bitch?' hissed in her ear. His breath was bitter with tobacco, he'd smoked more than usual. Rosy tried to collect her thoughts.

'Ssh George, you'll wake the kids. Come on, I'll make you a

nice cup of tea.' Their walls were paper thin. Jo, especially, slept lightly.

'I don't want any nice cup of tea,' he shouted, louder this time. 'What were you doing, down at the shops, gabbing with that good-for-nothing, Sam Greenby? Smoking his ciggies, were you, you whore? And with the babies in the pram next to you. I saw you all right. What else have you been doing while my back was turned, hey?' He grabbed her by the neck and twisted her arm, tight.

'Nothing, George, nothing really, I haven't been doing anything, honest I haven't. It's just 'cos he's on the Labour Party committee – he was telling me about his wife.'

'Oh, yeah.' George's grip tightened.

'And I suppose he said he was hard done by 'cos she's gone and left him, hey? I know all about him. Well, just remember that you're my wife, and you're not going to talk to him again, do you hear that? Never again. If you do, I'll throw you out, I swear I will.' He dug his nails into her wrist, so that a small line of ridges formed, like little dancing moons. Rosy bit her lips to stop herself from crying out.

'I was only talking to him, you know, George.'

He squeezed her arm. 'Yeah, but we all know what talking leads to, don't we?' He pushed her on to the floor, pulling roughly at her clothes.

'Whore. Tart. Slut. You're no better than you should be!

He kicked her legs apart.

'Had a good time with him, did you?'

'No, George, I was only talking.' Rosy cowered, trying to curl herself into a ball.

'Talking indeed. I'll show you talking.' His face leered over her, and then he forced his way in, there in the living-room, amongst the drying nappies and the pictures of the kids, thrusting harder and harder so that her insides ached and bruised with the pressure of him.

That night Rosy spent a long time in the bathroom, and carefully wiped away every trace of his presence, then lay in the bed looking at his large snoring figure. No matter what, she decided, no matter what, it wouldn't be he who came into her next time, it wouldn't be.

George, Liverpool, October 1953

'There's a letter here for you,' Rosy shouted through to the kitchen where George was eating his breakfast. She examined it curiously. They didn't get many letters and this one looked important: a long cream envelope, George's name and their address typed neatly. She ran her fingers over the black fancy characters on the back, feeling them raised under her touch. 'Mersey Docks and Harbour Board,' she mouthed as she walked back through the narrow dark hall to the kitchen, dropping the letter by the teapot.

She turned her back to George and began to busy herself at the sink.

'Must be from Goyley's appeal,' she called over her shoulder. No response from George.

'I hope he got off. It's hard for Dolly with him suspended, with the new baby an'all. It was only a few pounds of tea anyway, you'd think they wouldn't have bothered doing him.'

George ignored her, continuing to crunch steadily through three rounds of toast. Only the merest flicker of an eyelid betrayed the fact that he'd heard her. It wasn't until his second cup of tea that he picked up the letter. He wiped his fingers on the tablecloth, slit the letter with a clean knife and opened it neatly on to the patterned cotton that had once been white. From behind he could hear Rosy pause in her work as she waited for his reaction. He hunched over the paper as if to keep the secret for a while longer, then read the few brief lines, the letters hard edged and perfectly formed. He continued to stare at the dancing black words until a thin veil of tears made them blurred and ragged. He sniffed loudly, wiping his arm across his nose, then draining the last of the tea, folded the letter away neatly, laying it back beside the teapot. He stood up from the table and began to pull on his jacket. Rosy noted the thin line of his lips as he rummaged with his gasbag, so she was almost prepared for bad news when she too picked up the letter. No tears stung her eyes as she read the clear black type.

Dear Mr Conville,

We regret to inform you that Brother Michael McGoyle, whom you represented at his appeal last week in your capacity as part-time union official, had his tribunal's original finding confirmed and is henceforth suspended for a further five working days. He may surrender himself for work again on Monday 28th. Yours . . .

George was already buttoning up his overcoat when Rosy ran out to the front door, catching him by the arm.

'It's not your fault, you know,' she said. She patted him briefly, almost shyly on the elbow, then withdrew her hand. His cold grey eyes looked past her, defeated, as if he was staring at a future which held no hope.

'You did your best, it's not your fault he didn't get off just 'cos you've lost a few cases lately, you can only do so much.'

'Aye,' he answered, adjusting the scarf at his neck. She wasn't sure what she was agreeing with. As he put more clothes on, his body seemed to be slipping away into his silent, work-day self.

As she closed the door after him, a blast of cold wind rushed in through the house. Rosy shivered with cold and new fear. This morning, the kitchen seemed strangely quiet and empty without him. Instead of her usual relief, today she felt only tiredness. There was good reason now. She sat by the unmade fire and patted her belly.

No sun ever found its way into that little house, huddled as if for warmth against its neighbours, but that morning it was as if all the light had gone out of the sky and a blanket of greyness enveloped them. Rosy felt the roundness of her belly and hugged her knees to her chest. George was so bound up in his own affairs he wouldn't even notice for a while. She tightened her hands around her knees. Maybe this time the child would be born healthy, pink and strong and take great gulps of life-giving air. Maybe this time she wouldn't have to bury a cold blue body, a body so small clothes hardly fitted it. Over a year now but she'd never get over it.

'Have another baby quick,' the neighbours had said. 'It'll help you recover.' But George hadn't touched her, and they'd hardly spoken for months.

When they first married, the house had been full of his friends and union colleagues; laughter, excitement. But since the baby had died he'd gone into himself, and their sorrow, instead of bringing them together, had torn them apart. They'd never spoken of the boy's death, but it seemed as if George didn't trust anything anymore. He didn't come near her again until one late summer day when they'd gone for a picnic. There'd been beer in a jug, and laughter, and that night he'd come to her, tender and gentle as the day he first wooed her.

The change had started soon after the baby died when George lost his first case. His workmates taunted him, people stayed away from the house, as if to visit would bring bad luck. Increasingly isolated, in that year he became a different man. Now Rosy felt the first strong quickenings of her second-born inside her. She wanted another boy-child, she wanted it so badly. But losing this tribunal would hit him hard. Always lucky, always able to persuade people with his rich silver tongue, all that was over, like a door closing for ever. Rosy sat for a long time, holding the letter in her hand, before she even roused herself to the housework.

George held his head up high as he stood under the railway arches later that morning, waiting to be selected along with the other men. The tethered horses burrowed patiently at their nosebags, ready for their empty carts to be filled with the first loads off the ships. The air was thick with tension as the men prepared for the call. Some straightened up in an attempt to be chosen, others were unable to do so, bodies hunched and distorted from years of bending and lifting. George was aware of eyes that shifted as soon as they met his, and men edging away slightly as they stood ready for the foreman.

The last few months he'd felt the men turn against him. It all seemed so meaningless now. He'd worked all his life for the union, but the last few months he'd watched his work slip away like quicksilver. There were newer, harder elements at work, not bound by reason, nor ideals. Ideals didn't matter anymore. The dockers had been kings of the workers. Now he could feel their position slipping. There was talk that the employers wouldn't need so many men in future. George couldn't figure how that could happen, but doubt had set in like a canker.

The foreman approached. For a few wild moments George thought he would be passed over; but no, as always, the foreman, knowing he was a good steady worker, silently tapped him on the shoulder.

George walked through the dock gates with the rest of his gang, arriving at the side of the vast liner they were to work on. The men milled around waiting for the gang leader to size up the load, exchanging roll-ups and jokes. Nobody spoke to him. When he finally began work, using his hook to rip open the tough outer sacks, he felt sure two men deliberately pushed against him. But after that he was too intent on setting a good pace and shooing away flies from his hair, his eyes, his throat, to worry about that. The flies streamed out from the hold; they'd die soon enough in the cold autumn air.

It wasn't until they broke for food that the jibes started. George was last off the ship and when he finally joined the others in the cargo hut that doubled as their meeting-place, the noise stopped suddenly. Then Scotty the wag, the one who could never resist opening his mouth, shouted through the dust and smoke as George silently unwrapped the sandwiches Rosy had prepared for him.

'Lost your touch, Conny? Been fighting for the Red Army lately?' Laughter rippled round the hut. George stared at Scotty, willing him to silence, but then they all started, from every direction, like crows over a carcase.

'Over the top, Conny.'

'Too high and mighty.'

'You should have kow-towed to the bosses more, instead of telling them what to do. Goyley would have got off if it hadn't been for your big mouth, Conny.'

'They don't like that commy lark about the bosses being the enemy, you know that, you div.'

George rose quickly, stuffing the remaining sandwiches back in his gasbag. Tensing his shoulders against them and the long afternoon which lay ahead, he walked through their mocking assembly. Once outside, beyond their view, he strode purposefully for a few yards towards the dock gates, then, seeming to shrink, turned back and went past the hut. The air was filled with shouts, curt instructions, well-laden horses that trotted through impromptu games of football. George wandered towards the grey murky depths of water, trailing his feet along through the mud. Giant cranes surrounding their dock, normally such solid, familiar workhorses, seemed somehow menacing today, their cold metal harsh and ungiving in the dark late autumn day.

Presently he reached a quiet oasis of water, away from the bustle of the rest of the dock. George dipped his foot in and felt chill even through his boot. A newspaper package floated by, its urgent headlines now faded and sodden, its mass now spewing out chips. Seagulls squealed down, picking at them greedily. He circled his foot in the water, a trail of cigarette butts swirling out from under it. The ripples from his foot grew wider and wider, until the whole dirty expanse of water seemed to be vibrating with movement.

The horn blasted out for work to begin again just as George turned back towards the liner. Men hurried in companionable droves while he walked alone. And as he began work again, tensing his body to cope with the large heavy loads, their voices rang in his ears.

'You lost it, Conny, you bloody lost it. We don't want you defending us any more.'

2

June 1965. Kirkby.

'Gerroff me, gerroff me.' Jo heard the dull thud of slipper on flesh, and through a gap in the bannisters, saw her mother in a heap on the floor, blouse ridden up, back exposed. Her father stood over, head bent, drawing the slipper now up, bringing the slipper now down. Hands crept out from the heap, like the claws of a crab still finding itself live on the fishmonger's slab. Her mother's body twitched, hunched up in a ball. Jo hugged her knees and winced as the slipper came down again.

'Ssh,' she hissed to her sisters as they joined her on the stairs, high up, safe. Tina, skinny and pale, twisted her hands together.

'What's happening, Josephine?' she whispered.

'You know,' said Jo, and nodded for her to sit down. Tina stole a timid glance over Jo's shoulder and turned her head away. Pat took her place next to the bannister, and watched without a word.

'Gerroff me, I tell ya, gerroff me now.' Her mother was up on her elbows, struggling to her feet. She dusted herself down.

'You're not really a man,' she spat at Jo's father. He stepped back, as if hit by the words. His hands drummed on the table. He puffed his chest out, moved forward again.

'Oh, I'm not, am I? We'll see about that. You're not a proper mother, you can't talk.'

Jo felt herself stiffen as Tina cried softly in her ear. If Tina kept blubbering her father would twig they were there. Jo wanted to see this through.

'Oh, shut up, can't you? Get back to your room,' she said through clenched teeth. Her heart softened slightly when she saw Tina's miserable white face.

'Don't worry, it'll be all right. I'll come up in a minute, when they've finished.' Tina slid out, thin as a wraith, back up to her room. Jo felt sure that they'd finish soon. They'd been like this for years, arguing every night. She only had a misty recollection of early childhood, when her parents smiled sometimes and touched each other. Now they only hit each other. But they'd finish eventually, Jo knew that. Her father had to get up early next morning for work, regular as clockwork. Nothing would disturb that pattern, nothing. It was getting on for ten now.

But, and a small shadow of doubt crept into her mind, it had worsened lately. Raised voices early morning, pig-like snorts and sniffles at night; her mother out twice a week with Sam, that puny freckle-faced man with the ginger hair and missing teeth. Jo didn't know what her mother saw in him. He didn't seem any better than her dad, and he was stupid to boot. At least her dad had brains. Not that her mother would never admit to going out with Sam. It was almost as if, through lying to them, she was making the whole thing unreal. But why else did she tart herself up in front of the mirror? Why else did she put on blue eyeshadow, beige powder, pancake, dark lipstick? She'd never done that for their dad. Jo couldn't remember their ever going out together. Aware of silence, Jo leaned forward to see her father tearing at the alcove where they kept their coats.

Her mother's voice floated over, muffled as if she was trying hard not to cry. 'You can't do this, you know, George. You can't keep me from my kids.'

'I can and I will.'

'You know what I told you. I said you had to stop seeing him, you're making a fool of me Rosy.' Her parents stared at each other. Her father's eyes grew suspiciously bright. She'd never seen him cry, never. Could he be crying now? His eyes pleaded, like a dog wanting its dinner. And then, with no response from Rosy, his lips tightened into a thin cruel line. Jo knew that look. Once he made his mind up about something, there was no changing him.

'But George,' It was her mother's turn to plead now, desperate, 'you can't keep me from my kids.'

'Hurry up,' he said, 'get your bloody coat on. I haven't got all night you know. I wanna have my dinner.'

'But George, you can't do this. It's not right, it's not fair.'

'Who's talking about right, eh? Who's talking about fair? You're not bothered about right when you're sneaking off to meet your fancy man, are you? You bloody whore. Open your legs for him, do ya? Give him what he wants, do ya? That's more important than your kids to you, isn't it, eh? Well, you can bloody well go and stay with him, if you think he's so flamin' wonderful. Get the hell out of here.'

Jo looked round quickly. She didn't want Pat to hear those words. But it was too late. Pat, still sitting next to her, stared intently at her parents. Pat was only seven. Impossible to know if the words had registered their meaning. A tough one. It was always difficult to know what Pat felt, she hid it so well. You could punch and kick her and she wouldn't cry in front of you. But Jo noticed her bottom lip quiver and felt a sudden rush of sympathy. Pat was still only a little girl after all, in spite of her tough shell.

'Get to bed.' Jo spoke through a lump in her throat. She too wanted to cry but, as stubborn as Pat, forced the sobs down. Pat, who never usually obeyed her and, like a cat, padded through the world doing exactly as she wanted, rose without a word and walked slowly up to bed.

'I'll be up in a minute,' promised Jo. Pat turned away, silent. Jo watched her mother scrabble over the floor to gather up the contents of her handbag. She recognised the cracked, maroon leather, the shiny, gold-plated clasp. The lock had never been good. One day earlier that summer, Jo had stolen two shillings from it. The clasp opened with no pressure at all. The two coins meant freedom – five lucky bags – two for herself, one each for the kids. Inside the lucky bags were sweets, a balloon, a plastic mouse, a set of fangs, a false nose, a pair of glasses. When Jo came in from playing that evening, her mother said nothing about the money. But the punishment was the look on her face – puzzled and sad, disappointed somehow. Jo blushed at the memory. A wave of guilt passed over her.

'Come on, hurry up.' Her father's voice, gruff and hard, intruded. He shoved her mother aside and a lipstick rolled away under the small table.

'Leave it,' he ordered, voice stern now. He opened the front door. 'It's not right, George,' wailed her mother, feasting her eyes on the hall. Face purple with anger, he grabbed her by the arm and pushed her through.

'I gave you a chance, and you didn't want to take it. It's your own fault.'

Silence.

'And don't come back,' he yelled to the door. When he turned away, Jo saw him wipe one eye, but the movement was so swift, she thought she must have imagined it. He strode to the kitchen. Jo stood up and walked into Eamon's room. He hadn't come down for the argument; as usual he'd stayed in his room. But he was already half out of the window, watching their mother's slight figure slowly make her way down the street. Jo joined him by the ledge. Rosy stopped once and put her face in her hands, then straightened up and walked on. When she was only a dot at the bottom of the street, Eamon swung round.

'Gerrout!' he shouted to Jo, eyes cold as her father's. 'You've no right to be in here. Gerrout!' Jo turned, away from Eamon, away from her mother. It was no use arguing, she knew that. Eamon would never talk to her. Most of his life remained secret to her and revolved around school. They hadn't been close for years, she didn't feel she knew him any more. She left.

Downstairs, Jo drank tea at the small kitchen table, unsure of what to do. If she thought too hard, a circle of pain seared her head like a red-hot iron. She tried to clear her mind, think of nothing save the steaming brown liquid in her hands. She noticed, as if from afar, that her hands shook. Her father, shirt sleeves rolled up, washed his hands at a sink piled high with dishes. From the back, his trousers were streaked with dirt. He'd had them on since coming home from work but Jo knew he would make no move to change. He lived in the same shapeless, colourless clothes all week, after removing boots and overalls each night.

'There,' he said with satisfaction as he flung back the teatowel on to the kitchen door, as if disposing of a dead rat.

'That's better.' Seeming pleased with himself, he opened the oven door and drew out a plate dripping with gravy.

'Now, what's for dinner? Oh, good.' He put the plate down and began to tuck in. 'Breast of lamb. I like a bit of lamb.'

Jo watched her father as if he were an alien as he ate with every appearance of relish. He turned the pages of the evening paper with his left hand.

'Oh, there's a good programme on later,' he said pleasantly, 'about a man who goes up the Amazon single-handed. Why don't you watch it?' Jo stared back. She couldn't believe it. Hadn't he just thrown her mother out? To listen, you'd think nothing had changed. Was this some sort of grown-up game of which she didn't know the rules? Would he break into a laugh soon, say it was all a big joke and magic her mother back into the kitchen?

'I've gorra do my homework.' Jo rushed out of the kitchen, to vomit in the bathroom sink. For twenty minutes, maybe thirty, she sat in the bathroom trying to calm her quaking stomach. Homework was an excuse, her father must have known that – the kitchen was the only light, warm room, the room where she usually worked.

The evening drew on but Jo sat on in the cold dark bathroom. Although the lightbulb had gone, Jo made no move to put in a new one. She stared at the mottled dark-blue sky through the frosted glass window. The room was draughty, cheerless, as only an unheated bathroom can be.

When, a long time later, Jo finally forced herself to bed, the twins were still awake; Pat rigid on her back, staring at the ceiling, and Tina sniffing into a pillow.

'You said you'd come up soon,' Pat accused. 'That was hours ago.' Her new large teeth stuck out like a rabbit's.

'Oh, yeah, I forgot,' mumbled Jo. She felt like a sponge that had been wrung until it's dry. Such a long time since morning.

'Humph, where's my mother gone anyway?' Tina's voice was thin and frail as a reeds.

'Probably just over the road,' Jo lied.

'Where?'

'Ellen Mack's maybe.'

'When's she coming back?' Tina's voice was doubtful, but it was as if she wanted to believe the story. Ellen was, at times, their mother's best friend and sworn enemy. Ellen was the eyes on the street, nothing escaped her. She would have seen Rosy leave from her window.

'She'll be back later,' Jo said without conviction.

Pat began to cough, a choking, anxious cough that seemed to swallow all the oxygen in the room, and the subject was left. Jo turned the light out. Pat's cough ebbed away.

Jo was aware of them all sleeping fitfully that night. In her dreams, doors banged. It was dark when she woke, terrified, to a scraping, gnawing noise that sounded like the rat she'd heard once down at her uncle's house in Liverpool. Scrape, scrape, scrape, the noise came again. She imagined the rat with a dark sleek coat, and long pointed nose, ready to break through somewhere in the house. Her uncle had been decorating that time and had nailed up a new piece of hardboard to the bath, imprisoning the rat by accident. The scraping went on for days. By the time he levered off the hardboard the rat was dead. Grey, skinny, flea-bitten, smelly. Its mouth hung open, showing yellow, pointed teeth.

Jo lay rigid in bed, trying to dismiss the memory, but the scraping kept up. Eamon, she presumed, walking in his sleep. He'd done it a few times lately, eyes wide open as he wandered through the house. Then came a whispered voice. She couldn't make out the words. The noise seemed to come from Eamon's room at the front of the house, over the street.

Jo quietly padded in. A pale moon hung in the dark sky. The harsh yellow light from a streetlamp streamed through gaps in the curtains. Delicate tree-shadows waved eerily against the wall. It was as if the whole room, quiet save for Eamon's light snores, waited. Then the scraping resumed. Jo started. She thought of Cathy at the window in *Wuthering Heights*.

'Let me in, let me in.' What ghostly creature would lurk outside? In spite of the cold, sweat poured from her armpits, her breath came short and shallow. She wanted comfort and warmth.

'Come on, hurry up, what are you bloody playing at?' The

voice startled Jo. No ghost would talk like that. It sounded like her mother. Jo switched on the light. Eamon stirred in the bed. When she peered close through the window the harsh yellow showed her a face ravaged by tears, smudged mascara, wild hair. Her mother looked a sight.

'Hurry up, dozy arse. And turn that bloody light off.' Like an automaton, Jo obeyed and undid the squealing window-catch, fearful that her father might wake. Her mother tumbled out on to the floor, coat open, buttons missing. The streetlamp shone on her shoes, caked with mud.

Jo put her finger to her lips. Her father was only next door.

'Sod him,' said her mother, as she picked herself up. 'I don't care. And Eamon's no bother, he sleeps like a baby.'

'What kept you?' she asked, catching her breath. 'I've been knocking for ages.' She rummaged in her pocket, removed a cigarette and lit it in one swift movement. Inhaling deeply, she wiped her face with a scarf, then sat down on the edge of the bed and inspected her stockings.

'Look at that,' she said in annoyance. 'I've laddered my stockings getting up the drainpipe 'cos of that soft bastard.' Jo was too surprised to answer. She stood awkwardly, wondering what to do with her hands. Eamon slept soundly, arms flung out trustingly like a much younger child. His snores caressed the room, punctuated by her mother's swift puffs.

Jo stared at the bruise on her mother's forehead, bright blue and purple, pulsating. She couldn't think what her mother was doing, coming back at this hour of the night.

'How?' she whispered, pointed at the bruise, but the rest of the words wouldn't come out. She was cold, and tired of confrontation.

'How did I get that?' her mother jumped, glad of the question. 'Oh, that was your loving father. Really brave isn't he, hitting a woman?'

Jo felt tiredness overpower her. She yawned widely. The day had been too long, she wanted to sleep. Her head pounded.

'I've gorra get back to bed,' she said decisively. 'Are you going to bed then?' Jo twisted in embarrassment from one foot to the other as she waited for the answer.

'No, I think I'll just stay here for a bit,' said her mother, leaning back against the bottom of Eamon's bed. 'I might have a bit of a snooze.' She stubbed the half-finished cigarette into a cup on the floor.

'OK,' said Jo, confused. 'Tara then. See you in the morning.' She shuffled to the door.

'Jo,' called her mother softly.

'What?' Jo turned round, eager.

'Thanks,' said her mother. 'Goodnight.'

They grew used to the new set-up. At least twice a week for the next few weeks, Rosy would be thrown out. Twice a week for the next few weeks Jo woke late at night to let in her mother. She grew used to the scraping at the window, grew used to her mother's tired hard voice. She even woke sometimes before the scraping started. She was tired all the time and behind in her school work, maths especially. She wondered what would happen if she couldn't catch up. Would they put her in a different stream, not enter her for exams? Would she be stuck there for ever? Doing well at school was the only way out. But it was as if she had no control over anything any more. Each day, Jo woke to uncertainty. Her mother was living, yet not living there. Sometimes they'd arrive home to proper cooked meals – steak and kidney pie, or liver, or mince, with mashed potato, greens. They'd sit around together, with Tina on her father's knee. He'd crack jokes, and her mother would stay home for a few days. But, on other occasions, the icy blast of change would hit Jo as soon as she stepped in through the door. Tinned spaghetti, fried eggs, slices of rubbery, cold toast. OK for your dinner, but not for your tea. Her mother, dressed to go out, would put on pancake and lipstick, lacquer her hair.

'Tell your dad his food's in the oven,' she'd remind them. 'A chop and spuds on the plate.' Chop greasy and tough, tomatoes curled round it, potatoes floury and dry. And then the door slammed behind her, the house feeling empty until their father arrived home, tight-lipped, terse.

'Where's your mother gone?' he'd ask.

'The bingo,' they'd lie. 'Mrs Jones', 'Up the road.' Then followed long nights of argument and her mother locked out, to scrabble at the window once again.

One night Jo woke to a new sound – silence. Puzzled, she listened to a tap dripping downstairs. The argument that evening had been particularly fierce, but Jo expected her mother back at the window as usual. She always came back, Jo reasoned. Didn't she?

The sky had already lightened when Jo fell asleep to deep and troubled dreams in which no matter which way she turned, her mother was only a tiny dot in the distance.

In the morning over breakfast, Tina asked about Rosy.

'She had to go out.' Jo was quick with her answer.

'It's all right, she'll be here when you get home from school.' But she wasn't, nor the next day, nor the next. The days lengthened to weeks and the twins eventually stopped asking. A dead routine was established: get up, feed the kids, do the housework, go to school. Homework came at the end of the day, if Jo could manage it. Her insides felt empty. There was nothing worth hoping for, nothing worth aiming for. The maths teacher complained about her work and put her down a set. Jo didn't protest. He was right. The problems he gave made no sense at ten at night, when figures swam before her eyes.

The twins moaned and railed, and Tina especially clung to her like a leech. Each night Jo peeled them off, sensing her own vitality drain away. Pat's face grew harder, impenetrable, while Tina's dissolved, like glue, into tears. Her streaked white face made Jo furious. Eamon was like a ghost-figure; it was as if he'd removed himself from the family. He hung around with a gang at school, and, when at home, lived in his room. He didn't eat with them any more, but lived off chips, and meals at a friend's house sometimes; the mother seemed to have adopted him. Jo couldn't see why. At home, if Eamon spoke, it was only 'Yeah' and 'No', and the occasional 'Fuck off'. Never a proper sentence, never more than a few words, spat out one at a time. Once, they'd had an argument and he'd kicked Jo in the leg. She'd watched the bruise turn blue, then purple, then green and yellow. After that, he never touched her again and moved away when she came near.

Taking one day at a time, Jo felt a curtain of glass between herself and the world. Before her mother left and now were two different countries and, like a traveller who'd passed through

27

time zones, she'd forgotten the other side. Her father seemed more cheerful than ever. He often went out straight after tea, and came back covered with prickles and dandelion burrs, as if he'd been crawling through bushes. One night, she saw him talking at the gate to a man with dark glasses and a trilby with a short green feather; a small man, shifty, suspicious-looking.

'I think she goes to the Essoldo,' the man said, 'from what I've been able to observe.'

Observe? Essoldo? The words slid over her like a magic spell. The man looked like a private detective out of a forties film, one who was fated to be found gagged hand and foot at the side of a road somewhere. She questioned her father.

'You're too nosy,' he told her. 'Keep your beak out of my affairs. This is adult business.' She puzzled over the man for weeks until he stopped coming to the house and her father stopped his evening excursions. She never did find out the truth.

Jo told no-one at school about her mother. There was no point and nobody asked. Why should they? It wasn't their business, and there were too many kids always, too many problems. Jo remembered the school opening; new, purpose-built. 'A new era,' the local newspaper had claimed, 'our first comprehensive.' At the time, Jo hadn't known what comprehensive meant, but she'd been impressed by the word. The paper went on about a new world opening, a world of democracy and equality, the doors of the world prised open like a clam. But now the school buildings had a tattered, neglected air, rubbish blew in the playground. The young staff were often off, several teachers had been beaten up by ex-pupils, each morning the younger children had to protect themselves from a gauntlet of gangs who tried to rob them of their money.

If the school needed notes signing, she forged the signature in a neat careful hand. No-one suspected. If was as if all trace of her mother had been wiped from the earth, as if she'd never existed except in Jo's imagination. Her image grew hazy.

Not even Jackie, Jo's best friend, knew what had happened. They would lie on the floor in the room Jackie shared with her sister, and discuss their future careers. Jackie's house was one box among many on one of the oldest estates. Old that is, meant ten years, most of the estates had gone up in the last five.

'I want to be an artist,' Jackie claimed. She spent hours drawing her brothers and sisters, her mother, her father.

'Haven't you got anything better to do?' her mother would shout, shooing Jackie out, but Jo could tell that really she was proud of this daughter who might leap out into a life of her own, like a salmon leaping falls.

'I wanna be an Olympic swimmer and a runner and a writer and look after animals,' was Jo's breathless contribution whenever they discussed the future.

'I'll do some of them part-time. They don't have the Olympics in winter so that's all right.' In that cold pink room, their assault on the world seemed assured. Whenever Jo returned home, reality turned flat, grey, one-dimensional, the world and its possibilities shrank. With Jo's mother gone, the house had already descended to the basics. A cushion on the couch had split open and the horsehair spilt out. The small mirror over the fireplace had broken and her father had removed the small green glass animals that used to be on the mantelpiece.

'What do we want with this old rubbish?' he'd asked, and they'd shattered into a bucket. Jo felt the pain like a knife going in. She'd dreamed through those animals through a large part of childhood. Her favourite was the horse, with its long noble neck and legs poised for flight. Now her dreams lay in bits like the glass.

'My mother's at work,' Jo lied to Jackie whenever Jackie asked to go home with her. 'She does shifts. She doesn't like me bringing anyone home when she's not there.' Jackie, used to stability, and a mother who was there for her, accepted without comment. Whenever Jo lied, her heart beat so fast and loud, she was sure Jackie and the whole world could hear. One day the walls of her house would open up and she'd be swallowed up by a cavern of untruths.

They were all in the tangled web together. Eamon, proud like her, would never tell anyone about what was happening at home. But Jo feared for the twins. Tina looked so terrible that sooner or later, some nosy teacher would be bound to get concerned, and start asking questions. Then their cover would be blown. She'd have to warn Tina to keep her mouth shut. She didn't really know what would happen if anyone found out, but she had a vague idea that someone in authority – teachers, social workers, maybe, would move in on them.

School broke up for the holidays. That summer, while the twins played outside and got brown, Jo lay on the couch as much as possible, reading novels. She stayed white as milk through the long summer days. The summer disappeared like water swirling down a plug. Afterwards she couldn't remember the names of any of the books she'd read.

One morning, a crisp clear autumn morning, three months after her mother had left, Jo ran to school late. Latin today, and Raines hated lateness, he took it as a failure of character. Sure enough, he grabbed her when she arrived panting, and this time she couldn't slip to the back of the class.

'Come here, Conville,' he said, voice calm but firm. He had a crumpled grey suit on, and dark wisps of hair sprouted from his ears. His bald head shone in the fluorescent light. Thin ridges of black and grey hair near his ears offset his baldness. His chin, blue-black with stubble, gave him a seedy, unsavoury look.

Jo went to the front of the class. She hated being called Conville. She wasn't a boy, she had a first name.

'Could you tell me, Conville, why you are late yet again? This is the third time this week. If this goes on, I'll have to get your mother up here.'

Jo suppressed a smile.

'You'll have a job,' she thought.

'Well?' He stepped back to view her. Jo evaded his eyes, and wrung her hands uselessly. Why was he picking on her today? As she rubbed one foot behind the other, her toes chafed uncomfortably, her socks still wet from the washing.

'I'm waiting.' The clock ticked by, the class buzzed in expectation, sensing that Raines would go in for the kill, like a hawk aiming for prey.

'Dunno sir,' she mumbled.

'Dunno, dunno,' he mocked. 'You mean you don't know, my girl.'

'Yes, sir, I don't know.' She enunciated the words clearly.

'Well, that's a fine way to be. Eleven years old and you don't even know why you're late.' He smiled, enjoying himself now.

'Well, Conville,' he said dramatically, and paused as he

turned to the class. With his sense of melodrama, Jo thought wryly, he should have been on the stage. He was obviously a failed actor.

Jo looked back at Raines' face, listening to his words. He was red with impatience.

'Well, Conville, I presume your mother wakes you up.'

'Yes sir, of course sir.' Yes sir, yes sir, three bags full sir, my mother's not at home, sir. What would he do if she told him?

'Well, what time does she wake you up?'

'Seven o'clock, sir,' she lied. At seven, as grey light filtered through the dirt-stiff curtains, her father in his boots tramped a steady course through the house.

'And what time do you get up?'

'Eight-thirty, sir.' Dozing and dreaming on and off, on and off, until day pushed into the room like an unwanted guest, and Eamon yelled at them all to get up.

'Eight-thirty. Eight-thirty? Aha, I see. Do you mean to say that you get woken at seven, yet you don't get up till eight-thirty?'

'Yes, sir,' Jo repeated. She wanted to run away and disappear into her book, cloaking the pages around her. She stared at the curled script wriggling round on the page like snakes, trying to make sense of it.

'Why?' he asked. 'Why don't you get up earlier?'

'Dunno, sir,' she answered, truthful this time. What could you say? That in bed you could dream, hope, imagine? Once you got up the day hit you in the face like a wet flannel?

'And I assume your mother makes you breakfast?'

'Of course, sir,' she said dutifully. A mad scramble for tea and toast. A damp burnt smell as four pairs of socks dried in the oven and steam rose, misting the kitchen windows.

'Well, my advice to you, Conville, is to set your alarm a bit later and get up straightaway. You'd be much better off.'

Jo pursed her lips and looked down.

'We haven't got an alarm, you daft bugger, you, you don't know anything,' she thought. Her mouth stayed silent.

'You've obviously been watching too much late night TV, my girl. It's not good for you, you know, when you have to get up in the morning. You look tired.'

'We haven't got a TV any more, you stupid twat, it smashed

when my mother threw an ornament at my dad.' Jo was convinced that her thoughts flashed like neon bulbs around the room, but Raines seemed oblivious to them.

'After all, Conville, we've got to build good habits of discipline. If you don't while you're young, you won't be able to do it when you're older. We've got to start off the way we mean to go on. Give me a child of seven and I'll show you the man.' Jo mouthed the words along with him, wondering what on earth they had to do with her, female, eleven, with no alarm clock.

What did he know about anything?

The days continued in their endless monotony. School, home, school. It was best to have no expectations. Jo drifted through the days, and each night lay in the dark until sleep crept up through the silence. The autumn term wore on. Jo was due to go on a school trip with the hockey team, to a holiday home the school owned in Wales. After ranting for years that such trips weren't necessary, her father had had a change of heart; 'Especially as it's almost free,' he admitted. Before the summer she'd been looking forward to the trip, but now with her mother gone, all enthusiasm evaporated like steam. Two days before the trip, her father gave her two weeks' pocket money early, plus two pounds. Jo had never had so much money in her life. Was it cheaper for him not having a wife? she wondered, putting the money carefully away in the case he'd lent her. She packed and repacked that night. But her heart wasn't in it.

On the Friday morning before the trip, the geography teacher tried to interest them in the layout of the area they'd be staying in.

'It's a drowned glacial valley,' he said enthusiastically. 'Thousands of years ago mammoths were raging around those hills. The temperature was below freezing, the landscape a frozen waste.' Jo saw the earth warming up, glaciers melting into streams, ape-like hairy humans drawing matchstick figures on dark caves in long winter months, smouldering fires their only light. Yet the house they would stay in looked quite domestic from the photographs – mock tudor, with one dorm for the boys, one for the girls, and constant hot water from a wood-burning Aga. Ghosts of giant mammoths stalked the land. Their holiday home would be snug against chaos.

That afternoon she dragged her feet home from school. How did the mammoths get food into their mouths once they'd picked it up? she wondered. Really she was trying to put off thinking about what to cook for tea, when a sudden tap on her shoulder made her start. She swung around. Her mother, clean and smart in a camel coat with football buttons, faced her.

'Hello Josephine,' she yelled. 'All right there, love?' Jo gulped in amazement. She hadn't seen her mother for months. There'd been no word since that last awful night. They walked along companionably together, heading towards home. Jo nodded proudly at two girls from school, hoping they'd notice her mother. Let the rumours about her be quashed, let them see she did have a mother. Rosy babbled on about a new factory job she'd soon be starting.

'It's part-time you know, in Bird's Eye, evenings, so I can be here when you come home from school. It's packing fish fingers, so that's good, isn't it, Josephine?'

Jo's mind spun off, remembering a similar walk with her mother many years before. She had been five years old, the newborn twins back at the house with her father; a rare chance for Jo and her mother to be alone together. They held hands like sisters then. Neighbours stopped them along the way.

'How's the twins? How are you?'

'They've gained a pound. They're very alert, they're feeding well,' her mother answered with a sense of importance, first woman in the street to bear twins.

But when they walked back home, slowly spinning out the last few webs of freedom, her mother seemed to slump.

'I lost my teeth you know, they took all my calcium and I got pyorrhoea.' This confused Jo. Her mother's teeth looked fine and white and even, well polished. Jo had no idea what pyorrhoea was. She imagined piranha fish snapping round the edges of teeth. She'd seen a picture of piranhas once in the library. Ugly, nasty creatures, with teeth like scissors.

'They say you lose a tooth for every baby, but I was lucky until I had the twins. Then they all went, in one straight go. Look at me, only thirty-four and false teeth already!' They'd been united in a solid wall of resentment against the twins that time.

Jo came back to the present, scared. She looked at her

mother's teeth. Yellowing a bit now, but still small and neat and even. Her mother slowed down as they approached the house, unsure for a minute, but then unlocked the door as if she'd never been away. What would happen now? Jo wondered, but before she had time to think, the twins rushed up for hugs; small bundles of tousled hair, need and forgiveness. Jo watched them, oddly jealous of the way their bodies blended into her mother's. She'd never have that again; she was too big, hard, awkward.

'Eamon, go to the chippy,' her mother ordered when he came in. He turned round immediately. Later, as they attacked the fish and chips greedily, Jo stared at her mother out of the corner of her eye, trying to imprint the image on her mind. Her father appeared at the door just as Jo was savouring the last bite of orange crispy cod. She coughed and choked on the fish, washing it down with mouthfuls of water. When he came in she mopped at her face with a handkerchief, heart in mouth, petrified, waiting for the explosion. But as he stood at the door, a strange half-smile illuminated his face. Her mother drew up a seat, unwrapped a fish, and gathered chips from their plates.

'Come here, George, we're having fish and chips tonight; here's yours now.' Her language was as familiar as if she'd never been away.

'All right,' he answered, meek as a lamb. 'And how's my little girl today?' He put his arm round Tina, his favourite, and kissed her. He hadn't done that for weeks. Jo breathed out in relief.

'It's all right,' said her mother, noticing her anxious look. 'It's OK.' And it was all right, the rest of the day. It was all right telling their school news and hearing the details of her mother's new job; it was all right her father telling a story about a man on the docks. Oh, how they all laughed that day, relaxed and at home together.

That night Jo couldn't sleep, excited by the prospect of the trip and her mother's return. She thought of the house in Wales where she'd be staying. There was a river nearby; they could have early morning swims. They'd read by the light of log-fires and roam over green rolling countryside. She touched the stiff leather of her case, tracing the outline of the letters with her fingers. Was it true? Through the half-open door of her parents' room she could hear two distinct sounds – her father's deep steady breathing and her mother's higher, quicker breath. She stole in to check. Her father lay on his back, her mother curled into his side. He shifted his weight, and the bedsprings twanged. It was true. Her mother was back.

Jo woke to sunlight and the smell of toast, and rose to see the twins round the kitchen table. The whole place seemed cleaner, well scrubbed. The table was clear, the mound of dishes at the sink gone, streaks of congealed fat round the cooker disappeared. A bunch of chrysanthemums stood on the windowledge, bright hopeful suns of orange and yellow.

'Come on Josephine,' said her mother, standing over a frying-pan. 'I thought I'd let you sleep. Your dad told me you were going on the school trip today, you need your rest. Here, get a plate and I'll give you some scrambled eggs.'

The eggs were pale yellow with flecks of green mint, the toast sodden with margarine, the best she'd ever tasted. Jo had second helpings, then thirds, and a second cup of tea. Her father came in just as she was draining her cup and joined them round the table. Saturday morning he always worked, but he'd knocked off early, he told them. He looked old suddenly, with his bent back and grey, dust-splattered hair, but a smile cracked his hard, pinched face.

When Jo had finished breakfast, she stood, awkward at the kitchen door, surrounded by bags. Balancing on one foot, she watched her family. Heads down, intent on eating, they looked like one of those proper families in the adverts. Jo coughed, scared to break the peace.

'I've got to go a bit early, Mum.' The word 'Mum' sounded strange to her ears, she hadn't used it for so long. 'Will you be here when I get back?'

Both parents stood up. Her father leaned against the back door, smoking.

'It's all right,' answered her mother, serious. 'I'll be here, don't you worry. We've come to an arrangement about money, haven't we George?' Her father glared.

'Don't be telling her anything,' he said, his customary bad temper coming through. 'She's got too much imagination already, she doesn't need to know everything.' Then his face softened. 'Here take this with you.' He threw over half a crown. 'Get a few pressies.'

'And these,' added her mother thrusting a brown paper bag into her hand. 'There's a few egg sarnies and an apple.'

They waved goodbye from the gate and Jo ran to school, happy. Her mother was back, everything, just everything, was now OK.

On the trip, the feeling persisted all week, as cold misty mornings were followed by bright days of warm sun. An Indian summer had been forecast and an Indian summer came, mellow as an orange pumpkin. Jo dared her body to its limits, and plunged into the ice-cold river with the other girls, in spite of warnings from the soft-spoken Welsh housekeeper.

Jo knew nothing could touch her this week. She swam through clear water until her bones ached with tiredness and slept the sleep of the righteous at night, ensleeved by the hills, colours outside changing from light blue to grey to navy, and stars she never saw in the town. It was a week of magic.

When she leaped out of the coach, back from the holiday, and grunted a shy thanks, she ran up the remaining streets high with excitement, her case knocking against her sunburnt knees. No-one would recognise her, she was so brown. They wouldn't expect her to have a tan this time of year. Saturday afternoon. They'd have liver for tea and watch *World of Sport* on TV.

The house was quiet – no TV blaring out, no sound of children. She presumed the kids were out playing. There'd be time to unpack and get their presents out. She knocked again. If there was no-one in, she'd have to go through next door's back garden, their own back door was always left open. Then came footsteps down the stairs. Quicker, lighter than her father's usual walk. But it was he who opened the door, face blank, expressionless.

'Oh, hiya,' Jo said, 'I've just come back. I had a really good time. We went swimming in the sea when it was raining and we didn't even have any towels. And we played eight games of hockey. We lost most of them mind you. I mean, you can't expect to win every one, can you?' She threw her coat into the hall and began to lift up her bags.

'I'll just go and put these upstairs, I'll unpack now before they all come back. Are they still out playing? Is my mother in the kitchen? What time are they coming back? I've got some presents, you see.' She was about to walk up the stairs when something in the cold quiet atmosphere of the house made her turn round. Her father hadn't uttered one word, but stood at the door and looked out into the bright afternoon, as if searching for something. Fear tightened round Jo's stomach.

'Where is my mother?' she asked, not wanting to hear the answer. The kitchen door was closed. No sounds came.

He turned round slowly. She noticed his face, white now, a red angry spot on his big hooked nose. When he spoke, his eyes focused on her belly.

'She's gone,' he said, voice shaking, 'she's not coming back.'

Jo streaked up the stairs, threw her bag down and fell on the bed. Gone. The word hammered at her skull like a gong. Too late. Tears came easily, great sobs wracked from deep inside her. She lay for an hour, maybe two, and clutched the miniature travelling washing-line, the present for her mother, to her tight sweaty fist, until shadows lengthened, street lamps came on nd she could hear the twins' voices downstairs. She'd have to get up and give them their presents or they'd come up to the bedroom. She didn't want them to see her cry. She sat up in the bed and gripped the washing-line savagely. Then one by one, she pulled the multi-coloured pegs off, snapping them in half. With Pat's sharp scissors, she cut the line itself into one, two, three, countless thin strands, which fell like worms to the floor. By the open window, she gathered the pile up, then threw it as far as she could see, to a mud patch near the back of the garden. With her face set hard like a mask she picked up the bars of rock and went downstairs to meet the twins.

Hospital, Central Liverpool, November 17 1982. Night.

The sister had clear eyes and smooth pink skin. Head thrust forward, she tiptoed closer. Jo smelt the heady evocative mixture of perfume and cigarette smoke; it brought to mind her mother going out for the evening when she was a child. The ward was dark, with pinpoints of light down one end as they approached the nurses' office.

'If you wish to speak to someone, Mrs Conville, you can talk to the chaplain.' The nurse waited. She had a spot at the side of her nose which looked oddly out of place with the pink smoothness of her face, the clean crispness of her uniform.

'Uh?' Her mother was Mrs Conville, her mother lay prone on the bed. Her mother couldn't speak to the chaplain. Jo rubbed her eyes and looked at the clock. She must have slept for an hour, tiredness overcoming her in the warmth and darkness. She felt groggy and unfocused. It was very dark outside.

'The chaplain, Mrs Conville.'

Jo twigged at last she was talking to her.

'I'm not Mrs,' she wanted to say, 'I'm not married,' but remained silent. What difference did it make? If you had a child with someone, you were as good as married. Words like partner, lover, boyfriend or co-habitee never seemed right. One day she'd invent a word. But for now, partner was the best she could think of. Martin was her partner, Bobby her child. She'd left them at home eating beans on toast in front of the TV.

'He comes round every morning, you can see him first thing. Many relatives find it a comfort at a time like this. What denomination did you say you were?'

Jo looked blank-eyed at the nurse. Desperate to appear grateful so as not to offend the woman, but unable to lie, she admitted. 'I didn't. I'm not anything.' The Protestant god is a jealous god, the Protestant god keeps people to himself, the Protestant god provides for his own. 'Nothing.'

'Oh.' The nurse's eyes narrowed in confusion or disapproval, then brightened as suddenly.

'Well, he can give non-denominational counselling. He's really a very nice man. Would you like to see him?' The nurse, with a mission to perform, waited. Jo knew she wouldn't leave until she had an answer. Jo waved her hands vaguely.

'Yeah, of course, yeah, yeah. I'll see him in the morning,' she said enthusiastically. Mañana, mañana, everything tomorrow.

The nurse's dark eyes, enlivened now, bore into Jo.

'That's the spirit. We should take whatever help we can.'

She glided out, leaving an echo of footsteps on the tiled polished floor.

Jo checked her mother again and closed her eyes. That's the spirit. What spirit? The blood of Christ, rich, dark, pungent, as it flowed into your empty, early-morning stomach. The host, the wafer; 'melts in your mouth, not in your hands,' Sandra Ryan had whispered to her, the first time they'd received communion. It was Sandra Ryan who had turned her on to religion, after all, the summer they were twelve, the summer her mother left.

'If you go up to that new church with the trendy new vicar, you get free biscuits and coffee afterwards,' Sandra had told her. Jo took up religion with fervour. It was as if there was a great empty hole waiting to be filled, and religion slipped into it, easy as a glove. She and Sandra attended confirmation classes for months. Each week after class Jo sneaked home to the cupboard under the stairs, to gaze at the words in her prayer book. She read amongst her father's dusty magazines – *The Illustrated London News*, *National Geographic*, old copies of the *Daily Mirror*. There was also a copy of Nicholas Montserrat's *The Cruel Sea*. When you opened it, dust shot up your nose and tiny book-lice scurried across the page as if crossing a desert.

In contrast to the cupboard, the church was modern, light, clean as a whalebone. It had sprung up quick as a tent in an old ploughed field, where horses used to play, when they first moved to Kirkby. The rows and rows of white, brown and grey formula-made houses, all with neat handkerchiefs of gardens, had given them freedom to breathe, her mother said. All Jo remembered of Liverpool was a tiny dark house full of shadows, and a boy over the road marching proud beside her, carrying a rat on the end of a string. The streets around her new house became her world.

At confirmation, the young vicar, fresh-faced and earnest in his long frock, presented them with a brown cross, disappointing in its lack of ornament. A man she thought for a minute was the Pope, in a splendid high hat of purple green and white, carried a sceptre and tapped them on the head.

'I am the one true Catholic church,' chimed the vicar, to Jo's confusion. They were Protestants weren't they? She was reading *Villette* at the time and felt for Lucy Snowe, who, after collapsing on the steps of a Catholic church, had uttered 'They call me a Protestant, you know, but really I am not sure whether I am or not; I don't well know the difference between Romanism and Protestantism'.

'You were made for our faith,' the priest told Lucy. 'Depend upon it our faith alone could heal and help you – Protestantism is altogether too dry, cold, prosaic for you.' *Villette* and the man with the big hat had laid the seeds of doubt for Jo about where she stood, seeds which had sprouted and grown through all her adolescent years.

Jo's eyes flickered briefly open, but then the great black hole of sleep surrounded her, comforting in its velvety softness. She stretched her spine and settled back for the night in the hospital armchair.

3

Kirkby, March 1970.

'You'll have to leave school and get a bloody job,' he said, as he banged his fists down on the table. 'A proper job, work in Woolworth's like everybody else.'

Jo's hands tightened round the pen as her father continued his tirade.

She pressed down heavily on the paper, and drew box after box, then proceeded to shade them in. They'd been arguing for almost an hour and he'd threatened to go up the school.

'And I'll go up that school of yours and tell them I want you to leave.' His voice cut into her thoughts. She stabbed the pen into the paper and caught her thumb on a staple. Bright blood stained her hand.

'But I've got my exams soon.' Her voice quavered as she tried to control it. He snorted.

'A levels, O levels, where does all your fancy bloody learning get you, eh? You couldn't beat me at *University Challenge*, last night, could you?'

Jo reddened. It was true. Sixteen now, her mother gone for almost five years, and she still fluffed most of the questions, while he, with a memory like a computer, took every opportunity to show his superiority.

'See them flamin' ponces on that team – they've all had education, and how come I did better than them, eh?' he gloated, face red with satisfaction and belligerence.

Jo shrugged her shoulders.

'It's not for the likes of us, this education lark.'

'I educated myself,' he went on proudly. 'I never went to college. Except a Working Man's one,' he added.

'Yeah and look at you,' Jo replied and flinched away from his hand, which shot out, quick as a snake's tongue. 'You'd think it was something to be proud of.'

'I hate you, I wish you were dead,' she whispered under her breath.

'What did you say, you cheeky little monkey you? A working man *is* something to be proud of. One thing they don't teach you in that school of yours is manners, that's for sure. What did you say?' He thrust his purple face forward, and bared his few remaining brown teeth. Jo could smell hot sour breath. Veins stood out on his temples. Her hand traced circle after circle.

'Why don't you die?' she yelled and throwing the pen down, ran up to the bathroom. He followed and raged outside. The door vibrated with his kicks. Her words seemed to echo round the shadowy corners of the cold bare room.

'Why don't you die? Why don't you die?' She opened the window and put her hands over her ears. Clouds scuttled past as if keen to make their escape and a half-moon threw its light over the back garden. She breathed in cold damp air. Dull thuds bounced from the door, as if from a long way away. He couldn't keep it up forever, she reasoned – he'd said he wanted to watch a programme and, besides, it was freezing up there on the landing. The twins would be home soon; he still loved Tina best, she'd take his mind off her.

The noise died away, Jo shut the window and relaxed back on the toilet seat. She picked up a book and began to read. Her eyes scanned the page as she slid into the book, like slipping into an old familiar coat. It was Jane Austen, a world of order, and manners. Everything had a place, a purpose, there were certain ways of doing things.

It had grown dark when Jo stopped reading. She snapped the book to, and scrubbed her teeth vigorously. Dried pink paste, like the trial of a snail, was spread round the basin. Jo rubbed at the hard pink deposit, but it remained stuck fast. She put back the toothbrush, shut the door quietly and tiptoed to bed. The twins were already asleep.

The next few days passed without incident. Her father didn't mention the argument again, but each night Jo worried about what she would do if he forced her to leave school. All week she considered the choices. A job in Butlin's for the summer? A cruise ship or hotel? The need to get a job with somewhere to live meant the choice wasn't too wide. Her mind went round and round in circles. She saw herself washing dishes, scrubbing floors, smiling intently at customers as she served them food and drink, all the while hating their stupid sheep-faces. No, she resolved; she would set her mind to it, she wanted to stay on at school. If she could only get through these last few days of term, he might forget his threats after Easter.

Saturday morning, first day of the Easter holidays, Jo woke to a cold bright day, relieved at surviving the week. She dressed warmly. Today she was working at the town centre Chicken Roast shop. The manager had agreed to take her and Sandra on for two weeks over the holidays. Jo grinned to herself, her toes curled in expectation. She didn't care that the work was boring. She and Sandra would have a laugh; the money was handy, and, best of all, she got out of the house and out of looking after Eamon and the twins for a few hours. Being at home with the kids during the school holidays was like being locked in a cave.

'They're big enough and bloody soft enough to look after themselves,' her father had said when she told him about her job. Today was Saturday and he'd be back from work at lunchtime. Eamon was thirteen now, and the twins ten, babies no longer. They'd grown used to her mother being away; Jo was the mother now. Sometimes she felt about forty. Each night was the same, thinking of what to eat; tinned vegetables, tinned meat, boiled potatoes. Occasionally an apple or a tin of rice pudding. The dishes afterwards, the twins to send to bed. Lucky they had each other. Even though they fought and scratched like cats, the twins were close. Sometimes her father handed over money for Jo to buy clothes for them. This meant a trip down to St John's market to root amongst cut-price skirts and blouses, and after-school excursions to Curtess to shoe their growing feet. But mostly the twins seemed to look after themselves. They played out with their friends until the sky darkened and they were forced back home. They walked home from school trailing on the tail ends of tough loud gangs, and ignored her if she passed them. Jo felt like a landlord most of the time, with awkward rebellious tenants. She rolled her shoulders back, to try to shake off responsibility. Was this what old age would feel like?

Down in the kitchen that morning Jo felt uneasy. She lit the oven and drew her knees up, enjoying the warmth. To her surprise, the kitchen looked as sparse and uncluttered as it had the previous evening. No lukewarm pot of tea, no cup and plate draining from her father's early breakfast, no evidence that her father had been up at all. He worked half-day on a Saturday, regular as clockwork. It was now eight o'clock. Jo swallowed the tea and got up to check. With a cup in one hand, she knocked on the door of her father's room and pushed her way in.

The room smelt dusty and sweaty. Small chinks of light escaped through thin curtains pulled close. The grey pink eiderdown was now balded and skinny as a chicken after moulting feathers over the years. Jo breathed in stale close air. She'd hardly been in this room since her mother had left. Like in a neglected museum, her father hadn't changed anything, not even the sheets, it seemed.

'What do you want?' a hoarse voice rasped out. Jo adjusted her eyes to the dimness as she stood in the doorway. Her father lay flat on his back, trying to raise himself up on his elbows. His face looked grey and strained, and she could hear his deep bronchial breathing, like a horse snorting in winter.

'I've brought you some tea,' she said awkwardly, standing rigid. 'Do you want it?'

His hands waved at the air, and she put the cup on the small bedside table, spilling some on the eiderdown in the process. She rubbed at it with her hanky, but he tutted and waved her away. She edged backwards towards the door.

'I've got to go to work,' she said. He grunted.

'Aren't you going to work? Did you oversleep?' Her voice was hopeful, optimistic.

'I'm on holiday,' he said, voice muffled. Holiday? He never took holidays. Once, when she was a small child, they had stayed in a caravan at the seaside; there were pictures to prove it, she with a sun bonnet and bloomers to her knees. But since then, nothing. He worked all the time and never missed a day. Holiday?

'Buzz off then, didn't you say you had to go to work? Well, get going.' He pushed himself up on one elbow, forcing the words out. A fit of coughing overtook him. Jo watched, helpless and silent, as his body was racked with coughs, but his hands dismissed her impatiently. She could still hear him coughing as she left the house to walk through the cool morning to work, but as soon as she turned the corner and could hear him no longer, she put him out of her mind.

Jo spent the first few hours that morning with Sandra. They stacked pies, cut sandwiches, split breasts and wings off the hot greasy chickens Mr Rollings passed over in a steady, pungent stream. Sandra had long curly hair which she piled up under her blue hat; Sandra was loud and lively, good natured.

'What are you going to spend your wages on?' she asked Jo as they sat drinking tea during their break.

'I think I might use my money to go to a festival,' Jo replied.

Sandra looked startled at this news. 'What, one of them hippy festivals?' Sandra's eyes were round with horror. A lock of hair fell forward out of her hat.

'Yeah, why not?' answered Jo. She spoke fast, the words propelled like bullets out of her mouth.

'Jackie's asking her mum this weekend. There's one down in Derbyshire in a couple of weeks. She's got a tent, and we could always go by coach. Why not?' At the end of this speech she drew in a deep breath. Surprised, she hadn't realised that her mind was made up.

'But there's drugs and things at them festivals; my mum says they're not safe.' Sandra's voice shook, her face tinged with doubt.

'I thought you were the lively one,' said Jo, laughing. 'You're always going on about how you want a bit of adventure.'

'Yeah, but you don't know who you'll meet at them festivals, it's just not safe.' Sandra's usual carefree face crumpled into a frown.

'Maybe,' Jo conceded as she drained the dregs of her tea. It was no use getting into an argument with Sandra; there'd be no convincing her that festivals weren't full of drug fiends and mad rapists. They had fascinated her ever since she'd seen a production of *Hair*, down in Liverpool, with Jackie. Naked painted bodies had writhed on the stage while she sat stiff and unbending in her short tailored brown coat, black patent leather shoes and handbag. At the end of the show, as the audience leapt on to the stage to strip off their clothes, a man in a headband, fringed waistcoat and fringed trousers, pulled her arm and begged her to join them.

'Let it all hang out sister,' he'd shouted. But Jo was rooted to the spot, unable to move, and had clutched her handbag, tighter and tighter. Afterwards, it was as if she'd missed a chance to come alive.

Soon after, she and Jackie started braiding their hair. At Birkenhead market, they stocked up on curtain material which quick-fingered Jackie soon turned into dresses. On Jackie the dresses looked tropical, exotic. On Jo they looked like curtains. Something to do with Jackie's curves, she decided, and the sheen of her skin, compared to Jo's white-faced, beanpole looks.

'Hey, dreamer, you're not with us.' Sandra good-naturedly poked her in the ribs. 'Doesn't your mother mind you going down there?' she asked, puzzled. Jo hesitated, and was saved from spinning yet another story by the appearance of Mr Rollings.

'Can youse lovely girls help Nelly on the counter please?' he said. 'The rush's on,' he added, gleefully. His face shone at the thought of profits.

They rinsed their cups quickly, and sped down the grease-spattered staircase.

''Ere ya girls,' Nelly ordered them into position. 'Jo, you come this side of the counter and serve this queue here. San you stack the pies, we'll need to keep them coming. They'll go dead quick with this lot.'

Jo enjoyed serving behind the counter. It gave you a chance to get out of yourself, flirt, have a few laughs. She enjoyed the warmth of pies under her fingers, ripping off legs of whole chickens, squashing them on to greaseproof paper, pouring hot strong tea into cardboard cups.

Jo stood next to Nelly as she shoved pies into paper bags. She liked Nelly. Nelly was small, late middle-aged, with frizzy grey hair and a wide-boned face, the hardness of which cracked into a smile as soon as she spoke. She was like a tiny, withered nut, marked and lined by life. Her husband had recently had a stroke and sometimes she left early to look after him. But you never heard Nelly complaining. Once, after work, when Jo helped her carry shopping home, Nelly insisted she stay for a cup of tea. The bedroom door stayed shut.

'He gets embarrassed see, because of the paralysis – he slobbers down the front of his chin. He doesn't like to see too many people,' Nelly explained. Only that one time had Jo caught the cold light of despair in Nelly's eyes, and she had finished her tea and left, leaving Nelly to her privacy, giving her the respect with which she treated others, however young.

Jo rang up the till as she recalled Nelly's words of the previous week.

'It's great that you're getting an education – I wish I'd had one myself,' she'd said. Her face was wistful for a moment while she looked round the shops as if surprised to be suspended in this cage full of chicken pieces of strange shades of orange. Then her face cleared, like a rainbow brightening the sky.

'You keep on going girls, don't let anyone put you off, you get your exams, it's the only way out.'

That day, Nelly was as cheerful as always, bandying with the customers, exchanging a few words of comfort with the elderly woman who came in every week for 'A small piece of chicken, love.'

The rush passed quickly that day. They dished out pies, chicken pieces, cartons of hot soup. By late-afternoon, the smell of chicken grease was everywhere – in your hair, your overalls, your nose. At last, she and Sandra, dropping with tiredness, put on coats to leave. Nelly cornered them on the way out.

'Here you go, girls, I've divvied up the pies, there's five each, stick them in your bags, quick.' Grateful, Jo stuffed the pies into her bag. It would save cooking that night. She parted from Sandra, too tired to speak. Only as she reached her own front gate did Jo remember about her father. She shuddered. How would he be now? Still claiming he was on holiday?

The twins, small stick figures playing with friends, waved from further up the street. There was no sign of Eamon as Jo let herself in and put the pies straight into the oven. She knew the danger well. Once you took your coat off and collapsed, it was harder to get up.

She heard a low groan from the next room, poured two cups of tea and carried them in to where her father lay on the couch. It was almost as she expected. She wasn't even surprised – it was as if she'd been waiting for this moment. The room was dark and musty, the fire a small dead pile of ash. She opened the curtains. He flinched away from the dull grey light and silently accepted the tea. His skin looked flaky like paper, his breathing was stertorous and loud, his eyes bright blobs of pain. No point talking. Jo bent down to the grate and raked out the ashes, then built up a fire. Small flames licked the dark coals into life. As she put the guard on and rolled newspaper around the ashes, she saw that he had fallen asleep again, leaving the tea to grow a ring of cold skin.

Eamon crept in from upstairs, silent as a monk, and the twins came home ravenous. Jo busied herself in the kitchen, trying to forget the image of her father's still prone figure. But it seemed to fill her mind, like an old photograph rediscovered. They wolfed down pies, peas, potatoes, and afterwards Jo arranged a plate of the same for her father, then passed it to Pat to take in. Pat returned with the plate untouched.

'He doesn't want it,' she said bluntly. Her eyes were questioning, seeking reassurance. Jo blanked her out, and shared out the contents between them all. It was as if they were cannibals.

'What did my dad do today?' Jo ventured as they scraped up the remains of the glutinous gravy and tamed the last wild peas.

'Dunno,' answered Pat, 'I was playing out.' Pat's face remained hard and impassive as she looked away. Tina's bottom lip quivered.

'What's the matter with him?' she blurted out. 'Is he all right?'

'He's on holiday.' Silence. It felt as if they were marooned, no other houses close, no other people.

'So he says,' added Jo. Eamon snorted and walked out of the room, Pat stared at the floor. Tina began to sob, her shoulders heaving.

'Does that mean we'll go to the seaside?' asked Pat sarcastically, ignoring Tina.

'In March?' Jo laughed, and then they all fell about, hysterical, releasing the tension.

But later their mood grew sombre, and, in bed that night, Jo felt the cold grip of fear tighten in her belly. What would happen now? she wondered as she heard her father's wheezing echo through the house.

The chicken shop filled her week. By the end of each day, Jo's legs ached. The children ate pies until they were sick of them. She shopped in her break. Every day her father seemed worse. Each morning he rose later, the twins informed her, each night he lay on the living-room couch until the final dot disappeared on the TV, then dragged himself up to bed. On Wednesday she asked for food money. His hands tried to reach his pocket, then fell back against the pillows, empty.

'It's all right, I'll use my wages,' said Jo. On Thursday she asked him if should she call a doctor.

'What for?' he rasped, 'It's only a cold.'

Only a cold, only a cold. Time dragged, bones ached, but she got through the days. The old childhood magic beckoned – wish hard for a thing and it would come true. And what had she wished for?

'Why don't you die? Why don't you die?' Jo found herself saying in the shop. The customer, a regular, looked at her strangely.

'I knew you didn't like me, but this is ridiculous,' he said laughing, as Jo reddened in embarrassment.

On Saturday afternoon, in the lull after the rush, Mr Rollings told them to wash the walls at the back of the shop. They were brown with solid layers of grease, an accumulation of years. Sandra and Jo took a cloth, filled buckets with water and detergent and stood on two stepladders, to begin at the top. For a long while the walls refused to give up their grime. Only the water turned grey made them think that some muck had shifted. They perched on the ladder like two acrobats at the circus, and rubbed. The heat from the ovens rose in a great mass so that it pricked at their nostrils. As always, they talked.

'Are you going out tonight?' Sandra asked, pushing her hair back with her arm.

'I don't think so,' answered Jo. The cloth, like her body, felt slimy and greasy, as if it had been dipped in oil.

'Well, I'm going to the club with Liz, you can come if you want.'

'Thanks,' said Jo. The walls dissolved into a pale creamy colour like butter. Grease melted on the surface of the water.

'We've got a bottle of cider, we can drink it before we go.'

'No thanks, San, I think I'll stay in tonight and wash my hair,' she decided.

'Suit yourself,' Sandra looked disappointed. 'But you know where we'll be if you change your mind. You look like you could do with a good night out.'

'Maybe,' said Jo, and was saved from further discussion by Mr Rollings calling her back in to finish off the machines. They climbed down off their perches, emptied the buckets and went back into the front of the shop, now empty of customers. Mr Rollings, a self-important little man, was carrying the tray from a spit out to the kitchen. Jo was surprised to see him dirtying his hands. His job mainly consisted of telling others what to do, and carving up chickens. Nelly, Sandra and Jo were never allowed to do the carving.

'Youse ladies are too delicate,' he'd claimed once.

What a joke that myth was, Jo thought as she scraped off blackened bits of chicken flesh from an oven. The pieces dirtied your nails for days.

Mr Rollings stood and watched them, waving his arms about like a man directing traffic.

At last they finished, and Jo rushed out to breathe in great gulps of cold spring air. It had been raining, and the shopping centre glistened as if it had been polished.

'Look after yourself, love,' shouted Nelly. 'Enjoy yourself tonight.'

'You too,' shouted Jo, and waved. Jo knew that Nelly never left the house of a night because of her husband, but it was their standard parting.

Jo started home. Most shops had their grilles down, already closed. Rubbish blew haphazardly around the market square. A roadsweeper carefully swept some into a neat pile, the wind blew it away again. Lone dogs sniffed round plastic bags that spilt out from shops. A security guard passed her, cheerful in a chocolate-brown and yellow uniform.

'What's with your long face?' he asked. 'Don't worry love, it might never happen.'

Jo shuffled past the grey-shuttered shops, past the library where, years before, she'd queued since dawn with hundreds of other kids for the official opening. It had been like waiting for tickets to a football match, with thermoses of tea, blankets and periodic visits from parents. When the library finally opened at nine-thirty, a bouncer with shiny medals and bright military ribbons let them in to a light-filled cathedral of books. The library had plants, and private padded study boxes, and special new tickets to get books out. Jo sighed, remembering her wonder. Books had seemed the key to everything then. Books could take away pain, books could bring pleasure, fantasy, innocence. The library had become a haven, a safe harbour to berth in once a week. But now, with working Saturday, she hardly ever got there, and, besides, books didn't cover up everything any more. Books didn't cover up the rot, books didn't paper over the cracks. She glanced at the building as at a long lost friend, and crossed the main road to a private estate.

The houses were spacious, rambling, built with generosity, spare brick. Kids played on bikes out on neat pavements. When someone had first told her it was a 'private' estate, the word hadn't meant anything. She imagined the residents pulling curtains round their houses, or fences springing up, keeping them separate, apart. Now she knew what the word meant. The residents owned their houses. The residents could build extensions, sheds, porches, without asking the council. The residents could pass their houses on to their children.

The wide, clean streets seemed to narrow as she came into her own territory. Past the block of maisonettes, with the smashed-in windows and the broken-down drains, damp patches like great footprints all over the walls, the few families left living under siege. The council might knock the tops off the maisonettes, the local paper had hinted, turn them into houses. She tried to imagine them with their tops sliced off, like layered ice-cream. Why hadn't the council built houses in the first place?

The twins were in the kitchen when she got in, eyes bright with excitement like small lively animals.

'Can we go and stay at Margaret's tonight?' they caught her at once, before she sat down. 'She asked us to babysit for her.' Margaret was a neighbour up the road. The twins loved going there.

'You should see the baby,' said Tina, her face animated. 'She can pull herself round the furniture already, and she's only nine months.'

'That's nice,' said Jo without interest, as she put pies in the oven. They were dried out already from being on the counter all day. With sudden violence she swept them aside into the rubbish bin. They'd had pies four times that week already. She began to fry sausages, and slapped them around the pan.

'So is it all right if we go then?' Pat's face hung anxious, expectant, as Jo served up the sausages, burnt, black, funereal.

'I suppose so,' said Jo, through a mouthful of gristle. Pat looked eager to be gone, and really, Jo admitted, as she leant back in the chair, she didn't care what they did. They weren't small children any more, although she and Eamon still referred to them as 'the babies'.

'What's my dad eaten today?' The twins were almost out of the door at her question. It was a useless question, Jo knew. The answer was the congealed fried egg sitting on a plate on the draining-board, the half-filled, cold cups of tea. Heavy snores filtered through the partly open door. They heard Eamon walk downstairs, switch on the TV and shut the living-room door against them. The snoring grew muted under the drone of the TV. A tap dripped, the wind howled around the house.

'Go on then,' urged Jo, angry. 'If you're going, you better get a move on, it sounds like we're in for some rain.' The twins hesitated, guilt written on their faces. Rain squalls blew in as they banged the front door shut.

Eamon slid back upstairs, and the house grew silent save for snores. Jo pottered in the kitchen. She was frightened to go in the living-room, scared at what she might find. Would her father's body already be rotting away, ridden with maggots? Would the flesh fall off him? Would bluebottles eat him alive?

All week she'd immersed herself in work, but tonight she could see the house with a stranger's eyes, and it looked filthy and uncared for. Trying not to think of her father, she focused on grease-splattered cooker stains, layers of sticky dirt on the lino, curtains heavy with dust. Cobwebs covered every corner. In the food cupboard were a few ageing tins, two potatoes, green skin and sprouting eyes, a shrivelled-up onion. The cupboard smelt of disinfectant. Jo quickly shut the door and began to rub at a stubborn stain on the kitchen table with the rag that passed for a cloth. Her father had a thing about not buying cleaning cloths.

'Why waste good money,' he'd throw his arms out to ask, 'on things that are going to get dirty anyway?' Instead, a large box of ancient, ripped up sheets sat under the stairs. The rags were used until they smelt rank, then cast out. Jo stopped rubbing, the brown stain stared back. No matter how hard she tried, the place always looked dirty. It was like a black lead cloak around her shoulders, weighing her down at odd moments of the day. Jo threw the cloth down and sighed, smoothed out her skirt and flexed her tight-knotted shoulders. To lie flat without care on an airbed floating out to sea, sun burning into brown relaxed muscles, water soothing out ripples of pain, now that was a dream.

The image faded and instead, curious, she forced herself into the living-room. The fuzzy silent picture on the screen, lengthened and distorted like those in the Hall of Mirrors at Southport, took up part of her attention, but, out of the corner of her eye, Jo was aware of her father. The sound of his breath seemed to grow until it filled the whole room, a giant casting his spell. He lay on his back, as silent and still as a wounded animal, except for the rise and fall of his chest. Only his eyes seemed alive, bright and shining with fever. At times he leaned over sideways and, with great effort, sipped at a cup of water. Another cold cup of tea lay untouched under the couch. Jo wondered if she should take his temperature, but the thought of touching his pale, clammy flesh repulsed her. A smell of stale sweat permeated the room. They did not speak.

Jo turned off the TV and sat in the darkened room. It was like being in a cave, musty with only the glow of the died-down fire to illuminate the gloom. A dog barked, away in the distance. Jo shivered, rose up, and moved the thin blanket over her father. He said nothing. She stood at the door, awkward as always.

'I'm going to bed,' she said. 'Are you going?' He grunted, but did not turn his head. Jo hesitated for a moment, then walked up the dark, silent stairs. On the landing she paused. Should she say something to him? Do something? What could she do if he claimed it was only a cold? What was there to say? Through the frosted glass window she could make out vague, indistinct shapes in next-door's garden. 'Through a glass darkly,' the phrase repeated itself. Glass might shatter into millions and millions of tiny fragments of sparkling light and move through layers of endless space to stop suddenly, no longer whole. She was powerless to stop events, there were forces greater than her. She turned to go to her room, as a sudden gust of wind danced through the house and cold flurries of rain dashed against the windows.

Outside Eamon's room all was dark and quiet, as if he were asleep. Lonely, she ached to cuddle, talk, be near people. But she knew it was no point disturbing Eamon – he'd shout at her, tell her to get lost.

The bedroom seemed silent and empty without the twins; for once she missed their awkward adolescent bodies. In bed, she shivered under cold sheets and listened to the wind kick objects around the streets. There was laughter as people returned from the pub, and the noise of a can as it rolled along. Inside, their house felt like an island in a storm-lashed sea, far away from the rest of the world. It was a long time before sleep came.

Jo woke to cold rain splattering her cheeks, and a window blown open in the night. She dressed quickly and ran shivering into the kitchen. On with the kettle, wait while it boiled, then into the living-room for cups. There was a faint, sweet sickly smell in the air. Jo walked straight to the window and opened the curtains to another grey, dull day. She was aware of her father's bulk on the couch, but averted her eyes.

'Make the tea first, that's what I'll do,' she reassured herself. She remembered it was Palm Sunday. Reluctant to go back across the room, she leaned against the window. *And he rode towards Jerusalem on a donkey, and all around were crowds of people, happy, celebrating.* She'd have to pass her father.

The leaves on next-door's tree looked new, bright green,

vibrant. Soon it would be Easter, and long light days would come. Daffodils and new clothes and eggs and stones rolling out of caves on a hill and life would be reborn. She pulled her eyes away from the tree and rushed back into the kitchen, glancing neither right nor left. Safe there, she poured water into the teapot, took down a mirror and began to put on make up. Blue eyeshadow on the top lids, mascara on the lashes. Turning the mascara brush around, she smudged tiny dots of black under her eyes, the fashion with her and Jackie. Then came a second coat of mascara. The effect was spidery, whimsical. To look beautiful and mysterious today, that was the aim. All around was silence, and a knowledge that something was wrong, but Jo continued with her make up until new eyes, flirty and capricious, looked back. She heard Eamon get up, then go straight into the living-room.

'There's tea made,' she said. 'Ask my dad if he wants a cup.' Jo shouted, smudging her eyes. Luminous and sad, they stared out from the mirror as Eamon's voice floated back.

'He's dead.'

'Don't be stupid,' her own voice cracked an instant reply, coming as if from a million miles away. 'Don't be stupid.' Then the face in the mirror crumpled and tears black with mascara ran down her cheeks.

'He can't be dead, he can't be dead, he can't be.' She threw the mirror down and ran into the living-room. Eamon stood by the couch next to her father, who lay on his back, eyes closed, face lolled sideways, hooked nose prominent in the ashen face. His arms fell limply by his side, yet his legs were stiff and straight, and his chest, always so massive, seemed shruken, deflated. A small dribble of grey vomit, like gunge outpouring from an overflow pipe, fell from his mouth, staining the old maroon couch. Jo stared at the grey vomit, then turned her head abruptly away. The smell seemed more pronounced, a cloying smell that clung to your nostrils and made you want to plunge for fresh air and be sick. He wasn't dead, she didn't believe it. What if he sat up and criticised her, called her a whore for wearing make up, accused her of not even handling this, his death, right?

'I'll go and get an ambulance,' said Eamon decisively.

'No, you won't!' screamed Jo, alert now. 'You're not leaving me alone with him.'

'All right then,' said Eamon, calmly. 'You go.' He plonked himself down on the tattered old armchair next to the couch, drew out a comic from under the seat, then began to read as if today were a normal Sunday and nothing had happened.

'Go on, then, get going. I don't want to stay here for ever, he's beginning to smell.' Eamon's nose wrinkled as he pushed her towards the door. Jo resisted, reluctant to leave. Over the years she had spun elaborate tales of her mother working two shifts a day, concerned that no-one knew her secret. It helped that all her friends were from school, and a mile away from her immediate neighbourhood. Only Jackie had ever come home with her and, each time, Jo had said her mother was working. She had even managed to get Ellen Mack to believe that Rosy was still there from time to time. She refused to rise to Ellen's questions as to whether her mother's absences could be explained by the fact that she had found herself 'a fancy man'. Jo met these with silence. Eventually Ellen dropped the subject, to Jo's relief. She half expected her father to rise and demand a cup of tea; but no, the shell of him lay still, unmoving.

Down the street, through the windy wet Sunday morning, she flew. A few people stood at the bus stop, others huddled by the newsagent's, clutching great wads of papers. Jo reached the bottom of their street before it dawned on her that she was going to Jackie's house. Jackie's mother would know what to do, she'd had seven kids, she'd be able to help.

As Jo sped along, she was aware of people looking at her quizzically. She wiped away tears on the sleeve of her duffle-coat. By the time she reached Jackie's house she was puffing for breath, and racked by great sobs.

'Mrs Jones will know what to do,' she repeated to herself.

Mr Jones opened the door, in shirt sleeves and braces and baggy grey trousers. Jo had forgotten about him. He looked puzzled and lowered his eyes. Jo, speechless, became conscious of her unkempt clothes, her wild, uncombed hair, her coat done up wrong. She wiped her eyes; black streaks came off on her hand.

'Is Mrs Jones in?' He stood in the doorway, barring her entrance. 'Mrs Jones is in bed,' he said, with an air of finality that promised no leeway. Jo remembered now – Jackie had said her mum stayed in bed on a Sunday morning while her dad cooked breakfast of bacon, egg, tomatoes, fried bread.

'It's the only time she's got to lie in,' Jackie had told her, 'with us lot all week and the shopping on a Saturday.'

Jo turned to go. She couldn't disturb Mrs Jones, she'd have to go home. Mr Jones touched her shoulder.

'Here, Josephine, is anything the matter, girl?' and Jo realised that even he, a man, could see something was wrong.

Easy to say, 'No, it's all right,' keep her usual deadpan face and walk away, but words sprang out by themselves, dark, thudding, final. 'My dad's dead.'

He pulled her inside their sleepy, quiet, Sunday morning house and soon Mrs Jones rushed in, questioning her urgently as she combed out her hair.

'How do you know he's dead? Are you sure? What happened? How long ago? Where's your mother?'

Jo gave a mumbled, 'She's not there.'

'What do you mean she's not there?' Mrs Jones shook her, holding her by the shoulders, looking into her eyes.

'Where's is she, girl, where is she?'

'She's not there,' Jo repeated, and suddenly the relief of telling someone overwhelmed her. Tears welled up in her eyes.

'Has she gone away?'

'Hey, Jackie, come here. Where does Jo's mother work? She does shifts, doesn't she?'

'Yeah, but its Sunday, remember.' Jackie's voice came from a long way away.

'Did you ever see her?' The pair of them began whispering to each other, then Mrs Jones looked across with more sympathy. She thrust on a mac, scarf and boots and continued asking questions. Jo tried to concentrate and answer sensibly, but everything looked fuzzy and the words came out muddled.

'She's in shock,' whispered Mrs Jones. Then, 'Jackie,' she ordered, 'look after Josephine, and keep an eye on the kids. I'm going round to their house now.' She banged the door behind her and was out like a whirlwind.

'She's gone over the road to phone for an ambulance,' said Mr Jones ponderously, his words slow and awkward as the movement of a cow. Jackie, her dark hair hanging over her eyes, brought in sandwiches and refilled Jo's cup. They, normally so chatty, sat silent beside each other.

It seemed a long while later that Jo walked back home. Mr Jones had offered to walk with her and Jo, glad of the company, grew as silent as him. They walked very slowly, and everything she looked at seemed out of focus. She couldn't remember how much she'd told him and concentrated on placing one foot in front of another. The insides of her pumps were wet. Although the rain had stopped now, dampness hung in the air.

'Pride is the worst fault,' he said suddenly. 'You should have told someone, we would have helped you. You should have asked for help. We had no idea your mother wasn't at home.' Jo tried to concentrate on his words, but her mind was a hazy wash of unformed thoughts. Pride? How could she have told anyone? Would her father still be at home? Would they have moved him? Would the place feel different?

They arrived at her gate; a small crowd of kids milled round the ambulance outside. Tina, amongst them, grabbed hold of Jo's arm and looked up, beseechingly.

'What's happened Josephine?' she asked, her pale face even whiter than usual.

'He's dead,' said Jo. She licked the words with relish like a cat and pushed Tina away. It felt good to hurt Tina, her father's favourite. Ignoring her sister, she followed Mr Jones as he marched into the house. Inside the kitchen, Mrs Jones held on to their battered brown teapot. The kitchen was tidy, the previous night's dishes put away. Eamon was nowhere to be seen. She could hear someone walking backwards and forwards upstairs. She supposed it was him.

'Oh, where's your dishcloths, Jo?' Mrs Jones asked cheerfully, as if it were a normal day and she'd dropped in to visit. Jo felt a hot flush of shame in front of these strangers. She indicated the cupboards.

'There's some sheets in there,' she said. Then added very quickly, 'We haven't got any dishcloths.' Mrs Jones betrayed surprise, then her kind face lifted again.

'Never mind, I'll get Jackie to bring a few round later.' She began to bustle about with cups and teapot.

Two burly men in navy uniforms and pale shirts with shiny polished buttons stood against the wall as they filled in a form. Behind them, on the living-room floor, lay a stretcher covered with a clean white sheet. The lump underneath looked like a mummy in a museum exhibition.

'How old was he, love?' The ambulanceman, with dark curly hair and kind blue eyes, glanced up, pen poised, his foot wedged against the door.

'Can you hear me love? How old was he? What's your name, girl?' He seemed impatient to be off. A wave of disinfectant mixed with the familiar sickly smell wafted towards Jo. The sheet looked cool and comforting, she wanted to climb under it.

'I don't know,' answered Jo. He'd think she was stupid. There were so many things she didn't know. She drew in breath to prepare herself.

'Is he dead?' she asked, the words hard and tacky. There was a long silence. The man lowered his eyes and shrugged his shoulders. He glanced at his colleague, then at Mr Jones.

'We can't really say,' he answered at last, so low she strained to hear it. Then he reached down to pick up the front of stretcher. His mate took up the back.

'What a stupid, stupid answer,' Jo thought as she watched them manoeuvre through the door. Of course he was dead, it only needed him to say it to make it official. Why wouldn't he say it?

The men edged their way down the path. A door banged, the small crowd dispersed, children wandered off. Mrs Jones scrubbed away at the grey dribble on the couch, threw the curtains open wide, shined the windows, lit a fire. Jo stared into the flames. There were comings and goings, neighbours calling, whispered consultations in the kitchen. Mr Jones left without a word, Mrs Jones, with her sleeves rolled up, laid into the house.

Late in the afternoon, Jo stared as a key turned in the front door. When she turned round, it was her mother, grown older, with wrinkles like small spiders cracking through her make up, hair streaked with grey. Mrs Jones returned to the living-room, arms full of papers. The younger woman put the papers down and blushed, embarrassed.

'I was just looking for anything official,' Mrs Jones said stammering.

'They asked if we had his birth or marriage certificate. And there might be insurance,' she added, lamely.

Jo's mother ignored the intruder.

'Hello, Josephine,' she said, as if she'd only been away for a few minutes.

'What's happened? Sam had his arm discreetly on her shoulder, as if to show to whom she belonged. Upstairs, the ceiling vibrated as Eamon rocked on his bed. Outside, excited cries of children caught at the air. The world was alive, outside. In here, the air was leaden, thick as mud.

'Well, Josephine,' said her mother in her best telephone manner, 'what's happened?'

'You know what's bloody happened,' snapped Jo, hating her mother's hypocrisy, coming here with her fancy man as if she still owned the place. Sam's face twitched as he tried to look serious, but a smile cracked round the corners of his chin. Jo knew then that they were glad, and hated them for it, with their tight-enclosed coupledom and their air of good times. She pushed against the table, and a cup crashed on the floor. Mrs Jones crouched down to pick it up.

'You know what's happened. He's dead.' Jo's voice was wooden.

'Don't let her see I care, don't let her see I care,' she thought to herself. 'I don't wanna stay in this house with you. I hate you, I hate you both – there, the words were out before she could help it.

Jo ran to the door, blind with tears. Her mother grasped at her. Jo flinched from her touch.

'Leave her, she's had a shock,' were the last words Jo heard in Mrs Jones' low, sad voice.

It was dark when Mrs Jones came to her again. Jo had fallen asleep in the warm dusty airing-cupboard, amongst the spiders and cobwebs which normally frightened her so much. She stretched cramped limbs and felt her face creased and lined. She'd dreamed of her father. They'd been on a train together and she'd shouted for him to get off, but he'd taken no notice. Awake, she blinked her eyes. They smarted with tears.

'It's all right, Josephine,' said Mrs Jones. 'I've been talking to your mum. She's agreed it might be best if you stay round my house for a few days, until you settle down, like.'

Jo felt like a puppet suspended from strings as they stalked round the house together gathering up clothes, toothbrush, a book. As they left, she walked past her mother without speaking.

That night she curled up in a chair in front of the Jones' fireplace. The house was full of children, warmth, good food. They'd all been kind and left her alone, as much as you could in a house full of kids. The smallest boys rushed in to say goodnight, all clean and shining and peppermint breath. Peter, the youngest, clung on to his mother, who was trying to do the crossword down the other end of the room. Then he circled round Jo, curious like a cat.

'Is your dad dead?' he asked at last, a smile on his lips.

'Yes,' Jo answered slowly, supposing it to be true. His mother stormed over.

'I told you to leave poor Josephine alone,' she shouted. 'She's got enough to think about without you bothering her. Now get to bed.' Jo didn't mind. It was as if nothing could touch her any more. She studied the fire. There, fantastic creatures breathed flames of red and orange and blue. Their great long tongues lashed the coals. She was almost, almost content.

Later that evening, Mrs Jones insisted on giving Jo two tablets. 'Better to get a good night's sleep than to lie there worrying. I always use them myself – the doctor gives me them.'

Jo, curious, swallowed one and slipped another to Jackie. She thought of the next day. Tomorrow she'd go back to work, tell them what had happened. Mr Rollings would insist she take a few days off, but Jo didn't want to. She wanted to immerse herself in brown greasy walls and chicken breasts and legs and hot soup and warmth and people chatting. She didn't want to go back to that cave of a room and that sickly sweet smell and the lonely wind as it howled through the curtains.

The tablets began to take effect as she and Jackie giggled their way up to bed.

'To me, my hope in ages past,' sang Jackie.

'And me to him doth pray,' Jo joined in. The pair of them

61

collapsed, hysterical, halfway up the stairs. Mrs Jones stormed out, furious.

'You're waking Robert up, he's just gone off!' she yelled, her hand upraised to Jackie. Jo felt ashamed. Mrs Jones had done so much for her, and now here she was making more work. The older woman's face softened as she turned towards her.

'Look, Josephine, I'm surprised at you. I know you've had a terrible shock, but you've got to go to bed. You really need your sleep.'

'Yes, Mrs Jones,' Jo said meekly, and walked quietly up. She sat on the bed to wait for the bathroom. The room was cold, neat, small, with matching pink coverlets for Jackie and her younger sister who was already asleep in the top bunk. Her clear olive skin and dark hair were framed against the pillow. Jackie returned clean-faced in slippers and nightie, and Jo took her turn in the bathroom. She tried to quiet the rising excitement in her stomach as she closed the door behind her. Pink tiles, air lemony fresh, bath clean; it spoke of order, caring, ordinariness. More than anything else, Jo wanted to be ordinary, and live in a house with toilet rolls and air-freshener and food in a fridge and proper cooked breakfasts. A washing-machine maybe. She washed her face methodically, soaping her hands in the sweet-smelling lather, and stared in the mirror for signs of change. Her face was much the same but haunted, expectant, as if something momentous were about to happen.

'Come on Jo!' shouted Jackie from the bedroom, 'I wanna put the light out,' and then Jo flopped into bed, toes warm and cosy against Jackie's back. Perhaps everything would work out at last.

'Maybe now I'll be able to stay on at school after all,' were the last thoughts in her mind as she sank into the deep soft pillow.

Three days later, it was the day of her father's burial. Jo was in a café in town. She hadn't gone to the funeral.

'Are you sure, Josephine, are you sure?' her mother had asked repeatedly. 'I've got a black coat for you if you do wanna come.'

Instead, in the evening, rather than going home to her mother and the kids, and to curled up white, sliced sandwiches and bottles of beer in front of the TV, she'd opted to go out with

Jackie. It felt vaguely sacrilegious on the day of his burial, but she was in a defiant mood.

The café, El Kabbala, sounded exotic. They ordered two coffees, hot and bitter with grounds floating in them. Jo stirred in two sugars. Jackie was dressed in a black short dress, her hair braided, red and pink beads round her neck. Jo had a short, bright red dress, plain. When she moved, she knew, it hung tight against her bottom. They sipped their coffee and looked around. The café was full of mirrors, and triangular, thirties-style lamps, dimmed. Two old men sat at the front, slurping at tea. The proprietor was Somali – tall, thin, graceful, with a slight Liverpool accent.

'We'll just make eyes,' said Jackie, and they fixed their eyes on a group of four young men sitting in the corner. The group was loud and raucous but, occasionally, one with long dark hair and dark blue eyes would turn round and stare at Jackie.

'Make him look, make him look,' said Jo under her breath, 'and please God let me stay on at school.' Then, slowly, as if by magic, the fair-haired young man she'd focused on, with eyes as pale as the sea, turned round and fixed his glance on her. They locked eyes for an instant. 'It works,' thought Jo, 'it works. Damn my father.'

Hospital, Central Liverpool, November 18 1982. Morning.

It was morning when Jo woke again, with the taste of memories still upon her, like the remnants of honey on a spoon. She sighed heavily and stretched out her legs.

A brush scratched against her feet, like a small hungry animal wanting to be fed. She sat up with a start, expecting Eamon and the twins. Instead, she saw a nurse with a broom in her hand.

'Oh, I'm sorry, love, I didn't mean to wake you. Try and gerra bit more rest if you can. I was just cleaning up after the breakfast round.'

Jo forced herself awake to watch the young nurse finish sweeping, wash her hands and deftly straighten the bed. The nurse hardly looked out of school. Her face shone with rude good health. Jo felt old and worn out beside her as she folded up the blanket and drew the chair back in place. Her own body, in thermal vest and leggings, smelt sweaty in the warm, dry air, her back felt bruised and twisted. She checked her mother. No change. Still the merest rise of chest through bedclothes, still the faintest whoosh of air as it entered her nostrils. Her mother's hands lay splayed out beside her, useless as dead piano keys. Two nurses arrived. Expertly, they turned and washed her unresponsive body. Breakfast, Jo decided. After all, she had no idea when Eamon and the twins would arrive and there was nothing more she could do.

On her way to the canteen, Jo grew puzzled. There was something odd about the hospital this morning. Nurses, armed with mops and brushes tackled the floors, a job normally reserved for cleaners. Jo wondered what was happening. But as she walked down the pale grey corridors, through the old part of the hospital the public hardly saw, past pink rubbish bags and full green bags of linen, she realised it must be a work-to-rule over the ward closures.

On the first floor she spied a commotion through double glass doors. Men wheeled enormous cameras and other men with mikes and earphones gestured messages across a ward. A tall, suntanned man with greased back hair, aristocratic features which betray good food and money, addressed the cameras. His voice oozed authority and came from somewhere way back in his throat.

'And I want to say how grateful I am to all of you who have continued to work and who are doing such a magnificent job in such trying circumstances. Together, we will keep this hospital functioning. We will not be held to ransom.'

A few grey-suited administrators clapped politely as the important visitor shook an elderly lady's hand. A young nurse, burdened by a trolley laden with discarded food and dirty dishes, leaned against the door and rested for a moment. Fatigue reflected on her face, she held herself stiffly as if in pain.

'All right for some.' Her eyes shifted towards the visitor. The elderly lady held her hand aloft as if she'd been touched by a saint.

'I wonder what they paid her for that,' said the nurse.

'She looks like she'll never get over it.' Jo laughed. The nurse clanked along the corridor, her thin frame appearing too insubstantial to push the heavy trolley. Jo continued towards the canteen. She heard shouts at the window and saw banners wave, a megaphone, a man on a box. Another nurse went past, tutting in disapproval at the crowd outside. By the time Jo reached the canteen the air was electric with excitement, with office staff up for an early break.

'I've got it in for them cleaners.' The speaker was dressed in a smart tweed skirt and pearl-buttoned cardigan. 'They're just conning us. They know us lot couldn't come out, not us that keeps the records and handles the money. I mean, the hospital would collapse if we did, wouldn't it love? Selfish load of bloody scivers,' she went on, 'some of them get more than we do.' The woman looked around for approval. Her office mates murmured assent, punctuating their remarks with little clicks of sympathy. Jo caught the woman's eyes, then looked away. You traitor, she told herself, you should answer back, argue, not let her get away with it. The hospital workers were right; and if wards shut there'd be less work for this stupid woman, didn't she realise that? But tiredness clawed at Jo like a rangy beast. Each bone hung loose and weary. She turned away, silent.

In the canteen she was handed a plate chipped at one side, with a rasher of bacon, a dollop of scrambled egg and a piece of hard fried bread slapped on to it before she could protest.

'Come a bit earlier next time love,' said the large black woman behind the counter.

'We don't usually serve breakfast this late. But you're lucky today – there's a lot left.'

'No bloody wonder,' thought Jo, as she stared at the dried out deposits on her plate. But she smiled gratefully at the woman and held out a cup for the dirty grey slop that passed for tea. She sat alone at a tiny, crockery-filled table. The air was thick with smoke. It was ten o'clock.

She was on her second cup of tea when a hand gripped her shoulder.

'Josephine,' Jo swivelled round, as if stabbed in the stomach. No-one but her family ever called her Josephine. She'd been Jo since leaving home at eighteen, and she wasn't ready to become Josephine again.

'Josephine.' They were all there – Eamon her brother, and

Pat and Tina the twins. Her eyes searched over them, looking for signs of ageing, change. Eamon still had thick dark hair but his hairline was receding more, like the tide going out from the sea, and tiny lines skirted his intense grey eyes. He squinted at the cigarette smoke. His eyes had grown heavy-lidded and baggy since the last time she'd seen him and his belly had become flabby. Pat, dressed smartly in a pink jacket and trousers, had clear skin and eyes. Tina was pale and drawn as always, pasty faced, skinny legged, with a small neat lump of a belly. She was seven months pregnant.

'What happened to yous lot?' Instantly Jo addressed them in the plural, a gestalt creature with arms, legs, spines connected. Like worms with their heads sliced off, her family regrouped, regrew. It had been a year since she'd last seen the twins.

'I was waiting for you to come. I tried your house, Pat, loads of times, but there was no answer. Tina's as well.' Jo faced Pat and Tina, ignored Eamon. He had no phone number anyway, and she wasn't quite sure where he was living now. Eamon could never be relied on in emergencies, you could never get hold of him. But Pat?

'I was at work,' said Pat. 'I don't get in till seven'. There was unspoken criticism in her voice. 'And Tina had a hospital appointment. She's seven months you know. And she had to get someone to look after Jamie.' Jamie was Tina's first child. Jo felt Pat's comments were full of barbed innuendos. The implication was that she, Jo, didn't think enough about others.

'And I was in the pub.' Eamon leaned forward. 'I didn't get the message till late last night.' He defied her to say anything. Already Jo felt as if a whirlwind had hit her. The strain of being in hospital hit her suddenly. A nerve in her shoulder twitched, a bolt of pain travelled down her spine. An image of a perfect round circle in a field of wheat flashed into her mind. Scientists had recently examined whole fields with flattened down circles. Some said it was supernatural, some said it was just the wind. She would like to stand in one such perfect, cool, calm circle, untouched, untouchable.

'Anyway, how's Martin?' asked Pat. 'And Bobby? He must be growing up.'

'Yes, he's five now. You know what he said when I told him I had to come up to Liverpool?'

'What?'

'He asked did his grandmother still live in a swimming-pool? He thinks she lives in a swimming-pool, not Liverpool.'

Pat gave a wry smile. 'Kids say some funny things. Remember that time when you showed him the picture of a wombat from his cousin in Australia and he told the children in nursery his cousin was a wombat?'

'Yeah, he's funny.' The three of them laughed, together; Eamon walked on in front, silent.

'Anyway, worrabout my mother? How is she?' Pat moved closer as Jo filled in details. At every major word – stroke, damage, unconscious, Tina flinched, her hands clenched protectively round her belly. Pat's face grew grave and thoughtful. Eamon remained impassive. They walked back to the ward, silent. Eamon ground his cigarette into the floor, then lit another. Jo stared at large 'No Smoking' signs on the walls. Eamon's hands twitched. There was a faint odour of beer in the air. Had he been drinking already? Or was it the after-effects of the night before? She couldn't tell with him. Ever since they were kids, he'd been first at everything – first to drink, first to smoke, first to nick from Woolworth's. She was the little miss goody goody; clean, upright, with a reputation to uphold. He was the black sheep, the rebel. She was cloaked in the role of the boring, moral older sister; he'd helped wrap her in it.

They walked towards her mother.

'I don't think she's in pain,' said Jo, loudly. Tina started at the groans which came from behind curtains in the next bed. They arrived to find a new nurse taking her mother's temperature. The nurse shook the thermometer, wrote down a note on a clipboard attached to the bed. She frowned.

'Are these relatives?' she demanded, thin lips pursed.

'Yes,' said Jo meekly, like a naughty six-year-old. She watched the shock on the twins' and Eamon's faces as their eyes lapped her mother, who seemed to have grown frailer, more insubstantial since last night, as if she were already crumbling into dust.

'Well, you can only have two visitors at a time in this unit. Rules, you know.'

'But there are four of us,' Jo blurted out before she could help it. She wanted to shout.

'And your mother only dies once, you bitch,' but she didn't. One, two, three, four, keep your temper ever more.

'You'll not have four in here,' said the nurse, firmly. 'Sister's orders. There'd be no room for staff if an emergency rose.'

She replaced a chair in its position and hurried out of the room, leaving them stunned behind her. They stared stupidly at each other, blinking in the light like owls awake at the wrong time. Eamon broke the silence.

'I'll go, I'm starving anyway, I'll go.'

'No, you stay,' Jo pulled out the chair for him. 'You've only just come, I'll go out with Tina.'

'Yeah, let's go to see my mate up in the maternity ward – we can have a look around,' said Tina eagerly. 'Get genned up for when I come in.'

'We may as well take it in shifts,' said Jo. 'All right.'

Pat looked bemused at the thought of staying with Eamon but lolled back in her chair with a resigned air. The nurse from the night before walked in, and smiled ruefully in the direction of the door.

'One of yous lot has got to go. I'm sorry. Rules.' She shrugged her shoulders.

'It's all right' said Jo. She felt sorry for this nurse. It was the other one she didn't like.

'Don't worry love,' said Tina. 'A couple of us'll go.' The nurse seemed reassured by Tina's belly, as if a pregnant woman couldn't make trouble. She looked grateful. Eamon planted himself beside the bed. His eyes shone unnaturally bright. Pat, opposite, opened a magazine, her eyes shifting towards their mother. Tina pulled her head away. She linked Jo's arm as they left the ward. They walked in silence for a long time, Jo's pace adjusting to her sister's. Jo felt the warmth of Tina's arm. All she could think of was Eamon. What if Eamon tried to pull out the drip?

'Why stay alive if you're a vegetable?' he'd asked once, on one of those rare occasions when they'd made time to speak to each other. The old words hung in the air, a silent threat, as she and Tina made their way out of the safe, dim calm of the unit, up to the other wing of the hospital.

He's changed, my brother, that's for sure. He's fatter, older, paler skinned, hair stringing out on top of his head. He does not say as much. Normally it was off-the-cuff remarks, one-liners, flip sayings that cut you with his tongue. She, Pat, my sister, has clear pink skin, and shining, well-groomed hair. Have I shrunk, I wonder, or is she taller? Tina's so white and ill-looking – I can feel her bones through my arm. I want to take her, fill her with vegetables and fish, and make her breathe pure country air.

They asked about my mother. The drip gave its liquid in spasms, like a baby being rationed.

'Do you think she's in pain?' they asked. Pat's eyes grew sad – in adulthood she is the softest of us all, still the one least tainted by our childhood. She's generous to my mother while I'm mean, full of hurt. She touches my mother's hands, my mother's head.

'No, I don't think she's in pain,' I answered. Or at least I hope not. We walked the ward. I had an urge to laugh suddenly, to start a madcap dance of geriatric wheelchairs, to upset this house of clinical severity. But no, after our meeting in the café we walked po-faced, as if in a church, as we approached my mother's bed.

'Oh, put her teeth in,' said Pat, and flinched, unable to bear the pink hard gumminess of her.

'No,' I said, 'she might swallow them; the nurse told me.' I didn't believe that, however, I had no idea where the teeth were. I think it's easier for the staff to leave them out. Besides, she cannot eat or talk. When you're old, your mouth champs at air and nobody, nobody understands.

I walk with Tina. The nurses wear tight-fitting uniforms with metal belts clasped round their waists – the snake belts of my childhood. Pale, lilac, with peaked hats tied with hairpins. Most are neat, tidy, unfussy, only letting the smallest tendrils of hair escape from their hats. I must concentrate, take care, pay attention. Details, that is all I can absorb.

Pat, Kirkby, Spring 1971.

Pat was twelve when the blood started coming. It would be dark blood that came at night, like childbirth, Jenny Wong had warned her, and it felt that painful! She awoke to sticky legs and cramps in the gut, unable to make out shapes in the dark. She rose and walked round and round the room with her legs crossed. Tina and Jo slept, scrunched up, the bedclothes wound round them. Pat's knickers chafed and rubbed. She braced herself and tapped faintly on her mother's door. She took a sharp breath in. Her mother hated being woken.

'What's the matter?' The voice was surprisingly gentle. 'Come in.'

Her mother sat back against the pillows, with giant rollers sticking out from her head. The pillow beside her was empty.

'Sam's on night duty,' she said at Pat's surprise. 'He won't be back until morning.' The yellow-eyed clock ticked on in the silence. Outside, darkness and fear reigned. Pat shivered. She plunged in, swimming into a tide of words.

'I've started my period, Mum, I've started.' She sniffed, on the edge of tears, angry at herself for being so vulnerable.

'Yeah, I can see.' Her mother stared at Pat's legs where a thin strand of dark sticky liquid ran down.

'Go and get a towel from the drawer, put it on and get into bed with me.' Pat moved quickly towards the chest of drawers. No point pretending she didn't know where the towels were. She often stole in with Tina and they practised with the belt over their school uniforms, holding the soft white bulkiness of the towels between their legs. She picked up the packet, and handed it to her mother.

'What are you giving it to me for, you daft bugger, you? I don't need it, stick it on yourself.'

Pat lifted her nightie and adjusted the towel inside her knickers. She didn't dare ask for a belt. Awkward as an elephant beside her mother, she stumbled. Her mother was dainty, thin, delicate-looking. Pat felt like a mass of blubber compared to her. Her mother seemed angry. She puffed hard on a cigarette as Pat shifted from one foot to another. Then her hardness seemed to float away with the smoke.

'Come here, you stupid bugger, you, get into bed besides me. Sam won't be back tonight anyway, you might as well stay here.' Pat remembered that Sam had been working as a security guard for a few weeks.

It was the first time Pat had been in her mother's bed for years. Ever since that terrible day when her father was carried out stiff and cold, out through the door, out to the white ambulance waiting like a vulture out in the street, while she stood with Tina in a crowd of children as thick as flies, Sam had occupied the space in her mother's bed exclusively. She hesitated, then slid down under the warmth of the blankets and stretched her toes.

Bony as a chicken, her mother edged close, leaned over and adjusted the blankets. Pat felt her shoulders relax as she too sank back. It was like being a small child again, when everything was safe, before the world cracked open like an egg.

Her mother switched off the elderly bedside lamp and began to talk. In the dark, with the grey splats of rain falling down from the sky, and the clawing at Pat's belly, and the rest of the world asleep, her mother talked.

'I was a chubby little thing when I started, you know, just like you.' Pat leaned against her in disbelief. Her mother's face was as cavernous as a skull, heavy dark shadows stamped her eyes.

'I was scared when I started, you know . . . all that blood. I remember telling my aunty. She just gave me an ST and said "Mind not to smell". I was so scared.'

Her mother lay back and looked at the ceiling. Her face wrinkled.

'There was no point telling her I was scared. She was like a dragon. You couldn't get close to her. It wouldn't have worked.'

Pat cuddled closer, proud. Her mother wasn't a dragon. Her mother was real, and of now.

'So I put on an ST and went to bed. In the morning when I woke up it was down by my ankles and the sheets were splattered with blood. She went mad and made me wash them all by hand.' Her mother stopped. Her lips grew tight and thin at the memory. Angry, she wiped away a tear.

'Let's go to sleep.'

Pat lay awake for a long time that night, as the blood oozed out. It felt like a miracle, this talk, lying in bed.

Next morning, her mother was as bad tempered and removed as ever; no acknowledgement that she'd let out secrets, come closer. But it was two days later that the crunch came. Pat was home from school for her dinner. The packet of towels was at an end, but the dark blood kept coming. She cornered her mother alone. Sam was asleep upstairs.

'Mum, can I have some more sanitary towels? I've just used them all up.' And the blood's still coming, and the blood's still coming.

Her mother had red eyes and a cigarette in her hand. She'd been crying.

'No, I haven't got any more. That's all there is.'

'Well, can I have some money then, to buy some more? I can get them on the way to school.' If she took her bag and went early, there'd be time to nip into the toilets before class.

'No, you can't.'

Her mother's voice was dead, wooden.

She inhaled deeply on her cigarette and passed a plate of spaghetti over.

'Here's your food, get it down you, the others are late today.' Her face was blank, hard, uncaring. 'I haven't got any money,' she added.

'But I'm still bleeding. I've got my period. What do you expect me to do?'

'I don't sodding care what you do. Do what you like.' Her mother turned her back and carried on smoking.

Pat tried to eat the spaghetti but the salty moistness of it stuck in her throat. It felt like swallowing tadpoles.

Her mother lit another cigarette. Pat dashed to the toilet, away from her cruel hard figure.

The toilet paper was hard. It would make her blister, and catch nothing. She scrunched it up in a ball and threw it down the toilet bowl. Then, from the airing-cupboard, she extracted an old, ripped up sheet and stuffed it in her knickers.

That afternoon she walked to school, stiff as a pregnant duck. In the classroom, she sweated, terrified in case the teacher asked her to go up to the front of the class and write on the board. If a boy got close, he would smell her. Jammy rag, jammy rag, he'd chant and they'd gather round her as if she was a witch at the stake. They'd know her secret.

She was saved that evening by Jo lending her money for the towels. She stuffed the sheet under the pillow and promptly forgot about it. There was a faint smell of fish.

A few mornings later her mother stormed in. To Pat, her period now seemed part of the past, something you went through to brag about in the playground, to say 'When I started' so that you too could be part of a club. So it was a shock when her mother held the now foetid sheet aloft and, at first, Pat didn't realise what it was.

'What are you playing at, leaving this lying round, you dirty bugger?'

Sam's voice echoed from behind.

'You dirty cow.'

'Don't think you're staying on at school, you know, you're leaving as soon as you're able. We're not having another one like that bloody sister of yours lying round staying on for ever. She's cost us you know.'

'It's only, it's only . . . I'm sorry,' Pat managed, but then they laid into her like animals possessed, and kicked and punched her in the legs, the arms, the ribs, the side. She fell down to the floor, but her mother kept kicking.

In the midst of pain, as Pat held her head for protection, she had the feeling that although nothing had been explained, all this was nothing at all to do with her. She tensed herself against the blows, and waited.

As suddenly as it had come, the strength wilted out of her mother, her blows became light-fingered glances, insect wings beating against the skin. Pat stretched up and unfolded her body, now numb and bruised. As she stretched she saw, for a few seconds only, a glimpse of fear in her mother's eyes, before Sam led her gently away. Through her own discomfort and soreness, Pat staggered up the stairs to the sweet, dark, safety of her room.

4

Jo stared over the side of the enormous ship, down at her mother and sisters as they waved. Already their faces appeared to be growing smaller, even though the ship hadn't yet moved. A biting wind blew up from the water, the air bitter against her hot cheeks. Jo's stomach gurgled. She regretted the whisky her family had insisted she finish in the bar near the docks earlier that evening.

'I've always loved my daughter,' her mother had announced loudly to the pub at large, 'and I hope in God's name she'll come back safe and sound.' She hadn't said from where. It was as if naming Ireland would bring bad luck on them, remind her of Jo's father, bad memories. Sam, on the other hand, had no such qualms.

'Drop a bomb on the lot of them,' he'd said in a stage whisper, 'that'll solve the Irish problem.' In the dockside bar, people stared purposefully into their glasses and tried to ignore him. Soon after, Jo and her family had left in a ragged procession down to the ship. Jo had walked ahead but each in turn had linked arms with her, as if, after years of not touching, it was important to force themselves on her now. Jo was surprised at the display of feeling. Normally her family articulated nothing except anger.

The steps were wheeled away from the side of the ship and the blue hooded walkway hung empty in the air, connected to nothing.

'This is it,' thought Jo as she saw ropes untightened and heard the clank of chains. The ship's horn hooted and a cheer went up from the deck.

The engines roared into life, like a lion roused from its slumber. It had been so strange and rushed, the decision she'd made to go to Belfast. Hardly a rational decision, she recalled, rather a drunken inspiration after working a twelve-hour day in the Butlin's hamburger bar, her home for the summer.

'You must be mad,' Tony the cook had shouted next morning when she told him of her decision. She took the money, he fried hamburgers, their conversation stopped every time a customer appeared. They'd been going out together for a few weeks and spent hours discussing politics, hours wrestling on the bed, trying to get different parts of themselves into each other; neither very successful. Tony was in the IMG; any strike, demonstration or sit in and Tony was there. Forever lecturing her on her dreaminess and lack of awareness, and with an Irish father himself, he didn't mince words.

'You must be off your head to apply to Belfast. They'll have you, you know, they can't get anyone to go over there now, not after internment. No one in their right mind wants to go. Why do you wanna do a stupid thing like that?'

Jo hadn't really known why. Some connection with her father, she suspected, with his songs about 'Oul' Ireland', and the story floating round that he was really Irish, and the photo of him with his wide-boned face, and his uniform with the harp on, rifle across his chest.

'And didn't he fight for Ireland, Mum? Wasn't he Irish in spirit?' she'd pestered her mother. She'd desperately wanted to have a trace of Irish blood.

Her mother denied it a bit too vehemently. You always knew when there was something to hide.

'Liverpool as they come,' she pronounced. 'A romantic idiot in his young days, just thought he was Irish, daft like the lot of them. How could he be Irish if he was born in Liverpool? Just 'cos the family further back were.' She'd changed the subject and would speak no more. It was as if the past was a dark hole which threatened to swallow her up.

After posting off the application to Belfast, Jo had forgotten all

about it, lulled into calm by mind-numbing work. This illusion
ended when Tony was sacked for sailing a Pleasureland boat and
eight illegal passengers across to the Magic Isle at two in the
morning. Suddenly the first relationship she'd really built up was
snatched away, and she had a future to plan. It was as if she'd
been expecting it: the instant she reached out to people, wham,
they were gone. Tony camped out on the beach for a few days
with the other sacked Butlin's staff and Jo brought them food
from the café, but they couldn't keep it up of course, five
squashed into a two-person tent; it was the rain that finished
them. When Tony told her he was leaving, the news cut her like a
knife. With him it had been different from other boys, as if the
jigsaw pieces of her body and mind could slot together at last,
instead of being at permanant odds to each other.

'I've had enough of being a summertime hippy,' he said as
they walked along a wet cold beach. A driving wind, portent of
autumn, blew up off the sea. Summer was ending. A man played
a mournful guitar tune, a woman held an umbrella over him.
'I'll have to go back home, at least I'll be dry there. I'll get a job
for a couple of weeks before I go back to college, there'll be
something going. We'll keep in touch, you'll not get rid of me
that easy.'

He'd left so quickly she wondered later if she'd imagined him.
Afterwards, she couldn't remember his face, or hands which had
probed her, or eyes which had laughed at her. She couldn't
remember his smell, or imagine what they'd ever talked about.
Only a small photograph and a lock of hair confirmed that he'd
existed, and later, letters that ended in mysterious acronyms like
BURMA and SWALK. So she was glad, on the whole, when
Butlin's closed for the summer. There were too many memories.

Back home, in early September, the message was soon clear.

'I thought you were going to university; were the first words of
Sam's greeting. 'You told us you'd left home. I thought you were
supposed to be clever.' He'd now been entrenched with her
mother for two years and acted as if he owned the place.

'There's no room for you here, you know, not since you left
school. We don't have to be responsible for you any more. You're
eighteen, big enough and soft enough to look after yourself.' He
had the same phrases as her father. But he was not her father.

'Well, I don't know if I've got in yet, do I?' she'd lied, knowing well enough that most places had refused her. Belfast was the only choice left. Terms would start in October all over the country, and she'd be the only one of her year not fixed up. Some had definite places at university and college, others had jobs, and a few would redo their A levels at the local FE college. Jo knew she had no chance of that. Sam and her mother had made it quite clear.

'We've had enough of this education lark!' shouted Sam. 'We let you stay on this year, that's time enough. If you don't get in to college, you'll have to take a bloody job, work like the rest of us,' he'd snarled. Sam had three front teeth missing, the rest were yellow and brown. His breath smelt of drink. When he got mad, he hopped from one foot to another and punched at imaginary enemies.

After that, Jo fixated on Belfast, her only hope. On the news she watched cars burn in Belfast streets, learned of people being shot, homes raided.

Sam consented to her staying for two weeks. She slept in the living-room. One cold foggy night, she thought of her father. He'd died in the same room, alone, friendless. But the grey spot had long gone, and the couch was a new one, a studio design, green with brown legs, not quite long enough to be comfortable. Jo was ashamed of Sam. She considered him thick, coarse, a bore, and he'd taken over the house. He was loud-mouthed and rude when drunk, but, unlike her father, he'd agreed she should stay on at school, until after her A levels.

During the summer, a King Billy statue had appeared in the living-room, courtesy of Sam. Jo had closed the curtains, Sam opened them. Sam, proud to be an Orangeman, marched with the Lodge, and got drunk every July on the trip up to Southport, part of a caravan of coaches. Once there, he sat on the grass with his mates, sinking slowly into a stupor. Her father had never been like that. Sam was an alien, an unwanted intruder. Jo spent the two weeks catching up on old school friends. She felt torn – school was a discarded overcoat, the future a great black hole which threatened to swallow her whole. She imagined herself idling away hours on the couch, unable to sleep as the house grew silent each night. The days would tick away, unaccounted, empty.

'You better apply to the council,' her mother said. 'We can't have you lazing around here much longer.'

'They take young ones, you know, in some of these flats that nobody wants.'

'Great,' thought Jo, 'that's just what I want, a clapped out old flat over my head.'

'Of course, if you were pregnant you'd get a decent place up Tower Hill.' Her mother seemed unconscious of the irony. Jo knew Tower Hill, a collection of rabbit hutches, a few shops with steel grilles over them, a wasteland of single mothers. No buses, no hope, nothing. 'Even the rats wanna leave,' someone had remarked. There'd been an infestation of ants in the heating ducts, headlined in the local paper. The flats were new, modern from the outside, but if you touched the walls, the plaster crumbled into dust.

After that warning, Jo went to visit Jackie, who'd got pregnant, left school early, and ended up in Tower Hill. They sat in a patch of concrete by a thin line of swings, two of them broken, and swigged back White's lemonade. Jackie pushed the baby backwards and forwards with her foot and spoke of her flat.

'It's not too bad,' she said defensively. 'Brian's got a job now, and the flats are nice – once you're inside them,' she added. Brian was her husband, they'd married when Jackie was five months gone. Jackie, always artistic, always making things, always top in art, had gradually downgraded her ambitions from being an artist ('I'll go to college, do painting, I'll be like Michaelangelo'), to being a window-dresser. 'It takes a lot of skill to arrange windows – people train for years, and you can always get one of those top jobs in London.') She'd been sacked from window-dressing after arranging a display of black bras made up as bats.

'It's not the right image,' said the management, 'it might put people off.' She'd then turned to hairdressing.

'After all, I like talking to people,' she'd said cheerfully enough at the time.

Jackie had never done safe, small paintings, but big bold affairs where energy burst out from the paper. But that day in the grey concrete park, her spirit seemed to have dried up, like a tree wizened with cold. The shine on her face had gone – she looked as grey as the park, and, for the first time, Jo could see the seeds of Jackie's mother in her friend. A terrible realisation hit her then. They would both, eventually, turn into their mothers.

They finished their lemonades in companionable silence, Jackie's beautiful face tense and sad. The baby slept, wrapped in a winceyette sheet and blanket and wearing a blue pointed hat. Kids screamed and clambered over railings. A dog cocked its leg over the edge of the slide, ignoring the grass, weedy and uncared for. 'You could still try for college,' Jo blurted out.

Jackie laughed. 'Who'd look after the baby?'

'Some of them have créches,' said Jo.

'And what about Brian?'

Jo ignored the last remark.

'Your paintings were good, you know. Do you ever get out now?'

'No, we don't get out much,' Jackie admitted.

'Money's tight, with him only just starting work. We've just got the telly for company.'

Her face looked careworn, and she closed up, too proud to talk anymore. That look decided Jo. No way would she try for a flat in Tower Hill, no way would she make it her prison. She went to her mother's, unclear of the future, but sure of what she didn't want. And, like magic, later that day, she was saved unexpectedly by Ellen Mack, breathless from dashing across the road.

'There was a man on the 'phone for you from Belfast. Jesus, I could hardly understand his accent, but he's given me this number, and he says to 'phone him at two. He said something about being prepared to offer you a place.'

Raised from her sloth, Jo jumped up like a firecracker.

'Prepared to offer you a place' – powerful words writ against the sky, words which would release her. Jo fizzled with energy through the next few hours until she could contact him. When she finally got through, a light, optimistic Northern Irish voice described a choice of accommodation arrangements. He moved on to the term dates, contact addresses. Very little sank in. Yes, she said to everything, yes, yes, yes. When she put the phone down, Ellen Mack's family stared up at her, expectant.

'I've got a place at university,' she said proudly.

'That's nice,' said Ellen vaguely, as if she didn't quite know what it meant. Saying the words, it hit Jo that she'd decided her future for the next three years. It was like stepping off a cliff into space, there were no footholds anymore. From the dark, cave-like present, an open doored future beckoned, with bright shining light, flowers, people. She could hardly contain herself.

The rest of her family obviously had no idea what she was letting herself in for either. They acted as if she was about to sail to Australia and tumble off the edge of the world.

In the few short days before leaving, Jo wondered what Belfast would be like. She fixed in her mind's eye the image of her father with Tina on his knee, as he sang 'With a shillelagh under me arm and a twinkle in me eye.' His repertoire of Irish songs had diminished over the years, he sang less and less, so that by the time Tina was grown, only the popular, well-known ones were left. When he sang he seemed like a stage Irishman, mocking himself, and Jo thought then that his Irishness was false, a put on. It was not the Ireland of his songs she was going to, she reminded herself, nor the Ireland of postcards, with donkeys up the coast road and tiny cottages. The North would be different. The people in the North were harder, there was a war there.

Her mother became sentimental once Jo confirmed she was leaving. She slipped her money when Sam wasn't looking, and touched her tentatively, as you would a fine crystal teapot, or an egg. Jo wriggled away, hard as flint, embarrassed. Her mother handed over an old camel coat.

'It might come in handy – you never know.' Jo stuffed it to the bottom of her rucksack. She didn't want that manky old thing, probably infested with fleas – as soon as she had settled in she would dump it.

The past flew away like a shadow as Jo looked down over the ship. Already she sensed the suggestion of movement as the ship began to slip into the dark, dark night. Her mother cried, Sam theatrically mopped her face and squeezed his arm tighter. He was like a boa constrictor, Jo thought, wrapping his prey until all breath was gone. Jo saw Tina place her arm round her mother and the pair began swaying drunkenly.

'You'll never walk alone.' Their thin plaintive voices floated up to the ship, delicate as soap bubbles against its great bulk. Jo hunched her shoulders into her fur fabric jacket, the one with the shoulder pads that made her feel like Joan Crawford. The wind whistled through her thin trousers and she wished she'd worn tights. It was October, not spring.

Jo glanced round at her fellow passengers and hoped no one guessed the loud crowd below belonged to her. It would be 'Give Me the Moonlight' next. But people were oblivious, engrossed in dramas of their own. They leaned over the sides to blow kisses to small, huddled groups. The ship began to inch away from the shore. Jo's stomach seethed with a mixture of tension and relief. She breathed in deeply. No going back now, they were off.

A lump rose in her throat, as her glance lighted on Tina. Tina, small miserable Tina – how would she cope? Pat was substantial, her feet rooted on the earth. Tina was more easily bruised.

'Oh well,' Jo sighed, Tina was on her own now. She, Jo, was responsible no longer.

'Write to us Josephine!' Tina shouted, in a quavery thin voice.

'All right.'

Then the whole dockside became a mass of waving hands, like the seagulls that followed the ship, or white flecks of foam. Jo waved until her family looked like figures no longer and then at last walked inside with the cold.

Below it was bedlam. Soldiers were everywhere, in combat uniforms with berets on shoulders. They shouted and laughed with bravado, they spilt out of the bar carrying cans of Guinness and Newcastle Brown. Their accents were mainly from the North of England. Jo sat herself down in the tea bar, near a dark-haired girl, slightly older than her. She watched the girl munch her way through a Mars bar, a Kit-Kat, a Bounty, a packet of crisps and a big bar of fruit and nut as she herself demolished her mother's salty egg sandwiches. The girl had a stomach like cast iron, Jo decided. Already her own belly heaved and she doubted whether they were past New Brighton.

The rest of the night passed quickly, considering. Every time Jo looked up, with the egg sandwiches rising like tidal waves, the girl, Nora, was deep in a magazine, eating another bar of chocolate.

Morning came like a wet rag, with lights switched full on and a disembodied voice announcing that breakfast was now being served. People stumbled bleary-eyed to toilets and the tea bar, others slept on, flat out on the floor, regardless of the hundreds tramping by.

Jo walked down into an arrivals lounge bright with artificial light. People stood at the bottom of the steps, waiting for friends and relatives. Small groups hugged each other, talking rapidly. Men in dark-green uniforms and maroon flat hats with the letters RMP stood at the back of the lounge and stared hard at people as they disembarked.

Jo noticed other men with forties-style raincoats who also took a great interest in each new flux of passengers. She walked through without bother and stood at the large open doors to look out on the view – dark dilapidated warehouses, signs pointing to the city centre. The sky was clear, the air tangy with the whiff of autumn. Jo breathed in deeply. Cold, fresh air hit her lungs, shocking her into wakefulness.

A lorry petered to a halt a few yards ahead. A florid-faced man leaned out.

'Are ye lost, love?' he shouted over.

'Not exactly,' answered Jo, but then had to admit it. 'But I don't really know which way I'm going.' He laughed.

'Where are you heading for?'

'I'm going to the university.' Jo felt embarrassed. Maybe she shouldn't talk to strangers, maybe it wasn't safe.

'Hop in,' he said and opened the cabin door.

Soon she was gazing at quiet terraced streets, where milk floats deposited bottles on well scrubbed stone steps, her case wedged between her legs, her rucksack on her knee.

'New here? First time over?' he asked, concentrating on turning right.

'Yeah,' she answered, holding her breath. This stranger seemed harmless enough.

'Well, you have to be careful, you know, dear. There's some places not so safe and some folks not so friendly.' Jo smiled at his advice and settled back in the seat. He'd be OK.

'That there's Cromac Square.' He pointed vaguely in the direction of a row of run-down shops and houses. 'There's been a good few people shot there recently. You can still see some of the holes.'

Jo glanced over. It looked perfectly normal. She stayed silent as the steady stream of traffic from the docks gave way to red buses that congregated round a pillared stone building.

Soon they drew up outside a building that looked like a miniature Westminster Abbey; brown, neat. Solid arched doors with great black knockers, high arched windows. At any moment she expected someone to emerge and say 'Sorry, wrong place, wrong time'. How could this be Belfast, with its brilliant green lawns, and flowers, and order? Belfast meant crowds rioting in the streets, water cannons, homes raided at dead of night, funeral processions each day.

'This here's the university,' said the driver, opening the door. 'If you go in the porter's lodge just there, they'll see you rightly, OK? Cheerio now, have a grand time during your stay.'

Jo thanked him and waved goodbye. Her eyes and ears pricked like antennae, searching for clues.

She dropped her bags by the gate and walked the ten yards or so to a little glass-fronted shed where two men in black uniforms were playing cards.

'Excuse me,' she said in a loud voice. One of them came to the door of the hut. He held a ten of hearts.

'Hello, there,' he said, smiling, 'and what can we do for you, young lady?' His smile faded as he glanced towards the gate.

'Are those there your bags, love?' he asked, looking worried.

'Aye,' she answered, falling into the idiom.

'Well, could you move them please? People get a wee bit nervous with bags left lying round nowadays, you know how it is.'

Red-faced, Jo picked them up. No, she didn't know how it was, but she was sure she'd find out. She asked him the way to the address she'd been given. Accommodation had been found for her in a furnished house belonging to the university. With a fellow student as warden, it was halfway between halls and living out. She was to share with several other women, she'd forgotten how many. He pointed out directions, told her it was a ten-minute walk and retreated to his cards. Jo trudged up the road.

On her left were houses larger than she'd ever seen, with bay windows and the sun streaming into rooms which exuded wealth. Long, draped curtains exposed paintings, and full bookcases, candelabras, tables set for formal meals. Surely she wouldn't be living round here?

Jo finally reached the road she wanted. 'Sans Souci Park', she read, laughing, the name so ironic. But as she walked along the road, she saw the reason for its name, for the road was lined with sycamores, and the large elegant houses, set off from the road, were as detached from each other as they seemed from the rest of the city. They did seem without care.

'I'll be living in a park,' she laughed to herself 'they won't believe it back home.' When she finally reached the address she had written down, she checked her piece of paper once again. The house was enormous and turreted, large bay windows fronted a well-tended lawn, a lawn to play croquet on, a lawn to have picnics on. Blue-grey cypress trees framed the doorway. The door to the house was massive – solid oak, with a great iron knocker shaped like a lion. She presumed it was all a mistake. She couldn't be staying here. It was the biggest house she'd ever seen in her life, besides a stately home they'd visited one day with the school.

She put her cases down and rang the bell. A tall, heavy-boned girl with long wavy hair answered the door.

'Hi.' The girl smiled a large uneven grin and opened the door wider as Jo introduced herself.

'Come on in.' She confirmed it was the right place. Her voice was English, Northern, not unlike the soldiers on the boat.

'We've been expecting you – they 'phoned from the porter's lodge and said you were on your way up. You took longer than we expected. Fancy a cuppa? We're just having one.'

Jo followed the girl past well-scrubbed walls and half-opened doors into a large bare kitchen. She heard a voice float out from a room on the right – 'But what does it really mean?' then the door was slammed shut. When she turned round six pairs of eyes, six heads of hair bid welcome and the dark-haired girl waved her hands in introduction. Jo, still groggy from the boat and with legs that swayed from side to side, forgot their names instantly, but smiled vaguely.

'I'm Jenny. Would you like a wee sandwich?' The girl had

long brown hair. They all looked the same. Jo had difficulty telling them apart. 'I'm just after making one myself.'

'Oh, yeah, I'd love a butty.' There was a titter from the corner, and a small, pink-cheeked woman laughed. Rhona, that was her name, Rhona.

'Oh, sorry, I didn't mean to laugh. I just love your accent, so I do. From Liverpool, are you not?' The woman didn't seem hostile. Jo smiled in agreement.

A doorstep of a sandwich was thrust at her.

'I hope you like the Pan bread.'

'Yeah,' Jo grunted, her mouth full. She had no idea what Pan bread was, she just knew it tasted fresh, doughy, with strong pungent cheese.

'We're just talking about the discos that are on,' the woman who'd answered the door turned to Jo.

'There's a freshers' do on Friday, and then on Saturday there's a band on at the union. Do you like music?'

Jo nodded, uncomprehending. She puzzled over the word fresher. Daft to betray her ignorance, but she wasn't sure what the word meant. She'd seen it in connection with Oxford, Cambridge. It was a word associated with universities, she knew that.

The questions came thick and fast.

'What are you studying then?'

'Why did you pick here?'

'Do you think that you'll like it?'

'We don't get many English students. But then, I suppose you're not really English, coming from Liverpool, I mean.'

Jo answered them.

'I'll be studying English. It was all a bit of a rush coming over like, I'm still not sure what's going on.'

'Well, you won't regret it.' This woman had pale, baby-fine hair; 'You'll have a good time, so you will.'

'I hope so,' said Jo. She sat back to finish her sandwich and listen to the ebb and flow of conversation. It was hard to catch all the different accents. The effort began to exhaust her, and she felt her eyes drooping, so that when the small blond-haired girl offered to show her to her room, she jumped up gladly.

Jo followed the girl into a light, ground floor room with two beds diagonal to each other. A slight breeze blew through open French windows. There were two neat, bare desks complete with lamps, and two wardrobes along the centre at an angle. The bed near the door was made up already, with sheets turned down and a pretty flowered nightdress folded neatly at its foot. The adjoining desk had two containers filled with pens and a fuchsia branch that dripped pendulous flowers to the floor. The whole impression was of light and space.

'Anne, your room-mate, has been here for a few days,' said the woman. 'She's doing sociology. That's your bed over there.' She indicated the unmade bed.

'She's gone down to see a friend in Newcastle and she won't be back until this evening. Are you OK? Do you need anything? The bathroom's the first on the right upstairs.' Jo couldn't think of anything to say. She pondered over the woman's words – Newcastle? – on Tyne, or under Lyme?

Jo shook her head. 'No, I don't need anything,' she said, looking at the empty bed with its neat pile of blankets. Did she have to buy sheets? Where from? Would she have to go into town to get them? What was Belfast city centre like anyway? Was it safe? Would there be bombs, snipers on every corner? Would she find her way about? Then she remembered the only money she had the small amount her mother and thrust at her. The grant cheque wouldn't have arrived yet. Until it did, she'd have to do without.

'I'm fine,' she told the woman.

'I'll go and get a bath now, thanks for the tea and sandwich.'

'You're welcome. Cheerio for now. Have a good bath and try and get some sleep. Maybe you'd like to go out with us tonight, when we go down to the bar.'

'Maybe,' said Jo, 'thanks.' She shut the door with relief. Her jaw ached from smiling. She wanted to relax in her own company, and besides, she didn't want anyone to witness the contents of her bag. First, knickers and socks were thrown into one drawer. They seemed to fill a remarkably small corner. Two pairs of jeans, worn, three tee-shirts, one jumper with a hole in it, one bikini, red spotted, from Butlin's. It was obvious she'd have to buy some new clothes – what good was a red-spotted bikini in Belfast in autumn? Even her nightie had buttons coming off. In

Butlin's clothes hadn't mattered. They lived in blue overalls, and shorts and tee-shirts off duty. But here, everyone seemed so neat and well dressed. Clean and healthy, their cheeks glowed from an abundance of fresh air. She felt like a ghost in comparison, pale and ragged. She selected socks, vest, knickers, nightie and added a jumper. It could go over her nightie instead of a dressing-gown, it would cover up the holes. How much were dressing gowns? And slippers? Her head felt weary with effort.

The bathroom was old, large and clean, the type of impersonal cleanliness that she imagined came with hotels. The bath was deep with tarnished copper taps and feet at the bottom like in a Victorian drawing. When she turned on the water a gas heater lit up and water rushed through. Ancient plumbing clanked away, the bath filled up. She opened the window as the room grew thick with steam, and looked out on to a vista of deep browns, yellows and red tints of autumn. A willow tree spilt over from their garden to the next, knobs of yellow dangling from its branches to the earth. Blue tits picked at the deep red berries of an elderflower bush. The garden did look as big as a park back home, where a garden meant a rectangular patch of grass, a border of hollyhocks. She breathed in fresh air, sweet with the tang of woodsmoke, and watched an elderly silver-haired man dig up dahlia roots.

The bath was full and deep. She slid into it. Used to lukewarm, half-filled excuses for baths in Butlin's, the heat surprised her. Jo stretched to look at her body, skinny as always. She could hardly believe she'd managed to come here. Thoughts appeared one after another, stretched out like telegraph poles. Maybe she should 'phone Ellen to let them all know she'd arrived safely, they might be worried sick. No, she decided, she would send a postcard on Monday, it would be a good chance to explore, find her bearings in search of the post office.

Then tiredness took over and Jo didn't care about anything any more as she soaked aching limbs until they were heavy with relaxation. The water had grown cold before she was ready to get out. She quickly dried herself, on the small sparse towel she'd brought. Tatty and worn, it would be one of the first things to replace – she'd like a decent big towel, a soft one that covered you completely – fluffy and luxurious; she'd never had one before.

After dressing, she rubbed at the tide marks on the bath. In a shared household, she imagined, it'd be better not to get people's backs up straightaway, let them get to know her first before they discovered her sloth.

The smell of burnt toast hung in the air as she walked out into the cold hall. It was probably dinner-time now, but she felt no hunger and, besides, she had no food. Sleep was more necessary. She shuffled back to her room and flopped down on the bed, winding blankets around herself. When she woke it was evening. Clouds raced across a dark sky, past the uncurtained French windows. A figure fumbled with a lamp-switch by the other bed. Jo started.

'It's OK,' the figure said quickly, 'I'm your room-mate, Anne. Shall I shut this window? It's a bit chilly now.' She drew the curtain. 'There, no-one can see in now. Not that there's anyone to see anything, but just to be on the safe side.' Anne turned on a wallight. Jo could make out her large, hefty figure.

'I'm just about to make a sandwich and a drink. Would you like something?' She spoke in a clipped English accent, with a faint touch of West Country, and smiled a large shy smile. Jo smiled back gratefully.

'Yeah, I'd love something, but I haven't got anything in yet. I'll pay you back, I can get something at the shops tomorrow.'

'Don't worry,' said Anne dismissively. 'Cheese OK? And do you take sugar? It's OK, stay in bed, I'll bring it in, you must be tired from the boat. I've never been on it myself, but people say it's pretty bad.' How else could you get over the Irish Sea? Jo wondered sleepily while Anne was away, then realised the girl must have flown, of course. Some people had the money to travel quickly when they wanted, not tied to night crossings across choppy seas. She felt a wall of reserve shoot up, the resentment she felt instinctively against those who had never had to struggle. Then, with a pang, an image of Tony came back; his smell, his smile, as if he were here in the room. Tony thought he knew everything about Ireland. He'd always lectured her about 'the troubles'.

'It's a war situation over there you know,' he'd said to her once, only the week before she'd filled in the application form.

'Only when the Protestant and Catholic workers unite against their common oppressors will there be an end to class warfare and sectarianism.' Maybe he'd been the catalyst that had fixed Belfast in her subconscious.

'You, you're too bloody dreamy,' he'd told her.

'You think by imagining things better, you can make them better. That's not the way it works. There's a long hard struggle ahead. Ireland is a revolutionary situation – you wouldn't be able to handle it.' She'd have to write and tell him he was wrong, that it wasn't like how he thought it was. Belfast was quieter and a whole lot prettier than Butlin's, richer, peaceful.

Just then came a noise like thunder, and a distant series of cracks against the sky, followed by two more bangs. Jo drew the bedclothes tightly around herself. Her heart beat fast, beads of sweat erupted on her hands.

Anne walked in balancing a tray with pretty teacups arranged, two cheese and tomato sandwiches, a mound of digestive biscuits and two green apples. The tray shook slightly as another bang boomed out. She went over to the window to check it was shut.

'Don't worry about that,' she said, airily, waving her arms towards town. 'The Provos are bombing the city centre at the minute. A big one went off yesterday. It's got worse since internment, see, and there's been quite a few gun battles.'

'But it sounds so close.' Jo held her cup with shaking hands as she sipped at tea. 'And I thought it was so peaceful round here.'

'It is peaceful, touch wood, but you can hear all the shooting and bombs going off because we're not far from the city centre. Don't worry about it now. What course did you say you were doing?'

They talked for two hours, Anne filling up the teapot at periodical intervals. Jo found herself warming to the girl. There was no touch of snobbery about her, in spite of her accent.

'I'll cook for us both this weekend,' she said with ease. 'You won't have had time to get yourself organised yet. Besides, the shops are shut until Monday.' She was vague about having the favour returned, told Jo what to do to get her grant and where the laundry-room in the union was. She ended by producing an old clean pressed pair of sheets.

'It's OK, don't worry, they're a spare pair. You can wash and return them when you're ready. And don't worry about the washing up. I'm going up for a bath. See you later.'

When Anne had gone, Jo lay back contented. A distant crack hit the sky. Her pulse raced and her heart beat faster but she forced herseld to breathe deeply. Anne had said it was miles away, hadn't she? And she'd have to get used to such things if she was going to stay here. This house was safe, and snug and warm as a blanket. The night grew quiet again. Jo's breathing slowly relaxed as the cracks died off, to leave only trees rustling in the wind. Jo slid back down the bedclothes to dream of packs of cards falling down, one after the other, as endless doors opened and a long long road stretched ahead.

November 18, 1982. Hospital, Central Liverpool. Late morning.

Tina and Jo left the hospital by the main entrance, then out round the side to the annexe. On the way they had to pass bins which were overfull: pink and white plastic bags spilling from the top, like toothpaste from a tube.

They trailed up and down narrow high beds, looking for Tina's friend. A nurse directed them to a bed they'd missed on entering. Curtains were half closed around it.

'Hiya,' they both greeted Sheila. She looked like Tina, pale and badly nourished, as if cut from the same mould. A touch of red in her hair, a slightly upturned nose, but the same general impression. Her lump was lower, visible through the bedclothes. Jo remembered her as a freckle faced third-year, smoking behind the bike shed at school. But now, aged twenty-five, she already had two kids. Her wrist was strapped to wires which were attached to a machine.

'They're monitoring the heartbeat,' she said in greeting. She gratefully gobbled up one of the proffered bananas and leafed through the magazine Tina had brought.

Jo stood back as Tina and her friend chatted about pregnancy. Her eyes drifted to the window, where a black threatening sky engulfed the frame. An aeroplane flew past. Somewhere, way way down below, a train shunted back towards her old home, her old life.

Opposite was a graveyard, next to it a playground. There,

women pushed children on swings, lively stars of energy, strong legs, proud chests, sprouted next to crushed bones, dark earth, cold marble.

'I've never really buried him, you know,' she said in a low voice. The older woman opposite caught her whispered words, stared, then tactfully went back to her magazine. Jo looked towards Tina and her friend, animated and involved in their discussion. She felt disconnected, far away, removed.

'No, I've never really buried him,' she whispered.

Young mothers pushed their children higher and higher. The cries of children beat against the glass like the wings of an insect. The noise seemed to grow louder.

'If I close my eyes, I can touch the sky,' Bobby had said a few days previously. 'Are you the strongest mother in the whole wide world?'

And then, she knew with a sudden, certain knowledge, like she'd never known anything in her life before, that she had to visit her father's grave. It was simple, easy, necessary, and time. The smell of fertile women had become too cloying. She wanted out.

'I'm going for a walk.' Tina looked up in surprise, nodded, and turned back to Sheila.

'I won't be long,' added Jo. They did not stir.

'Good luck Sheila.'

Sheila grinned. 'Thanks,' she said. 'If I have my way, I'll have had it by the time you come back.' 'I'm beginning to get a few pains. And do you know what, I feel like going for a walk. Do you fancy a walk, Tina?' Tina laughed, and Jo left them huddled, animated, oblivious to the world.

Then away through the city she travelled, walking down streets only half remembered, taking wrong buses, pointing herself northwards, like a homing pigeon beamed on its flightpath.

5

Belfast, March 1972.

Jo entered the small, wood-panelled philosphy
seminar-room. Books lined the walls, dappled sunshine shone
through the long, velvet-curtained French windows, bare
branches brushed against the glass. Father Foley sat immersed at
the head of the table, near the blackboard, reading a book. He
lookd up and smiled hello, then shifted his eyes down again to his
book. Jo was surprised to see him. Nolan usually took this
seminar.

In gloves and hats against the wind, the others arrived puffing
and panting. Father Foley closed his book, then stood up.

'Mr Nolan will not be here this week courtesy of the British
government. You may note that he has been imprisoned for
refusal to fill in census forms.' A frisson of excitement rippled
round the room, table-mates whispered to each other. Father
Foyle quelled them with the look a new teacher gives to a class of
six-year-olds.

'I hope,' he went on, walking round the room, 'that he will be
back in the near future. I will take over the class until his return.'
He paused, snapping his sheaf of notes shut. 'This week we are
going to discuss moral stands, and whether one sort of violence is
justified against another. 'What's your opinion Anne-Marie?'
He addressed Anne-Marie on the back row. Jo could only
vaguely hear her answer.

'State violence . . . economic targets . . . defending ourselves,'
and recorded the tut-tuts of the Protestant contingent in the

front row, but really she was thinking about Nolan.

That tiny, polite, hesitant man in prison.

Always the intellectual, so reserved and enclosed, he handed out lengthy references and was a stickler about getting their work in on time. Sure, she'd known his wife was active politically, but him? It didn't seem possible.

'But where do you draw the line?' she heard Father Foley say, as if from a long way away.

Nolan had been on the students' Bloody Sunday demo, near the Donegal Pass army barracks the month before, but then so had many of them. Out of outrage, disgust and anger, they'd marched down the streets, to jeers from Sandy Row residents, and sat down in the Dublin Road. Jo had been frightened then, with the RUC Land Rover and the army jeep waiting in the wings, and the student leaders arguing with the police at the front. They'd sang songs and stretched out their legs in the freezing cold Belfast day, and it had sunk into Jo at last that they weren't playing any more. They were all moved on, roughly but efficiently by RUC men with impassive Paisleyite faces. The leaders and the Revolutionary Marxists, who protested at this, were promptly arrested. There'd been scuffles and screams and someone had pinched her arm. Jo fingered the faint purple bruise. Nolan hadn't been up near the front, she was almost sure of that.

Throughout the seminar, Jo felt unable to participate, but had to listen to discussions and assess arguments.

'Josephine do you not think Plato, Aristotle, other philosphers would have had an opinion?'

Jo blushed red and fumbled with her notebook. Several months into the course, she'd learned to keep her head down, get through seminars hardly speaking. It was easy enough if you sat at the back, and did the essays on time.

By the end of the class Jo felt as if they'd been put through a steamroller. Father Foley recommended further reading, some references in French, some in German.

'But I can't speak German,' one student protested.

'Well, if you're going to be a true scholar,' snapped the priest, 'you should learn at least two other languages in your spare time here, or you'll never be able to read as widely as you ought to.' He shuffled papers into a briefcase and dismissed the students.

Jo remained seated while everyone rushed out. She fiddled with her notes, and soon she was the only student left. She made no move to go. It was important to talk to this man, he held the key to some answers. He banged his briefcase shut, wiped the blackboard dry, turned round and saw her.

'Are you OK there, Jo?' His pale eyes penetrated her like lasers.

'Yeah, well, no, not really,' Jo mumbled.

'Do you want to talk then?' He looked concerned, yet detached. She liked that quality about him. Detachment was what she needed, the cold eye of reason.

'Yeah,' she answered eagerly.

'OK,' he said briskly, as if he was used to this role, 'fine I've got three quarters of an hour until my next seminar. Coffee?'

She nodded mutely and followed him obediently through the quadrangle into the Great Hall. Father Foley threw his bags on a small square table in the self-service section, selected coffee and scones from the counter, then joined her and sat back. Jo spread butter and jam on the scones, and bit into the rough wheaten texture.

'Now Jo, what is it that worries you?' he asked. His mouth was full of crumbs, pale brown nuggets caught in the crevices of his teeth. She took a slurp of coffee, bitter and hot against her tongue. He stared.

'Is something the matter? You've been very quiet lately in my class, when at the beginning you used to speak up all the time.' It was true – when she'd first attended his history of philosphy classes, she'd been garrulous and eager. But as the months went by, and Belfast soaked into her skin like a chemical, her enthusiasm waned. It seemed so ridiculous sometimes to be alive and studying, while others lay dead, and the city collapsed around you and, at home, her family sucked each other dry.

The priest ignored her glazed eyes, and resumed speaking.

'I wasn't meaning to put you on the spot today, it's just that if I don't start the class off everybody stays quiet and nobody ever learns anything. I have to get you all to talk.' He looked almost plaintive.

'No, I don't mind,' said Jo. 'Your class was good. It was really livening up near the end. I have to start thinking sometime.' She paused, and watched his delicate fingers clasp the cup as he sipped coffee. He seemed to be waiting. Give a person silence, she thought, and they'll fill it.

'Come to think of it, I haven't been doing too much of that lately – thinking I mean. At least not very constructive thinking. I seem to be going round and round in circles.'

'Well, we all do that at times,' said Father Foley. He pushed his crumb-filled plate away, lit a cigarette and flicked ash into the ashtray.

'Well?' he asked, blowing smoke away from the table.

'Oh, yeah, I wanted to talk. Well, really, all I wanted to say was I don't know what I'm doing here.' He waited, willing her on.

Down the other end of the room, a waitress served coffee in a silver pot to two tall men in suits. Loud guffaws reverberated dully against wooden panels. The room was like a vacuum, as if no air entered from outside. Only the muted clatter of cups, only droning conversations like a distant mass of bees.

'You see, when I arrived here, I just wanted to get away from where I came from.'

'We can never do that,' said the priest gently.

'I never really thought past that,' said Jo. 'It all happened so quick. I wanted to forget everything that had gone before. I thought I could start to live.' Father Foley nodded encouragingly.

'I was going to be quiet and enjoy myself. Besides, I was so scared of this place – the university, the lecturers, the whole set up. I was overawed, everyone seemed to know so much. I accepted practically everything they told me, at first.'

'Aye, that happens,' he commented wryly.

'But then after a little while I realised it wasn't enough. Don't get me wrong – I've been enjoying myself with the best of them. But I don't feel right. Lots of the students round here seem so smug. All they want to do is go the library and work like robots. They don't really want to question anything, they don't really want to know.

The priest smiled.

'But you've got to question things,' Jo shouted. She was angry now at this priest. Like a sponge, he soaked up questions, unable to give concrete replies.

'Why are a lot of the lecturers English?'

'You tell me,' he said, mildly.

'And why do so many students come here with their friends they've already made from school? What's the point of that, eh? I thought the whole idea of university was to get to know new people.'

'Some of them can't get grants to leave home, you know.'

'What about the departments?' Jo yelled back. 'Sometimes you'd think this was a cosy little Oxford college from the way they ignore what's going on around us, while down the road people are getting shot and tortured. I can't take it. Yet we all seem more worried by the library shutting early than anything else. There's people dying round here, yet we all go on as if nothing was happening.'

Father Foley, white-faced now, spoke very quietly and clearly.

'Do I not know it Jo? You should only speak for yourself, you know. One of my cousins was in Derry on Bloody Sunday. He was lucky – he was only hurt in the arm. He saw people running and heard shots and saw one man on his stomach trying to crawl to safety before collapsing. Do I not know it? I've got students who've been interned, trying to keep up their studies when they can't get hold of any books. I've got students afraid to walk home at night. I've got others who are head of the family while a parent is inside. Do I not know it?' The breath came out of him in small gasps. He too banged the table. Jo flinched back as if struck.

'I'm sorry,' she said, 'sorry.' Her hands shook round an almost empty cup. Bitter coffee grounds stuck to the roof of her mouth. She could hardly speak. Father Foley, calmer now, touched her arm.

'I'm sorry too – for getting carried away. It's not your fault, I'm not blaming you. But don't you see, you've got better problems than the lemmings who sit in the library all day? You're doing OK.'

'But I don't know what I'm doing here.'

'Do any of us?' he answered quietly.

'I don't belong here,' Jo went on, 'I'll never belong here. But I can't go back to where I came from anymore.'

Father Foley leaned forward and almost spat the words out, exasperated.

'You're learning,' he said. 'You've got this time to learn things you've never known before and will never have the chance to again.' He lit another cigarette and inhaled deeply.

'But I'm so confused,' said Jo, on the verge of tears. 'There was a girl from one of our tutorials in Derry on Bloody Sunday as well. And when I asked her whether she hated the soldiers, she said no, not the wee lads, the young boys, they were just lads following orders. It was the ones at the top she hated, the big ones, the faceless ones. How can she be so forgiving?'

'Well, she's right, is she not?' asked the priest. 'They're cannon-fodder, just like some of ours – they've had no choice in their lives. What do you want out of this place, anyway? Ready-made answers to help you forget your past? Well, you're not going to get that, not now, not in Belfast. You have to make your own mind up on things.' Then his face softened.

'Catch yourself on, don't take yourself so seriously. You're young. Enjoy yourself, it's not wrong to do so, but if you want more, you'll have to work at it. Of course you're confused. Who isn't? Just look around you and you'll learn soon enough. Maybe you should get away for a few days, get everything in perspective, it gets us all down sometimes.'

'I was thinking of that,' Jo volunteered. 'There's a music festival on near Birmingham. I was thinking of going.'

'Grand,' he said, smiling. 'Grand idea'.

They drained the remains of their coffee in silence. He gave her a friendly pat on the shoulder and left. Josephine continued to stare into the dregs of her cup for a while after he'd gone. He was right, of course, he was right.

That night Jo munched bread and hard white cabbage in the kitchen with the other women. Ever since Sue, permanently on a diet, had discovered there were hardly any calories in cabbage, the whole house had gone mad on it. The food cupboards were full of cabbages – dark green, red, white shrunken heads on bare wooden shelves. Jo didn't even question that she had no need of a diet, she just followed the rest.

'Have you decided whether you're coming to the festival yet?'

Jo asked Sue through a mouthful of cabbage. Earlier that week, Sue had half promised to go with her. She'd said she wanted to try acid. A restlessness permeated them all lately, a belief that somewhere 'out there' a party was going on, a party to which they weren't invited.

'I want to live, try everything,' Sue had said. But from the look on her face now, she was clearly having second thoughts. Jo crunched her way through the sandwich, waiting for an answer. After the session with Father Foley, she'd made her mind up quickly. He'd given her permission to enjoy herself. The festival began next day. They'd have to get an early boat over and hitch all day.

'Direct experience, that's what's important, not just all this book learning,' Sue had announced. So what was she playing at? Jo grew impatient.

'Well, are you coming then, Sue, yes or no?'

'I'm not sure,' Sue answered in her measured North Country tones. She could never be hurried. It was like trying to hurry the sea – it would rise up when it was time.

'I don't know about this acid business. I know it was me who was keen to try it, but what happened last week has put me off.'

'It's put me off as well,' said Jo. The fateful day was still vivid in her mind. It started innocently enough, with the whole household, plus Sue's engineer boyfriend from Antrim, round the kitchen table late one Sunday morning. Sue offered Jo a shortbread biscuit. Jo thought it strange for breakfast, but bit in. It tasted sour against her tongue, but she downed it with her morning tea. Only later did Sue tell her it was full of dope. Jo had gone through various stages: elation, panic, paranoia. Finally, she walked over to her friend Gerry's house and he had taken her around the city, waiting for the effects of the drugs to abate.

Once home, they'd discovered Sue spewing up in the first floor bathroom. All night Gerry sat with the pair of them, ensuring they didn't choke on their own vomit.

'You're right,' Jo agreed to Sue, 'we did overdo it that time.' It was an experience she could have done without. Sue tried to dismiss the memory.

'Besides,' Sue went on, sticking her jaw out in a determined manner, 'I know someone down the Lisburn Road who says they can get me acid if I really want some. Maybe I'll just do that – stay here and take it in comfort. It seems an awful long way to go just for one small tab. What about the weather anyway? It says on the forecast it's going to stay cold, and rain maybe.'

It was obvious Sue wouldn't come. Once Sue started talking about the weather, all was lost. She was the only person Jo knew who ever listened to weather forecasts. She liked her comforts, and had a thick dressing-gown, an electric blanket and not one hot water bottle, but two. Jo swallowed hard to hide her disappointment. She picked at pieces of cabbage on her plate.

'Well, if you change your mind, I'll be aiming for the eleven o'clock boat. I'll walk into town, and get the bus to York Road.'

Sue said nothing.

'I'll be back on Tuesday. Besides, I have to go,' Jo added quickly, 'I said I'd meet a mate from Liverpool. And I'll probably see our Eamon,' she added.

'Sorry,' mumbled Sue. Shamefaced, she avoided Jo's eyes. 'But I just can't face the journey. And I've got this sociology essay – "The value of kinship ties in a modern society".'

'Aye.' Jo wouldn't let Sue know how disappointed she was, and how scared of going on her own.

'Bloody kinship ties' she thought angrily, the things they gave them to write about – ridiculous. An image of Eamon, her brother, with his heated, scowling expression, formed in her mind. Eamon and the twins were her kinship ties, a tangled skein of wool with the strands all running into each other. Eamon had always held it against her, that she, as the eldest, had been able to leave home first. What would he be like now? Rude and arrogant as before? Or softened? There was no way of knowing.

Jo went to bed early that night. She woke next morning at half past five. She lay in the dark for fifteen minutes, then tiptoed out of bed, threw a few clothes into a bag and walked into the dark silent kitchen. Shutters creaked as she downed tea and an orange and extracted a tin of pilchards from the cupboard. There was nothing else except cabbage.

The day was grey but dry. The wind frisked along dark brooding clouds. Patches of blue opened up, like a quilt, bright with expectation in the fresh cool air. A ring of pale green buds inched out along a grass verge, like a fat swollen necklace.

'Man injured in Markets area gun blast', Jo read with a shiver. 'Leisure centre corruption row'.

Jo walked on, trying to put the headlines out of her mind. Every day someone was injured, killed, every day another bomb went off. You scoured the papers to see if it was close to home, or close to places you frequented, made a mental note of the incident and hoped that lightening didn't strike twice. And so your area contracted – University Street, Malone Road, Stranmillis, Botanic Avenue, the Lisburn Road.

Outside the dozing Students' Union, a minibus unloaded a group of women, the Union cleaners. Students Union, Union, Unionist. All the cleaners were solid Protestant, Unionist she knew, the porters as well. That knowledge seeped into your bones unconsciously, through placing a person's accent, their name, their school.

'What part of Belfast do you come from?' you'd ask innocently enough at first, but soon you wised up.

'You can tell from the eyebrows,' a Derry friend claimed; 'Catholics eyebrows are closer together.' Ridiculous, you knew, yet you found yourself watching faces for the crinkles round the eyes, the space between their brows. Most names you learnt quick enough. Sadie, and Helen, and Ida and Rhona, you knew which camp they were in. And Dympna, Rosetta, Brigid and Dierdre – those names were clear Catholic. Yet others were confusing – Anne belonged to both sides, and John at times. And all the while the confusion of your own place. Transplanted lecturers who'd carved a niche for themselves in Northern Ireland academia thought you too were Fenian. One had complained of your big, bushy, Afro-style perm.

'You don't look Irish anymore.'

'I'm not,' Jo answered, but he hadn't heard.

'You're different from most of the other English ones', a Protestant friend had claimed, 'you're not like them. You seem to have a chip on your shoulder just like the Irish.' Class was on the tip of your tongue, but you didn't have the theories right, and class had been commandeered by the Revolutionary Marxists. And you were English weren't you? Were you? From Liverpool?

The women tumbled out. Jo heard their harsh downbeat tones and averted her face. Sadie, who cleaned their house once a week, had a cousin who worked in the Union early mornings. Jo had only met the woman once; she was unlikely to bump into her again, but, even so, Jo hunched her shoulders and hurried past, guilty, embarrassed that she was off for pleasure and people like Sadie's cousin were ready to start work. What had Father Foley said? 'Look around you and you'll learn?' Jo squashed the guilt down, and carried on towards the city centre. Past flattened buildings she walked, past shattered windows hastily boarded up, orange tape surronding them, like wrapped up Christmas presents, slivers of glass still filling the pavement. Bombings had intensified after Bloody Sunday; night after night, the city had gone off until now it looked blitzed.

She caught a bus to York Road station. The bus brimmed with people, the air thick with smoke and periodic laughter. Most had paint-splashed overalls or headscarfs and over-large shopping bags and got off at Gallaghers, near the myriads of small warehouses down by the docks, leaving the bus almost empty and silent.

As she boarded the Larne train, Jo's last view of Belfast was of smoke curling up from factory chimneys to join the grey rain clouds above Cave Hill.

On the boat the sea was grey and choppy, the air misty. Jo stayed inside, engrossed in a thriller. Scotland loomed, lonely with sheep, before she'd got used to the rolling, stomach-clenching motion. With the boat nearly docked, she looked round; it would be hard to find a lift, and no fun being stuck for hours in Stranraer waiting for the traffic off the next boat. Eventually, she found a small group of lorry drivers near the bar, their ears strained for tannoy announcements. Bulky, fleshy men, they directed her on to another table where two men sat playing cards. These two were skinny, with wily, suspicious faces, like weasels. She forced herself forward.

'Excuse me.'

'Get her.' One dug the other in the ribs, mimicking her voice.

'Excuse me, excuse me,' he repeated. He had a Lancashire accent she couldn't place exactly. Jo took an instant dislike to him, but bit her tongue. She needed the lift.

'I was wondering if you were going anywhere near Carlisle.'

Carlisle was the first stage. After that it was motorway, the roads widened and you were pulled south, like a magnet, away from the cold, cold North.

'Well, we might be.' His eyes skimmed her body, and Jo pulled her jacket closer. She hated this part.

'Oh, give over messing, Arthur,' said the second one, thinner and shorter than the first. 'Give the lass what she wants.' A smile played around his lips. He intimated she should be grateful for his intervention. Jo avoided his gaze and fixed her eyes ahead, towards the bar, where stewards frantically wiped down slop-covered surfaces.

'All right,' said Arthur. 'Follow us down the car-deck when the tannoy goes. We're third from the front – a blue van – Atkinson's the name. You'd better not be late because we can't wait. If you miss it, you miss it.'

'Thanks,' muttered Jo under her breath.

'She's not too grateful, is she now?' said Arthur to his mate as if she didn't exist. They went back to their cards.

Jo sat a few tables away where she could still see their movements. When the drivers' announcement came, she was halfway through a cup of strong stewed tea. She pushed it aside to follow the throng of people.

The cab was high. They offered her no hand to get in. Jo hitched herself up on to the left-hand seat, near the window. They joined the stream of lorries and cars away from the port and, for an hour or two, the driver, Bill, concentrated hard, and said very little. Then he relaxed into negotiating the small tight bends, and began to make conversation. Jo answered him in monosyllables. She didn't like this greasy little man, nor did she feel comfortable alone with the two of them in the cab. He offered lemonade out of a bottle. Jo, repulsed by his red rubbery lips, refused politely. Arthur slouched sideways against her and dozed. They passed through small grey-stoned villages. She saw caravans moored on beaches by the lochside and the distant turret of a castle or two through the dense thickness of trees. The names rolled by like poetry – Newton Stewart, Gatehouse of Fleet, Castle Douglas.

By the time they arrived at Southwaite service station, Jo felt less scared and relaxed her hold on the door. She told them she'd get out. They said they were going further, towards Manchester.

'That's all right, I've got a mate here,' she lied. They didn't push, as if they too were glad to be relieved of the strain of making conversation. They skidded into the lorry park. She jumped out, waited until they'd disappeared into the café, then walked up to the beginning of the motorway. Eight-thirty already, dark.

Half an hour later, cold and miserable and losing her confidence, she gave up and trudged towards the café. Their lorry roared past her with a beep.

Jo spent the night alternating between the tiled white toilets and the two cafés – one on each side of the motorway. Each drink could last an hour. Only a thin trickle of people seeped in until three-thirty, when four coaches discharged, and travellers with soft Scottish accents, grey with sleep, loaded trays full of Danish pastries and bacon rolls. By the time Jo came full circle, the shift had changed and the cashier, blank-faced and uncaring, didn't even look at her as she rang up her purchase. Like the rest of the staff, she looked pale, uninterested in anything around her. Her bright orange uniform dazzled Jo's sleep-crusted eyes.

Then somehow it was morning and first light struggled through dark threatening sky, visible through the panorama of glass at the end of the café. Cars became shapes again instead of disembodied headlights. A quiet hum began as the morning traffic picked up. In the toilets, women put mascara on pale lashes, rubbed fake tan into skins that had never seen the sun and pursed lips daubed with bright lipstick. Jo splashed her face with water and stared back at pink, puffy, dark-circled eyes and a skin sallow and pasty from lack of sun. She brushed hair back from her forehead, but it seemed to emphasise the bony squareness of her face, so she let it hang forward again, loose and unruly. Then she left to join three people already perched at the beginning of the motorway.

Time passed quickly that morning. The first lift, a sales director in a Jaguar, on his way to London, cruised down the motorway at a steady seventy, and ate up the miles. He dropped her on a B road near Preston, and glided away. Next came a middle-aged couple in a battered old car, going to visit their niece. The last lift was in a tractor with an empty trailer. The trailer smelled of animals, there was cow dung on the floor. Straw stuck into her trousers, rain lashed against her face, but Jo didn't mind, grateful for the lift.

The farmer dropped her at the end of a lane, and pointed towards a small hill. Jo could already hear music. She waved thanks and walked the last half mile up, over and then down towards a large hollow, like an old, scooped-out lake. You could smell the mud, oozing out like chocolate from cracks between tents. The air was damp, acrid with smoke. People walked around with plastic bags on their heads, wellies on their feet. Others wore sandals and had bare legs spattered with mud. Women with long, complicated braids stirred gigantic pots on fires piled up with wood. There was a smell of incense in the air. Small children rolled about in the mud. On stage a group warmed up, odd twangs and tweaks bursting from their guitars. Drops of water dripped down off the edge of tents. Everything felt damp. Steam rose as wet clothes dried above fires on improvised washing-lines. A figure loomed up out of the dark, like a cow out of mist, the figure recognisable suddenly as her brother Eamon and next to him, Lyn, her mate. They greeted each other, showing no surprise at meeting amongst thousands of people.

Afterwards, when Jo looked back at that time, she could not remember the events clearly. It was as if, later, she saw things through a filter, a smoked-glass screen, behind which she, as a principal character, had a part but no substance. She knew the three of them stopped at a large blue tent which said 'Bukta – defies the elements' in heady black letters. She knew Eamon bought acid from a dim figure in the smoky interior, she knew the hairy, pot-bellied minder with the misty brown eyes offered her and Lyn a joint while they waited. The floor of the tent was covered in a Persian rug with intricate coloured birds and animal designs; once vivid and bright, now faded. All this she knew, but after Eamon split the tiny tabs of acid, after she'd eaten half a tab, the rest was like a dream. French, German, Spanish voices surrounded her, the sky filled with stars. Heavy rock drifted from the stage, candles were lit, the hesitant mournful tones of a clarinet resonated through the air.

Then colours began to change and run into other colours and everything Jo looked at became fluid and without edges. On the stage, one performer began his act. High pitched and loud, he screeched into the microphone. Jo heard the yammering of thousands, and pressed fingers tightly against her skull. On stage a giant television screen showed a car crash, again and again. The screeching rose higher. Then came soft noises, whisperings, rainbows darting in at the corner of her eye. One image merged into another, like a child's watercolour painting. A woman's face became her mother's, her head half eaten by maggots. Then Jo knew it was her own screams she could hear and ran and ran until she reached a lonely bare field. A man stood there and she hugged him.

'I love you, I love everybody!' she shouted. Only when the heat of his penis rubbed against her skirt did a desolate shadow descend. She escaped to a harsh landscape, jagged with rocks, bare of trees. It was as if the rest of the world had died, she was the only one left. Sleep of a sort came that night, with waking and crying and dozing again and lights all around, so many lights. Then it was grey drizzly morning: reality; and Lyn, sitting white-faced by the edge of Jo's sleeping-bag, spewed up into a plastic bag. Rain dropped relentlessly down the back of the tent; a small puddle had formed where Jo had pushed against it in the night. Everything was damp, sodden. Jo felt a deep bronchial cough beginning.

'I think we should go home.' Lyn looked up. Jo nodded. 'I think we should take Eamon home, he's in a bad way.'

Jo nodded again and ran the few yards to Eamon's tent. In the night, she'd forgotten about him. She vaguely remembered his prizing the man in the field away from her.

'Con-merchant, con-merchant!' he'd shouted. And to her 'You're so gullible.' Now he lay rigid on his back, and stared at the tent roof.

'Eamon,' she murmured softly, but there was no response. He shivered, as if in fever. Stupid bugger, Jo thought, the first clear idea she'd had all night, 'he was part of the reason I came here. He was the reason why I took the half tab.' He'd given Lyn and her half each and he'd taken one.

'You're not used to it, I am,' he'd announced, confident as

always. He'd told them he'd been taking acid for years. Now it looked like half his brain had been blown away. 'Stupid bugger!' she spat, angry at him for being her brother, awkward, a bother. This weekend was supposed to have been a rest, enjoyment.

'How are we going to do this?' Her head pounded in her skull, she felt helpless. It was difficult to formulate sentences, the words seemed to wriggle away, like tadpoles with a life of their own.

'I don't know,' answered Lyn, shrugging her shoulders. Her hair lay damp and frizzy, her eyes looked vacant, red-rimmed. She had an air of resignation, all energy knocked out by the emotional storms of the night.

But they managed somehow, folding up blankets around Eamon and shifting him from side to side, propping him up against their bags while they took down the tent. Eamon, his face drained of blood, stared into space, with no spirit left inside his body. He looked like an empty shell. If you touched him, Jo thought, he might shatter into pieces, like the glass balls on Christmas trees.

Eventually they joined the crowds of people waiting for lifts at the main gate. The camp site was deep in mud now, and great plops of rain fell from the sky.

'It's been raining for three days,' remarked one girl in front of them. 'I've had enough.' She and her friend were dressed in identical long flowing skirts and white Indian blouses spattered with mud. She turned to her friend. 'How was your trip?'

'Too much,' answered the other.

Too much, too much; the phrase drummed into Jo's brain as she shifted Eamon forward. If nothing else, it had definitely been that, too much to cope with, too much to take in, grasp. She smoothed back his hair. Well, she'd experienced this acid business now. At least, she reflected with satisfaction, she'd have something to tell them back in Belfast. The thought of Belfast hit her with a pang. Home, friends, things to do, a place to live. She wanted to go back.

Later, Lyn wangled them a lift nearly all the way home with two men, three women and two babies in a van. The van was hazy with smoke, a large joint did the rounds. Jo, who still couldn't inhale properly, was glad when they were dropped off on an East Lancs road grey with driving rain. Eamon's eyes, though open, responded to nothing. They bundled him out like a corpse.

After Lyn had helped get Eamon home, she waved Jo off with a cheery goodbye and a promise to write.

'Take care.' Her voice floated through the quiet, empty streets.

Jo knocked at the door of her mother's house. Ellen Mack's curtains twitched on the other side of the road. The watchers were in position.

'Let it not be Sam, please not Sam, please, please not Sam,' Jo prayed. It was two o'clock, Sunday afternoon. Sam might be out. If not, she couldn't explain what was wrong with Eamon, not yet.

Tina opened the door. She looked taller, but as pale as ever.

'Hiya, Josephine!' she shouted. A smile broke out over her face, she showed stained, uneven teeth.

'What are you doing here?' her face alighted on Eamon. 'And what's wrong with him?'

Pat, behind her, surged forward.

'Hiya, surprise, surprise, look what the cat's dragged in.'

'Quick, is Sam about?' Jo asked anxiously. They shook their heads.

'What about my mother?'

'Are you kidding?' cried Pat in scorn, 'It's Sunday afternoon, remember, they're down the pub getting bevvied. They won't be back till gone half three. What's the matter with soft lad?'

She prodded Eamon with her fingers, inspecting him as if he were a piece of meat.

'He looks in a bad way.'

'Yeah, he is,' said Jo. 'You could say he's had a bit too much'.

'Quick, let's get him upstairs before they come back. Sam'll probably kill him if he finds out what happened.'

'Dope again?' asked Pat nonchalantly. 'He's gonna blow half his brains out one of these days. The school's been sending letters to my mother'. She supported Eamon with her hands and stared at him as if he was a stranger.

'How do you know?' asked Jo, pausing.

'I know, because I opened one of them.'

'How come you opened it?' asked Jo. She felt the old curiosity come back. How? Why? When? She would never get to the bottom of her family.

'I thought it was about me, I had to stick it back together again quick!'

'Why would they be writing about you?' Jo stopped, in spite of her hurry, and leaned Eamon against the door, like a storeroom mannequin. It was as if she was swimming into a net. Trapped, your family's claws clutch at you again.

'What have you been doing?'

'Oh, things,' Pat looked mysterious.

'What things?' Jo sat down, but kept her arm out to hold Eamon.

'Come on, tell us what you've been doing. Eamon'll be all right for a minute.' Pat's mouth set in a silent, thin, hard line.

'She ran away from home, went to Southport, never went to school for two days and the police had to bring her back in a police car.' Tina imparted the news without taking a breath.

'Is it true?' Jo asked, but she knew the answer already from looking at Pat, who hung her head and avoided Jo's eyes. Pat, big Pat, strong Pat, who could always take what life threw at her, driven to running away.

'Yeah, kind of.'

'What do you mean?'

'I mean I went with Jenny Wong, my mate. She said we'd run away, we'd get a job in Southport, she said. She chickened out, though. Oh, it was all right while we were legging round, going on the fair, and she was flirting with the fellas, she didn't mind that a bit.' Pat's lips tightened, her mouth turned down at the edges. 'But later, when the money ran out, and we were going to have to sleep on the beach and steal food, then she chickened out. She said it wasn't worth it, she said she wanted to go home to her mum.'

'I don't blame her,' said Jo, 'but what did you do?' Eamon flopped like a sandbag, and slipped down a few inches. His breath came deep and loud.

'Well, we walked around for hours but she was whining so much by this time I couldn't stick it. We'd gone all along the beach, some man had chased us away from his boat. I didn't know what else we could do. So I found a bench in front of a police-station, sat her on it and lit a fire in the 'phone box.'

'You what?' Jo couldn't keep up with the story. She watched Eamon's eyelids. They didn't flicker an inch.

'I lit a fire in the 'phone box. You should have seen the flames go. Mind you, the yellow pages took a long time to catch. It got quite warm. The police were a bit slow, though, they took ages to come out, and it was right on their doorstep. No wonder they never catch anyone, dozy arses.'

'What happened then?' Jo leaned out to support Eamon, who was slowly sliding down the wall.

'They asked me why I did it. I didn't answer them, which seemed to get them really mad. Jenny gave them our addresses and they got her mother on the 'phone. She was screaming and crying as if Jenny had been away for ten years instead of one night, and said I'd always been a bad influence on her. Then they brought us all the way home in the police car.'

'What happened when you got home?'

'Nothing,' Pat answered, looking bored. 'Nothing. Sam wouldn't open the door. He took one look out the window and said, "Fuck off coppers." He didn't seem to be bothered about me.' There was a few seconds' silence, and the merest suggestion of sadness on Pat's face.

'It was all right though, I had a key,' Pat added, then changed the subject. 'Shall we try and get him upstairs?' She had the familiar hard look on her face: closed off, she'd said enough.

Jo felt stunned. But there was no time to ponder. Pat was already humping Eamon up the stairs. Jo grabbed hold of his legs, dead weights. They manoeuvred him into the room and threw him on the bed. His eyes closed. Jo pulled down the bedclothes, switched off the light and shut the door. She sat with the twins in the kitchen, while Tina made tea and toast. The kitchen was muggy, with the oven on for warmth, and steam on the windows. Tina opened the oven to inspect a shrunken joint of meat on the bottom shelf. Greasy potatoes surrounded it. On the stove was a pan of cabbage and carrots, already cooked.

'Do you think it'll be all right for me to stay tonight?' asked Jo. 'You see, there's no boat back, I wouldn't make it tonight anyway.'

'Yeah, I suppose so,' said Tina 'Sam'll moan, but take no

notice of him, you know what he's like. You can squash in with me and Pat.' They spoke about school, which Tina condemned as 'boring'. Pat refused to say more about the fire; it was like trying to prize open a clam. They were reticent about Eamon save saying that he'd bunked off a lot and had got in with some older crowd. At four o'clock, Sam and Rosy came in, merry and effusive and 'Yeah, of course you can stay Josephine. You can sleep in the living-room' and 'How are you Josephine?' and 'Is there any trouble where you are?' 'Mrs Smith over the road had to go into hospital and old Mr Jones died you know, shame, but best thing really,' and 'Doreen Mack's pregnant, but what can you expect with a girl like her?'

'Dirty bugger,' added Sam.

Both drunk and happy, their smoke-reddened eyes took in every detail of her appearance, she knew, capturing her loose blouse and wide trousers. Their hands gestured in all directions, like a composite buddha.

Afterwards she could hardly remember anything of what they'd said, but they'd smiled and gone to bed without once raising their voices. Later that night Jo walked round the living-room, restless, unable to sleep. They'd even given her a sheet, and Sam had lent her his alarm clock that glowed in the dark. The orange figures stood out. One o'clock. Five and a half hours more before she'd have to start out if she wanted to make the boat. It was a long hitch up to Scotland. She crept up to Eamon's room. His eyes were open as he stared into space like a zombie. Light flooded through the open curtains from the street lamp outside. His eyes were as opaque, impenetrable as thick cloth. The room smelt of stale smoke and old urine. When she pulled the bedclothes back to look at him, the undersheets were wet and soaking. She threw the blankets back roughly and addressed the wall.

'Well, Eamon,' the wall stared back, 'I don't know if you can understand me, but I'm going back in the morning, I've got lectures tomorrow; besides, Sam would probably kick up a fuss about my staying longer.' A taxi drew up further down the street, there was a clatter of heels, a door slammed shut, a light went off. Eamon's face stayed impassive. He didn't disagree.

'Well, it wasn't such a big idea,' she went on, 'taking the acid.

And you shouldn't have taken so much, you shouldn't have made out you knew what you were doing, you stupid bugger you. You're always like that, making out you're bigger than you are.' She poked him. His body, as flabby as jelly, offered no resistance. 'Maybe they cut it with strychnine or something, like you first thought.'

Both eyelids closed, deep snores issued from his body. Jo sat on in silence. The streetlamp flickered, like a damsel fly about to exhaust its alloted life span, and went out. The room, dark, shadowy, spooky, seemed full of cobwebs and dragon flies as it had when she was a child. She remembered Tina's request to visit her some time, Pat's hard hurt look when she spoke of the fire. They too wanted out, they too were desperate.

Back in the living-room, she lay scrunched up on the couch and tried to sleep. The newish grey studio settee had a seeped-in smell of tobacco smoke, and the musty, dirty odour of unwashed clothes. She sniffed the air. Wet dog. Sam's hound howled outside in the back yard: an ugly looking thing, with pepper and black markings and great yellow teeth.

She gave up on sleep, and tried to read, but the pale yellow bulb emphasised the bare sparsenesss of the room and her eyes kept drifting from the book to take in the curtains, worn and frayed, the table scratched and marked, bare of tablecloth. A bunch of plastic flowers adorned the mantelpiece, the butterfly mirror above the fire was the same one from her childhood. Worn and flaking now, it gave you back a mottled, bitty reflection. Her mother's improvements hadn't lasted long. The house had sunk again into its tatty interior. Outside, through the gap in the curtains, a jungle of weeds faced her. Jo sighed, thinking of the long journey back. And as the light burned into her eyes, making them smart and itch so that at last she was forced to turn away, she knew she had no choice. She switched off the light. No, she couldn't come back here, she didn't belong here any more. Tina and Pat were right – she was lucky to get away. And anything, including war-torn Belfast, was better than this, anything.

November 18 1982, Central Liverpool. Afternoon.

When Jo found the graveyard, the air seemed fresh after the stifling heat of the hospital. The light drizzle of rain didn't bother her. She walked down the narrow, faintly trodden paths beside the graves, carefully noting the plot numbers on the mimeographed sheet the attendant had given her. It was difficult to find your way about down this end of the cemetery; the attendant had told her that no one had been buried there for years, and many of the graves were tangled and overgrown.

'You'll have a job finding it,' he'd warned her, 'it's like a jungle down that end. We don't get many people visiting that patch now. Loads of families have moved away, see.'

Strange job to have, to spend most of your life looking out over a graveyard. The inside of his cottage had been bright with pink and red geraniums and outside his door was a neat bed of Michaelmas daisies and asters.

Jo gazed at the inscriptions.

> *And all the angels shall shout their triumph*
> *A new dawn will break on that day of redemption*
> *To my beloved Joe, who drowned at sea*
> *Into the arms of the Great Mariner*

And then a small, poignant *Mary, aged three.*

Trickles of rain began to seep through her jacket, making her jumper damp and uncomfortable. She thought she was never going to find it. Her legs ached, she'd have to get back soon, she'd told Tina she wouldn't be long.

The long pencil shape of a cypress tree swayed slightly, inching up towards the sky. Rain settled on its dark drooping branches. Time for endings. Endings were necessary before beginnings could be made.

Edging her way along the last section, where headstones rested against a small wall, Jo banged her foot against a large broken urn fallen on the path. Looking up, she saw 'ville', peeping out from behind ivy like a coy face behind a mask. She scraped away layers of moss and greenery and then underneath was the name she'd been searching.

'George Conville,' she read, 'Dear husband and father'. No

pearly gates, no shining doorways to heaven, no new dawns flourishing, only 'Dear husband and father'. That was a joke. Black eyes and fights every morning, lips tightening in anger each night. A few words veiling over whole aeons of history.

Jo carefully removed a winter jasmine from its pot, shook the roots out over the spiky long grass and patted it into the crumbly damp earth. Maybe the plant wouldn't take; it might be too dark for it here and it would nave to compete with the ivy to survive, but it was a bit of colour at least. Swaying thin and spindly in the wind, its yellow flowers were bright points of light.

Then she turned out the bulbs from her pocket, some with white shoots already lengthening from their fatness. She scooped out handfuls of friable soil, some of which stuck in small clods to her damp woollen gloves, and planted a circle of bulbs in front of the headstone. It was too late for planting, but what the hell?

'Various, mixed,' the man in the shop had promised. She stepped back and surveyed her work. Pale short shoots pushed their way upwards. Soon, with only winter's brief light to nourish them, the tips would turn green and, in the lengthening days of spring, fresh colour would erupt from the dark earth. New dawns would break. But all shall be well, and all shall be well, all manner of things shall be well.

Jo faced the headstone squarely. In her mind, her father's face hovered close, young, unlined, like in an early photo, eyes smiling. But her mother's words stung her ears.

'He was a bastard, remember, he never gave me any money. Why should I want to remember him?' But, 'Aye, he had a great sense of humour when young,' stole in, 'before you lot came along.' And, 'dead romantic he was, bringing me roses when we were courting. No, he wasn't Irish, you daft bugger. Just thought he was, like thousands of other romantics before and since. Changed his name to an Irish one and fought in the civil war.' The voice and face now faded away. And then in her mind's eye, she saw the friendly short letter from the former trade union chief, when she, obsessed by the past, had tried to find out about her father.

'Your father supported progressive ideas,' the man had replied. Had he? When? While he was dragging dead weights from bowels of ships that swarmed with insects and rodents?

Piling them up, day after day, by the side of vast great liners? Staving off thirst that could never be quenched by strong, black, milkless tea? Spending his breaks alone. Dying alone on a cold windy night when speech couldn't bind him to his children? When had he changed? At what point had he turned from a smiling, unlined man to the silent bitter father that she had known?

'Aye, he had the gift of the gab, your dad. He was a great speaker once.' It was the family doctor's voice, admiring, years after her father had died. Did he? She searched back. Four years old. They were in a large park, she didn't know where. Her father stood on a soapbox, she by his side.

'All religion is rubbish,' he shouted, the words imprinted on her mind for ever, 'they only want to keep us in our place and divide us.'

'Don't give us that socialism lark,' someone had shouted from the crowd. She remembered the words, without knowing, at that time, what they meant. And then they'd all started heckling, the mood turning ugly. Her father lifted her on to his strong and powerful shoulders and turned to walk, purposeful as always, towards the lake at the other end of the park. His grey suit, shiny with age, smelt of soap and tobacco, and his shoulders heaved strangely under her. When he put her down near the ducks his face was streaked with tears. She took his hand, wanting in her childish way to make everything all right again. She didn't want him to cry. The image faded. Jo brought herself back to the present, fixing her eyes on the gravestone as if to reassure herself that yes he was dead, yes he was gone. But all shall be well, and all shall be well, all manner of things shall be well. Different parts of the same man, fitting only now into the jigsaw. All equal and similar parts of the truth. Jo put the bulb wrappers away, trod the earth in flatter and stood back. Time to go. She left the grave, feeling quieter than before, as if she'd kept her half of a bargain.

6

Belfast, May 1974.

Jo was dreaming about ice-cream when the doorbell rang. She hadn't eaten ice-cream in weeks and the local shop on the corner had run out as soon as the Loyalist strike had started two days before.

'Ice-cream's not high on the list of essential goods,' the woman in the grocer's had told her. Jo smiled. What was? Petrol? Toilet rolls? Baby foods? Who decided the priorities? She stumbled downstairs, throwing the covers back over Dermot. He huddled into a corner and carried on snoring.

Jo pursed her lips in anger and tiredness as she stomped past a first-floor landing of tightly closed doors. The ring went again as she reached the ground floor. Siobhan's bedroom, next to the door, stayed resolutely shut. They'd all, especially Siobhan, taken to drinking more heavily than usual in the last few days. Impromptu parties after the pub, ghost stories round the fire, late-night fry-ups – the evenings had never been so sociable. They'd talked much more than usual, and she'd found out more about her fellow tenants in the last few weeks than she had in the previous seven months they'd lived together. There were six of them; always someone about, but with coming and going, sitting down to talk had been quite rare, until the strike that is. So, in a strange way, Jo had enjoyed the last two days.

Jo reached the hall, saw two figures through the glass, stopped and sidestepped away. Best to be careful. Pleasant thoughts left her, and panic started up – sweating palms, forehead on fire, a gurgling in her stomach. Assasinations had escalated in the last few weeks: doorstep shootings in front of family and friends, people followed home, their bodies found on wasteground next day, the area sealed off for booby-traps. You had to be careful.

'Who is it?' Jo called out. She stood to the side, preparing to run.

'It's us, Tina and Pat,' said Pat's deep familiar voice. Jo opened the door in astonishment, ushered them down the long hall into the back kitchen and rubbed sleep from her eyes. She could hardly believe it.

'What are you doing here?' she yawned, then, seeing the hurt look on their faces, added 'Oh, I didn't mean it like that. Come on, sit down, I'll put the kettle on. How did you get here anyway?' She moved to the sink.

'The Larne ferries are off, I know, it was on the news.' She stared at them as if, like ghosts, they might disappear.

'The Liverpool one of course, you dimbo,' said Pat, contemptuously. 'That's still running all right.'

Jo felt the familiar prickle of irritation at the back of her neck. Instantly, her shoulders hung tense and heavy. Responsibility loomed, and she hated it. She rinsed cups through. In her mind's eye, she saw the boat again. Orange plastic seats that stuck to you all night, the smell of vomit from blocked up toilets, children screaming, stewed tea bright orange with tannin. The last time Jo had travelled on the Liverpool boat, two summers before, a terrific storm had made a lorry turn over on the car deck below. Next day, the *Belfast Telegraph* had led with the storm – a front page spread with the lorry centre stage, upturned like a giant beetle, taking precedence over the usual bombings and shootings. Never again, Jo had vowed, never again. Since then, she'd travelled the long way round, via Scotland.

'Was the journey all right?'

'Fine,' answered Pat. Their faces were battered like potatoes. They didn't look fine.

'We brought you some fudge.' They produced a gooey mass with 'Carefully handmade in England' written on the box.

'Thanks,' Jo muttered, depositing it in a kitchen cupboard as she waited for the kettle.

'Well, I hope you'll be able to get back home again before the strike gets worse.'

'We've only just got here,' said Pat acidly. 'Are you trying to get rid of us already?' She flopped down on the cushions, and threw her rucksack onto the floor. Nervous as a small bird, Tina perched on the edge of the table. She clutched a pink case and glanced round furtively at a Paul Klee poster of a woman with an umbrella. Jo stiffened. A bolt of anger hit her. They'd never visited before. Why now? When she'd gone over at Christmas, they'd said nothing about coming. Mind you, she'd hardly had a chance to speak to them. Sam wouldn't let her in the house.

'I don't want you here with your fancy ways and your boyfriends,' he'd shouted, his top teeth out. 'Get yourself married like Julie Green. Look after yourself and stop sponging off us. Student indeed. Lazy good-for-nothing more like.' Julie Green was nineteen, with two kids already, lines round her eyes and the grey, passive look of the prematurely middle-aged. Christmas that year became two days on the sofa at Jackie's house. Jackie's mother made her feelings known.

'He must be a bloody animal that Sam, not to let you in the house to see your mum and sisters. What's your mam doing with him anyway? I wouldn't stick with a man like that.' Jo had met the twins in the concrete park, now bare of swings, behind the house.

'My mother's stuck to Sam like glue,' Pat had said then, and Jo, proud as ever, unwilling to chance rejection, had given up trying to see her. She wondered why the twins had come. Had Sam flipped at last, and thrown the twins out? They sat impassive, volunteering nothing. Jo poured boiling water into the teapot and waved airily at cushions stacked against the benches. Questions could wait until later. Breakfast now.

'Make yourselves at home.' She removed three ashtrays and a clutch of beer cans from the low coffee table that Siobhan's mother had donated.

'We had a few people round last night,' she explained. 'Everyone's getting a bit nervous about walking home late, so some people waited until it got light.' She'd seen Belfast early that morning. Red-brick streets, the stinking river winding its way under the city, the gasworks outlined against the first pink rays of dawn. A burnt-out car near the bridge. Still quiet light, cats mewing. Possibilities. It was always so hopeful in the morning. The twins nodded as if they understood. Jo thrust four slices of thick white bread under the grill. They toasted quickly to a deep golden brown. She buttered the toast, carried the tray over to the table, poured out steaming tea with one hand, and threw a week's supply of papers onto the floor.

'Now tell us,' she said, 'what brings yous lot here? I didn't know you were coming. Did you send us a card or something? The post has been a bit funny.'

The twins exchanged sheepish glances.

'Nah, we didn't Josephine, it all happened a bit quick like, we didn't really have time to write.'

'What do you mean?' Jo settled back further into her chair. She had the feeling this was going to be a long story. Wrong of course; she'd forgotten that Pat never wasted words.

'Sam threw a wobbler, chucked Eamon out and said we were next, as soon as we finished school this summer. He was going crazy 'cos the dog got run over and he had to take it to the vet – it might have to have one leg cut off. So we decided to do a bunk for a while.'

Pat delivered all this in a monotone, and laughed, but Tina didn't. Her face looked tight and pinched. Jo imagined Sam, red-faced, hopping from foot to foot, like an out-of-condition boxer. Sam had threatened to throw Eamon out for ages. Eamon had hit Sam in the jaw at Christmas. Sam, a jealous, insecure little man, used to having Rosy on his own, couldn't take competition. Jo knew Eamon's A levels were due in two months.

'So what's Eamon doing? Where's he living?' she asked. It wouldn't be easy for him to get a place.

'He's staying at his maths teacher's for a bit.' Tina chipped in. 'He's got a place at Bristol University if he passes his exams; he's just got to hang on till then.'

'Jammy sod,' added Pat belligerently. 'It always works out for him. And you,' she added under her breath.

Jo ignored her remarks.

'But don't they know where you are?' She turned to Tina.

'Dunno,' Tina sounded bored. 'We said we were going to stay

with a mate for a few days – we didn't say which mate or where.' She sipped her tea.

'It was only sitting round at Jenny Wong's that we decided. I've always wanted to come to Ireland anyhow – see how you're living, and we both had our wages from our Saturday jobs. I'm in the chicken shop now you know, Nelly put a word in for me.'

The smell of chicken grease and the heat slap as you walked through the shop door, came back to Jo. She tried to push the memory down.

'But what about school? And what about my mother? Won't she be worried?'

'Her, worried?' Tina laughed, as she bit into a piece of toast. 'They'll be so glad they can stay down the pub without coming home for us, they won't care.'

'And the school doesn't give a damn. They're gonna get shot of us this summer, remember. They don't want us dimbos anyway, it's not like you clever dicks. Crawling up to yous lot just to get you to stay on so they can improve their exam results.'

Jo blushed. They were right of course. The school was supposed to be comprehensive, but everyone knew if you weren't in the top streams, you'd had it; the only jobs left stripping chickens, boxing fish fingers or putting tops on margarine tubs in Bird's Eye or Kraft, or maybe, if you were lucky, getting taken on as an overworked, underpaid nursing auxiliary. In her first few months in Belfast, she'd done a sociology option, and had come across a report about 'Europe's Outer Estates'. It spoke of problems for the future as young people voted with their feet, moved away *en masse* and estates, depleted of a generation, of life and talent and hope for the future, became ageing, single-class ghettoes. The report had forecast that nearly half of the young people would move away from these estates by the end of the seventies.

'And I'm one of them,' Jo thought, guiltily. What choice had there been? And what future would there be for the twins? She bit savagely at a piece of toast.

'I better let my mother know where you are.' Tina's teeth nibbled like a mouse along the edge of a crust. Jo stood up.

'I'll get dressed, go to the 'phone and leave a message with Ellen Mack. My mother might be worried sick.' She put her cup down.

'I doubt it,' snorted Pat.

'Even so,' Jo asserted herself and ran to dress. The weight of the big sister role fell on her again like a cloak. Filled with resentment, she dressed quickly. When she came down they were in the same position. Jo poured another drink, acutely aware of overflowing ashtrays and dishes piled in the sink. She was conscious of Tina staring at a poster which advertised a women's conference in London. 'We're not bad, we're not mad, we're angry!' it said, in big black letters, juxtaposed with another one promising 'Planxty's latest tour'. Next to it, a 'Season of French films'. Alongside, a man carrying a white handkerchief approached a prone figure. The Bloody Sunday commemoration poster dripped thin red letters like blood. Jo emptied her cup and cleared plates away. Probably the twins saw all this student mess and politics as a joke. They thought her scruffy, with her wild permed hair and long skirt. At Christmas they'd refused to go out with her, claiming she was still 'too much of a hippy'. They were into short skirts, neat acrylic jumpers, long straight brushed hair, careful make-up. When they finally walked down the street together, she in a long flowered skirt, a gang of kids followed them, dancing and skipping round their heels, like rats after the Pied Piper.

'Still got your nightie on, girl?' the kids teased. The twins had blushed red, embarrassed, angry at her drawing attention to them, signalling them different.

'I'm not going out with you again until you smarten yourself up,' Pat threatened. They seemed to have forgotten all that.

Jo put the bread away, wiped the knife. It was her turn to be angry at their infringing on the careful separateness of her life away from home. She banged the knife down. Their startled eyes looked up but before she could speak, Dermot walked in, tousle-haired, sleepy. Unfazed by strangers, he put his arm around her and began to kiss her on the lips. Jo pushed him away, embarrassed.

'These are my sisters,' she indicated. He nodded, yawning.

'How's about ye then?' They nodded back.

'This is Dermot . . . my friend,' Jo added.

'What's happened to Niall?' Tina asked, all wide-eyed innocence, 'I thought yous two were going steady. Serious it

120

was, you told me.' She paused for breath. Jo could have throttled her.

'Oh, we're not into monogamy,' she muttered at last.

Pat laughed. 'Oh, you mean you're screwing around.'

Jo drew her jacket tight and tried to make herself as tall as possible. 'I'm going to make that 'phone call,' she said haughtily. 'Dermot, will you look after them for me? Give them another cup of tea.'

'It's all right,' Pat leaped up. 'We're not babies, you know. We know where everything is.' It sounded like a snub. Jo felt their claws going in deep. She wanted out.

Jo's anger subsided as she walked through the unnaturally quiet streets. Yes, the twins got on her nerves, but they might not stay long. Who could take to Belfast at a time like this?

The first two 'phone boxes were out of order, Ulster workers' stickers plastered all over them. The river lay dirty and still through railings. Over the bridge a few cars roared past. She found a 'phone box a few streets away near the embankment.

The 'phone call was madness: the mindless cheerfulness of test card music in the background, a baby screaming close to the earphone.

'What did you say?' asked Billy, Ellen Mack's husband. 'I'm on shifts you see. I've only just got up, I'm a bit tired, like. Could you say it again?'

'Could you tell my mother that the twins are staying with me?' she repeated for the second time. 'They're all right, and they can stay here for a while.'

'Oh, is that Josephine?' he said suddenly, as if something had finally clicked. She'd been on the 'phone for several minutes. Who the hell did he think he'd been talking to?

'How are ya? All right there girl? Ay, I hear there's some trouble over there, isn't there? Some strike or something. Are you all right?'

'Yeah, I'm fine, 'will you tell my mother . . . .' The pips started going. She shoved in more money, cursing herself for not waiting until after one, when it would have meant fewer coins.

'Is everyone on strike then?' Billy shouted, then went on without waiting for an answer. 'The dockers have been on strike here again. Mind you, they're always on bloody strike aren't they? No offence meant, girl, I know your dad was one. Anyway, nice to talk to you, the twins are staying with you, right. Ah, you're a good girl. I'll pass the message on, I'll get our Ellen to nip over later and tell your mam. I think . . .' His last words were drowned out by the sound of the pips. Jo replaced the receiver and walked back towards the grocer's. Two men in khaki jackets stood menacingly outside the shop, eyeing people as they went in. The door was propped half open. Jo put two cartons of milk, a loaf and half a pound of butter on the counter, but the shopkeeper took hold of one carton.

'You're only allowed one, see, love. Supplies, you know. It's rationed. Unless you've got more than two wains of course,' she added. 'But you're only a student, sure?' She glanced across at the two men guarding the shop. Jo added a tin of powdered milk and waited for the woman to ring up the price. Someone would have to come back and buy proper food later; she couldn't think this early in the morning. The woman named a figure. Jo handed over money.

'Are you open the same time as usual?'

'Well, I'm not too sure of our times,' the woman answered quietly. She glanced again at the two men ranged like statues against the wall and threw her arms out wide.

'It depends on circumstances, sure. They're saying as how it should be two until six for food shops, so they are.' The woman's face was tinged with regret, as if she was personally responsible for letting down her customers.

'Never mind,' Jo reassured her, 'I don't think we'll starve, we've got enough tins to last us a fortnight. Tara.'

'Cheerio there, love,' said the woman.

Jo walked back to the house. Dermot had a Purple Haze record on loud. The windows vibrated with the noise. Siobhan, with eyes puffed up like a hamster, was making coffee. She collected her cup and stumbled back to her room. The twins sat round crosslegged, looking uncomfortable. Jo felt embarrassed. What would her friends think of them? They both had tight, white leather mini-skirts. When Pat bent over, the tops of her thighs wobbled. Her enormous breasts flopped through her teeshirt in spite of her bra. Tina's hair hung straggly and greasy. her breasts were small and unnaturally pointy, pulled tight.

As if to read her thoughts, Pat asked, 'Don't you wear a bra anymore, Josephine?'

'I haven't worn one for years, you know that,' Jo blushed. It seemed like she'd only just learned how to arrange herself in a bra when the fashion came to throw them off. She remembered how six of them in a gang at school had set the pace; granny vests, mini-skirts, braless, they thought they looked great. But in a class discussion with the English teacher one day, her confidence was shattered.

'What's your idea of a real woman?' Sandra McGarrigle had asked the teacher. They, leggy adolescents, obsessed by the idea of 'real women', adored this particular teacher because he treated them like adults.

'Sophia Loren,' he answered without hesitation, 'because she keeps her mystery.'

That night Jo went home, put a picture of Sophia Loren on the wall, pouted her lips and stuck her hips out. It was a losing battle. Her legs looked skinnier than ever, and her newly developed curves were like pimples compared to Sophia Loren's bosom. She gave up the struggle pretty quickly. And now Jo still didn't wear a bra; there wasn't much to uphold on her beanpole figure. Dermot tittered and turned the record down.

'Well, I'm away off,' he said grinning. 'I'll see you tomorrow, OK?'

'Yeah,' Jo answered, embarrassed, 'I think so.'

'Cheerio there, girls'. Dermot waved his hand, and was gone.

'He fancies himself,' said Pat bluntly, as soon as the door banged shut. 'He's a big-headed sod, isn't he?' Did you see the way he was looking at you?'

Jo ground her teeth. Had they come to spoil her life, when she was getting on so well, working on the student newspaper, getting to know Dermot, keeping up with her studies? Sex was in the air, lust reared its head constantly, her knickers were permanently wet with excitement. And now they'd come to spoil it.

'Come on, let's sort out what you're doing,' she said angrily. 'How long do you want to stay?'

'I dunno.' Tina looked sheepish. 'A week, maybe two,' she added.

'OK,' said Jo reluctantly. 'That should be all right. It depends on the strike of course, we'll have to see how it goes. But I can't be with you all the time. I've got lots to do, you've gorra realise that.'

'Oh, yeah, we know that, you're always dead busy.' Pat's face was deadpan. Jo bustled on, ignoring her.

'Today, for instance, I've got to go down the Students' Union to finish off an article. You know I'm working on the newspaper? You can come if you like. We're getting all the features ready. Then, if the trains are still running, Monday we can send the articles down to the printer's. You can sit round there for a bit. Now, what do you want to do? Lie down for a while?'

It came out like an order rather than a request. They meekly assented. Jo became aware of their eyes ringed by papery dark circles and the white skin of those who stay up late and rarely see the sun.

'I'll fix the bedroom up and you can lie down for a couple of hours. I can work on my article while you're asleep, then it won't take so long when we go down the union.'

They nodded, passive with tiredness, and followed. Glad Niall was away for a few days, she ushered them quickly past his room. It was getting awkward with Niall and Dermot. Last time she brought Dermot home, Niall had barged in on them.

'You're my woman,' he'd shouted, dramatic, loud, so the rest of the household could hear.

'You bloody hypocrite,' she'd yelled, sheets wrapped round her.

'You said we wouldn't own each other. You said.'

'But this is different,' he'd cried, storming out of the bedroom.

'Different?' Dermot had hidden under the bedclothes. He'd wanted a quiet night.

'Worrabout when you slept with Annie, that woman from Newry, hey?' Jo had countered, following Niall into the living-room.

'That was different . . .' Niall's eyes had pleaded.

'That was . . . spiritual . . . and I was helping her with her exams. She's very nervous you know. We sat up all night and talked about Marcuse.'

'Spiritual my arse,' Jo retaliated.

'You screwed when it got light – I can tell because I found her bloody knickers under my bed a few days later.' She'd dragged the bedclothes off Dermot to throw at Niall. Through the door, Dermot was exposed, his goose-pimpled bottom and bare legs looking like those of a stick insect found under a stone.

Niall slunk off crying, 'I love you.'

Niall was a bloody liar.

'That's Niall's room,' she hissed as they went past. 'He's away in England at the minute.'

'Well, that's bloody handy, isn't it?' commented Pat. A trickle of sweat dripped down Jo's spine. What made them so superior and wise? They banged into the room, Jo quickly smoothed out blankets and turned down sheets at each end of her single bed. The room at least was tidy. She beamed proprietorily, like a hotel-keeper showing off her best. She loved this hideaway at the top of the house, her single virginal bed, so different to the cold sparse room, the crowded double bed she'd shared with the twins. From the velvet-curtained window, you could see the tops of trees in the park, peeping up behind the rooftops. And in a gap between the roofs, the palm house glinted, the reflected light of the glass so intense it hurt her eyes.

Her room was full of odd angles, cubby-holes with jars of flowers, postcards, tiny teddy-bears. A large film poster showed King Kong grasping a young woman. Her desk, neat against the wall, was ringed with postcards. A new typewriter sat proudly on it. She and Niall had bought it between them. She paid her share with the first-ever cheque in her first-ever chequebook. Neither of them could type properly yet but they'd agreed. 'It would come in useful for the paper', with which they were both obsessed. As editor, Jo was caught up in the day-to-day running – writing, pruning, finding advertisers, liasing with the printers. Niall, on the other hand, fancied himself as a 'proper writer', and produced wordy literary reviews once a fortnight. Jo felt he didn't need to live in the real, practical world. As the twins stared at the room, taking in everything, she felt as if they owned a part of her soul. She didn't like it.

'Yeah, we'll have a good sleep, Josephine. Thanks,' said Tina.

Jo shut the door firmly and went back downstairs. It was quiet again in the kitchen. She wiped crumbs into a corner of the table, then began on her article. It was already drafted, and she was supposed to check it for facts and tidy it up, but her interest had gone. At the moment, it felt like just another few columns of newsprint that nobody would comment on, nobody would even read.

She was still scribbling furiously when Siobhan walked in, wide awake this time. It was half past one. Siobhan held her head as if in pain. They compared notes about the night before. Jo woke the twins, gave them more tea and thick slices of cheese on toast, the cheese taken from a huge block in the fridge. Someone in the house had stocked up for a siege.

Later, the three walked down to the Students' Union. Tina, eyes wide with surprise, commented on how rich the houses were. Jo saw bay windows, solid doors. She hadn't paid much attention to her surroundings for a while.

'We hardly know the neighbours,' she said defensively, as if somehow, that insulated her from the wealth around her.

'Only the old lady next-door. She's got a cat that keeps getting stuck up the tree. And there's a young couple with a baby at the greengrocer's. They're quite friendly.' Emphasis on quite. It had taken her months to work out, but the young couple, though friendly, treated most of their customers as social superiors, calling you 'Madam', asking 'What would you like?' Jo had never got used to that deference. Back home, of course, anyone who owned a shop was better than you, and soon let you know it.

'Yeah?' – raised eyebrows, curtness, a bored disdain.

'These are all student houses,' she added, quickly. Big old bay-windowed houses, solid, handsome outside, but inside were lengths of unheated halls you ran through to get to your room, and bare kitchens with grease-splashed cookers and multiple separate stashes of tea-bags.

They passed the Botanic Gardens. The palm house glinted in the early afternoon sun, like a thousand mirrors reflecting the sky. Jo showed them the bus stops, the newsagents, the other shops.

'Shutdown almost total', said a billboard. An old man with white hair and a thin overcoat waited hopefully at a bus stop, eyes straining anxiously into the distance.

'The buses are off this afternoon,' Jo informed him bluntly. 'It was on the news last night.' The man stared blankly, shifting position from one foot to another.

'Is that right then, love?' he said at last. 'It's a terrible business, terrible business, so it is. I'll have to walk into town, so I will. Thanks for telling me. A terrible business, a terrible business.' He started to walk.

'And I've had a hip replacement,' he shouted back, a slow stumbling figure.

They bought take-away teas from Smoky Joe's next to the union. The café, almost empty, save for two tramps who slept in the Botanic Gardens, wasn't living up to its name today. No groups of overalled workmen, no workers out for a quick break.

A single porter greeted them at the entrance to the union. He didn't look up as they entered. The building, like the café, felt empty. In the office, Stuart, the sports editor, typed manically in one corner, Tommy the advertising manager gesticulated wildly on the 'phone, and Kevin, who liked watching films but never managed to produce a review, stared into space.

Tommy finished his conversation and all three men came over to greet the twins, amused at their timing.

'A grand time to come,' Tommy laughed. They were used to Australians, Americans, Canadians, turning up at particularly tense times, asking for the Falls Road, Andersonstown, the Ardoyne. Tommy had threatened once to open up a travel agency 'guided walking tours a speciality'.

Tommy and Stuart drifted back. Kevin brought the twins coffee and passed over old copies of the paper to read.

Jo plunged into work, trying to ignore the noise. Usually she felt at home in the office; as in a second skin. Today, however, aware of the twins as they fidgeted in bored indifference, she felt tense and jumpy. A band of pain stretched like elastic round her head. She gritted her teeth and ruffled through a pile of copy.

A pretty uninspiring bunch, she decided, subbed them quickly and put them in the 'To the printer's' envelope. They'd decide what was going in later, when it came to layout. For now, they'd get it all typeset. There'd be plenty of time to decide, with the strike slowing everything down.

'How about a cup of tea?' She turned to the twins.

'OK,' said Pat, and everyone broke off for a break. They

clutched cups of strong tea. Kevin's shoulders heaved with laughter.

'What are you pissing yourself for?' asked Jo. He held a book in his hands. She saw the title – *General Prospectus of the University*. He had a weird sense of humour, read comics all the time and watched cartoons on TV.

'Have you seen this? Did any of you ever read it?' He held up the prospectus.

'Look at the bloody bumph they give out to the poor sods who are thinking of coming here.'

'I'll read you some out. I think we should print it. It's a classic,' said Kevin. 'Here, look at this, "The language of symbols has its own eloquence, and transcends the barriers of nationalism".'

'Oh, aye,' said Stuart.

'It then goes on about stained-glass windows and great medieval cathedrals.'

'Yeah, this place is medieval,' agreed Jo.

'But this is the best bit,' Kevin could hardly contain himself. ' "Our aspirants have performed the prescribed rites and face the door that will admit them to the inner sanctum." '

'The Club Bar?' asked Tommy quizzically.

' "The *ianua vera* will always guard the access to the inner mysteries".'

'What's a "*ianua vera*"?' asked Pat.

'I haven't the faintest,' replied Kevin. 'It wasn't in my dictionary.'

' "Its massiveness is the guarantee of their inestimable worth and its own wooden structure suggests precious caskets beyond containing the accumulated wisdom of many generations." What?' Keven looked at the words again. ' "The archway is Romanesque to indicate that the entrant should bow his head and lower his eyes as a mark of respect. The great stained-glass window which he will see in the hall, will be the sign to him that the Gothic painted arch must henceforth awaken his ascensional dynamism".'

'Get your ascensional dynamism today,' shouted Tommy, as they collapsed into laughter. The twins looked puzzled and confused.

'To whomsoever knocks,' added Kevin with a flourish, 'so shall it be opened.'

'Who are they bloody kidding? They don't let as many Catholics in as Prods, we all know that. God, they've even got two philosophy departments, one for each side, so they have.' They passed the paper round, giggling.

Jo felt a stab of guilt. The twins had no idea what they were all talking about. The twins couldn't get into their easy cynical way of relating. The twins didn't possess a dictionary, never mind one with such words in it. The twins were left out. Jo was angry at them again, angry for showing themselves different, angry for being themselves. She turned away.

'I've got to work on some layout with Stuart here. How about going for a walk?' They flinched back, hurt, and shifted uncomfortably in their seats. Tina slipped the back of her white leather slingbacks off, then on again in nervousness. Pat started back unblinking, like a night-owl awaiting its prey. Jo shrugged her shoulder in frustration as if to cast them off. Entertaining them would be a bore – they'd had none of her experience now, and couldn't even share a sense of humour. Trying to entertain them was already becoming a strain. What would it be like after another two weeks? They seemed so passive, like blobs of jelly stuck fast to the floor. Kevin, seeing her dilemma, jumped up.

'Catch yourself on,' he butted in. 'I'll take your wee sisters off for a while. I finished my work a long time ago, and I don't want to go home. It's so quiet round our way at the minute it makes me nervous. I can escort these two lovely ladies sure, take them for a wee dander down town. I've still got a wee bit of petrol, may as well us it for a good cause. Are you ready then ladies?' The twins brows furrowed as they tried to decipher Kevin's accent, but, getting the general drift, they perked up like flowers just watered.

'Yeah, great,' they said in unison, and roared off in Kevin's clapped-out mini.

Two hours later Jo had finished work. Stuart and Tommy had gone and Jo paced the office, growing increasingly annoyed. Her throat thirsted for a cup of tea, but the coffee bar was shut, and she didn't dare leave in case the twins returned. She stared out at the road drained of cars. A few people walked by, heads thrust into coats, like tortoises. Elm trees swayed. Suddenly Kevin's car broke the silence, like a bronchitic old man. Jo watched from behind the curtain as the twins got out, clutching a loaf of bread each, their arms linked through Kevin's. Jo ducked in embarrassment. She was ashamed of them and hoped no-one would figure out their relationship. They walked the short distance to the union building. Pat's podgy knees, their white legs and cheap insubstantial skirts, seemed to grow into a giant image.

'This is what you are,' the image seemed to say, 'This is what you'll stay.'

Jo pulled the curtain back just as Pat looked up and saw her. Jo blushed. Pat could often read her thoughts. She would know Jo was ashamed of them.

The twins were flushed with excitement when they arrived in.

'Oh, we had a great time, Josephine,' Tina said, her pale face now glowing.

'Was there any trouble? I haven't heard the news yet.'

'Only a few big fellas down at the City Hall, but once we got past them it was fine. The town's deserted, sure. I looked after them, so I did,' said Kevin, crossing his heart and grinning. 'I never let them out of my sight, your honour.'

He leaned back as if waiting to be hit. Jo flicked at him, good-naturedly.

'Well, thanks for looking after them.'

'It's a pleasure, love,' he laughed, mimicking their accent.

'Well, I'm away home, before the barricades go up again. I'll see you all another time. Cheerio.'

The twins, more lively after their outing, kept up a steady stream of chat all the way home. They filled her in on their friends. One was a hairdresser, another worked in a betting-shop, another had enrolled as a nurse.

'There's quite a few without jobs, though – there's not much going round our way now,' added Pat. 'I don't know what we're going to do when we leave.' She went silent.

'Well, you're not coming here,' was the only thought Jo had as they neared the house. 'You're not coming here.' Her head felt fuzzy with fever.

They spent the rest of the day at home, boiling water and cooking whenever the electricity came on. Late afternoon the TV showed buses being burned and Loyalist gangs stoning shops in the city centre.

'But that's just where we were,' said Tina, white, as she recognised the street. She remained quiet and thoughtful, and nervously twisted a ring on her finger.

They lit candles as the light faded and the electricity went off again. The dark lent itself to storytelling. Jo, only half attentive, probed them about Sam. Her ears hurt now, and her throat was raw.

'He's going screwy,' Pat vouched. 'He's always in the pub. My mother goes drinking to keep him company, so she says, but she's just as bad as him really. We never seem to see her on her own, she won't put her foot down to him anyway, she always agrees with everything he says. When he threw Eamon out, I thought Eamon would kill him, but nothing happened. Eamon just left and my mother never tried to stop him. She just lets Sam get his own way with everything. That was only the other week, and we haven't seen Eamon since. You're dead lucky for getting out when you did, dead lucky.' Pat leant back in the flickering light, withdrawing into herself again. Jo shut her eyes. When she half opened them, she could see two Pats. One swam back into focus. Jo stared at the twins tired, strained, old beyond their years. They gazed at the flickering gas fire and the ebbing candles, saying nothing. The elephant presence of Siobhan interrupted the quiet.

'Let's away off to the pub for last orders,' she said. 'The lights are coming on again soon.'

'I'm getting the flu' said Jo. 'My throat's killing me.' When she opened her mouth, it was difficult to swallow.

'A hot whisky'll do you good,' said Siobhan. 'Besides, you've got to show your wee sisters some of the Belfast night-life, have you not?'

Jo shrugged her shoulders, defeated. They put on coats, walked out. Street-lamps came on.

'It's like the Blackpool illuminations,' said Pat, sarcastically. They passed curtains drawn tight against the night, as the city braced itself for siege. The Catholic pub on the Ormeau Road was full and rowdy, and Jo forgot herself as singing started up. But when later, much later, long after the pubs should have closed, they had to walk back through sleep-dark streets with eerie waiting shadows of men always just around the corner, Jo wished she hadn't ventured out. Her eyes felt like red-hot coals, and their voices seemed too loud and raucous in the silence. Only when they were safe inside again did her heart stop beating fast with terror.

'Come up to bed if you're feeling sick,' said Pat. 'You look done in.' Jo shrugged her off.

'I've just got to do this.' She felt the need to be alone, and roamed around restless as a cat, obsessively emptying plastic bags into already overflowing bins in the yard. Normally she wasn't that keen on housework, but the binmen had already stopped coming, and if the strike kept up, she reasoned, hygiene would become important. They'd have to burn rubbish to fend off the rats bound to appear. The yard would be dotted with bonfires, pinpoints of light against disorder.

The future was uncertain. Loyalists controlled the power stations, 'the key to everything', people in the pub had said. How would the twins get back? And what if they couldn't, and instead worried away at her like terriers all the time? She tied up the bags and squashed them into the bins. A black canvas of sky mocked her, leaden, ungiving.

That night Jo couldn't sleep in the threatening darkness. Her heart kept up a relentless fast beat, her hands were clammy with sweat. Nerves poised on edge, she waited for sounds. When breaking glass shattered in next door's yard and flames leapt up high, reflected against the windows, it was almost a relief. People carrying torches appeared in backyards. Jo heard a scream, a front door slam and the old lady's cries next door. She looked out the window, and saw the old woman being led to safety. Sirens echoed through the night. Then came sleep, and dreams of hooded men and stones clattering against her window and the twins attached to her back like humps so that everywhere she turned there was no escape and her body was heavy with effort.

Later, she woke sweating in her own bed. Pains like a red-hot poker tore at her stomach. Through the open door, she could hear whispering on the landing. Siobhan talking to Pat.

'Student killed just up the road,' she heard Siobhan say,

'through the head.' Jo shivered, in spite of the warmth. 'waste ground . . . hitching back to hall . . .'

'That's terrible,' said Pat. 'Why would anyone want to shoot him?'

'Catholic,' answered Siobhan, 'enough at the minute. I'm away off home myself tomorrow. What about yourselves?'

'We'll try and get a boat home tomorrow,' came Pat's clear voice. 'With Jo being sick, there's not much point being here, anyway. I think we'll take her home. I didn't realise she'd get worse so quickly.'

'Aye, you're better off going,' Siobhan's voice had grown louder. 'With us all leaving, she can't stay in the house on her own.'

'Yeah, we'll get a taxi to the boat,' said Pat, decisively, 'and we'll probably have to get one the other end, with her in this state. My mother'll just have to let her stay until she gets better.'

Their voices grew faint again as Jo drifted back off to sleep. There were bangs, explosions, shatterings of glass in her dreams, a dolphin's long, mournful cry. She howled with the dolphin, until high-pitched screams filled her skull and she woke with her fingers in her ears. The night was black, blacker than she'd ever thought possible, and she was afraid.

November 18, Graveyard, Liverpool. Afternoon.

Jo walked slowly down to the newer part of the cemetery, glancing back at the jasmine blowing fitfully in the wind, its delicate flowers tiny dots of colour. The graves were wider apart down this end, headstones marbled and shiny. 10,271, Sam's space, and next to it, 10,272, her mother's plot – booked. Strange that her mother had arranged the plot as soon as Sam died, she who never liked to talk of death, whose nearest phrases skirted round the issue as 'something might happen'. It was as if she wanted to make sure that, even in death, nobody forced her to lie next to Jo's father again.

'Darling, beloved husband', was etched on Sam's headstone. 'We shall be united'. Next to its sparse neatness, a small empty patch of died-down grass, a tiny flag marking the number. An empty plot waiting to be filled by her mother, lying now in the

133

hospital. Jo looked towards her father's grave, melted now into the dark backdrop of the wall, and then back to her mother's and Sam's space. Three graves, three lives, passion creating all the trouble, and now passion stilled in death as the two lovers made ready to lie next to each other. Her mother would die soon, it was obvious. Everything passed, even passion.

Stillness crept over Jo. She felt light, energetic, prepared. She retraced her steps back to the road and walked to the bus stop. Ahead, at the hospital, lay waiting, uncertainty.

Eamon, Bristol, Spring 1978.

Calm now, Eamon smoked as he waited. He pulled his jacket around him, for the room was cold, and cluttered with the debris of their life – empty beer cans, ashtrays full of cigarette stubs, a few clothes strewn over the floor. Steady breathing came from an open door. The rest of the house slept. He waited as the sound of police sirens grew higher and higher and a car screeched to a halt. As car doors slammed and heavy footsteps ran closer, he thought of the pristine white walls of the new civic centre, now marked by his graffiti, of the clean, unused windows, now shattered and lying like daggers on the pavement. It gave him satisfaction, of a sort.

'Open up.' The police banged at the door. 'Open up.'

He rose from the chair. In spite of the muggy heat, he shivered. They'd taken long enough to come, he thought with annoyance – he'd practically signed his name and address, in neat, careful, bright polished pink, in a corner of the wall, so that there'd be no mistake. They'd taken long enough.

The solicitor had a pointed nose and a thick Lancashire accent.

'Three months I reckon.' He would not catch Eamon's eye. 'There was a lot of damage. They don't like that.'

'Aye,' agreed Eamon.

When the magistrate gave him four, and spoke of 'making an example of people like you', it didn't sink in; not until the heavy cell door closed that first night and the square of light receded.

The weekly sessions with the local shrink were the worst of the ordeal. The man had the sensitivity of an ape. During the first week, Eamon imagined they might talk properly, speak of dreams and desires, but the man was not interested. He cut him short on childhood.

'Any odd feelings?' he asked.

'Only a bit of diarrhoea.'

That provoked a laugh.

'Hallucinations?'

'Yes, that I'm out of here.' Ha ha ha, ha ha ha.

The crunch question he repeated each week, 'Do you know why you did this?' (This act, this deed, this anti-social manifestation of your dis-ease).

'I thought it might have something to do with my childhood, you know. We never had no money, and my mother left us. And my sister hated me.'

'Oh really,' the man would say, uninterested, and lean back in his chair to wait for more. But there was never more, never. It was something to do with the smell of the room, the atmosphere, the intonation in the man's voice. It wasn't the right time. So they'd sit in silence and scratch with pens, or smoke, until their time was up, funnelled away like excess gas. A pile of pills, a note –

Much improved, but liable to paranoid delusions. Advise continue medication for next two years, inform of change of address, register with doctor.

And then they shed him like a winter coat.

He told them of his change of address: her London house, in summer. She big-breasted, maternal. Heat steamed off pavements, petrol fumes hung in the air. The whole city seemed to have slowed down, ground to a lethargic halt. Sunshine, but still the black-coloured treacle reached down into his skull, like a bad tooth spreading its rottenness to taint all around it.

They'd cured nothing.

In a tiny house in East London, he drank his tea, hands shaking.

'A week,' he asked, 'or two?'

'Maybe,' she said, 'I suppose so.'

And so he stayed through that heat-tinged summer, that summer of flies and insects and the cat infested with fleas, and little lumps that rose like mountains on his leg.

'How do you feel?' she asked.

'Fine,' he said, 'fine.'

'Was it awful in the prison and the psychiatric hospital?'

'Awful,' he agreed.

'Do you still take medicine?' A shade of grey fell over her eyes as she asked, a shadow, a filter. She wanted her house safe, warm, sane for the baby.

'Yes,' he said, 'I'm sane, you know.'

'I know, I know.' Her arms enfolded the baby, a six-week blob of pale face and mouth.

'I still have flashbacks you know.'

Her eyes looked puzzled, grey, with dark shadows under them, fine lines like spiders painted round the edges.

'I still see things, hear things.'

'What things?' she asked brightly, her mind elsewhere. He didn't elaborate.

They left him alone, he heard them talking.

'He must be tired,' whispered Jo. He knew it was a front, her trying to be solicitous.

And so that time he pulled out the mirror he carried around, examining it closely for cracks in his face. Once, in the prison, he'd thought it shattered into a thousand pieces in his hand, because his face had split apart.

What did she know? Nothing. She had a warm home, a baby, a man to love her. He had nothing.

On the third day she asked him to have a bath.

'It's our home, you know. You smell.'

'I know, I know.'

But she wasn't aware that his clothes bound him together and kept him whole. He didn't want to take them off. Each time he sniffed himself he knew he was real. Would she destroy that? If he bathed he would fall apart.

They threw him out eventually, one warm September morning when the leaves glinted gold, and freshness hit the air, like an upside-down spring.

''Phone,' they said.

'Keep in touch,' she pleaded. He didn't.

136

7

Bristol, late spring, 1979.

Jo settled back on the clean, wide grey steps, and lengthened her spine against the warm brick wall. Beside her, separating the flat from next-door's spacious, undivided house was a railing, painted black with intricate designs of leaves twisting round its uprights. She brushed against the railing, where she'd hung five nappies, now slowly being bleached by the afternoon sun. The sun burned into her bare arms as she lazily watched the slow trail of traffic round the square of Georgian houses: tall, thin houses with narrow rectangular doors and solid grey columns outside, bright clean windows that glinted with sun. Soon the traffic would thicken and choke up the square, like a spider wrapping up its victim. But for now, Bobby, her child, was asleep and she had maybe one precious hour to herself. She began to read the letter from her sisters.

Dear Josephine,

Hope you're keeping well. We knew you'd be visiting Eamon and Mary this week so we're writing there. Life is looking up – me and Tina have both got jobs – me in a lorry firm and Tina in a playgroup. Neither of them is much money, but it's a start. Tina wants to take her exams at evening class and there's a chance I might be able to move out from office work and learn how to drive. Anyway, we're much better off than a year ago when we were still on the dole and staying on my mate's floor. I don't think I could have stood it any more if we hadn't got this flat. I was even going to ask my mother if we could go back and stay at her's for a while; it shows how desperate we were. Anyway, the flat's fixed up really nice now and there's a spare bed, so if you ever want to come up with the baby, you're welcome. He's a lovely little boy, and it was great to see him again the other week.

Well, that's all for now. Look after yourself, and keep in touch.

See ya,

Pat.

Jo folded the letter away, and stretched out her bare, freckled legs. A pang of jealousy, real as a stomach ache, tore at her insides. Hard to credit it, when she'd always been the lucky one; but she was jealous of the twins, jealous of the seemingly easy freedom of their lives. She'd spent her free years in Belfast, that time wouldn't come again. She was a mother now, not free, not a teenager. Maybe she too would sink like Jackie her friend from school, her world bounded by children. Jo almost closed her eyes, and stared at the rainbow colours that glinted through her eyelashes. Her brain felt fuzzy, light-headed; maybe just the sun, she suspected not. It had been the same ever since Bobby's birth – vagueness and confusion, as if she'd never be able to think clearly again. For months, she reflected, with all the paraphernalia having a baby entailed, a trip to Woolworth's was the furthest she'd got. She grinned. Well, at least her first trip away with Bobby seemed to be going OK. She'd managed to get to Eamon's in one piece, leaving Martin at home. Like a dog straining at the leash, she'd itched to leave.

There'd be time enough at home to come. Since Bobby's birth, time, a strange creature, had a different quality about it. Everything had to slow down, so that you too became fascinated by a flower, or a feather, or an animal. You spent time giggling and seeing the pattern in things; the chink of light through a door, shaped like the moon, shadows dancing on the wall, a flame that burned bright in a candle. Then there was 'free' time for herself; concentrated, dense, it never stretched far enough. Free time was like gold; at home the wall was full of lists calculating her and Martin's due. She was earning herself a free weekend by bringing Bobby here, a free weekend in the long distant future when Bobby was no longer so dependent.

'We've both got jobs now.' The words rubbed in like salt to a wound. She had no job, she was merely a mother. She imagined the twins rushing in from work, getting ready for discos. Her last such outing had been when Bobby was three weeks old, to a music pub with a friend. It was the first serious stage of motherhood. Her friend had danced and tried to entice Jo, but milk had leaked out through her jumper and all Jo could think of was Bobby crying. She went home sson after. Spontaneity certainly went out the window with motherhood, everything had to be planned, even visits to the toilet whilst Bobby slept.

Jo slipped down the straps of her top. The sun felt so healing and delicious, it was impossible to resist. Ridiculous really, to be jealous of Pat! she concluded. Pat had never been one for discos; she'd be more likely watching TV, or babysitting for a friend. Tina was the one who often went out, dressed up, determined to enjoy herself. And why not? It was such a brief flowering. At fourteen, some were radiant, confident in their burgeoning sexuality, yet a few years later, you'd see them prematurely aged, weighed down by kids. Despite that, Tina wanted to hold on to her youth.

The twins needed some luck. They'd stayed at her mother's house for three years after she left. Sam's temper had got worse, not better, until finally, when they were sixteen, he'd kicked them out. Tina took a live-in hotel job for the summer, and Pat had stayed with Jo and friends who'd squatted a large house in Barnsbury, North London. Jo didn't know the women, but a Belfast friend of a friend had arranged it all. It had been a shock, after living in Ireland, to find that they were all English.

'What do you expect in England?' asked one. In fact on closer inspection there were two German women in the house, and one white South African; it was just they weren't Irish, or from the North. The accents, the endless discussions, the formal arrangements for meals, remembering which foods were no-go, which foods were classed as healthy, all took some getting used to. Back in Belfast, a green pepper, garlic, or a wholefood shop was a miracle. In Barnsbury there were all varieties of vegetables, and sunflower seeds, and Greek bread and olives. They took turns making meals; a rota on the wall showed different colours for their names.

Jo couldn't get used to all the cars in the street at first, or the small patch of green called a park. Cars backfiring startled her, which made the others look at her strangely. Didn't they know what was going on in Ireland? she would ask herself. Their neighbours in the square were film producers, media people who never spoke to them.

It hadn't worked out, with Pat staying, not with the collective household and the revolutionary posters on the wall and the people sitting round discussing their feelings.

'But why does your sister need to live with you? We've allocated all our places – you won't have enough space if she stays – it's important that we all have our own room, that we're all equal.' The woman who'd spoken was an over-ripe ballet dancer whose face glowed with health, whose family, Jo knew, dripped with money. They lived in an enormous house up on The Bishops Avenue. Her father was a doctor in private practice. Jo always had the feeling back in those days that the woman was playing at being left-wing. If anything went wrong, she could hop back up to Highgate like a frog, straight into the bosom of her family. It was obvious, thought Jo, that Pat had to stay with her because she had nowhere else to go, but the woman seemed unable to comprehend.

The same woman would come home with stories from the refuge she worked in, commenting on the awfulness of the refuge-dwellers lives, and how brave they were to put up with such things.

'What things?' Jo asked once, curious.

'Violence, incest, poverty,' she answered grimly.

'Oh, those things,' said Jo. She felt worlds apart from the woman, as if a great silent language barrier grew like a forest between them. After that exchange, she was too proud to betray family secrets, and, in answer as to why Pat should stay, merely mentioned 'circumstances'. But, soon after, she deliberately picked a fight with Pat.

'Why don't you speak when people ask you questions? Why don't you ever have any ideas? Why don't you join in the discussions?'

140

'They're a load of divos,' answered Pat, 'faffing on about nothing.' Jo half knew she was right. Those earnest young middle-class people wore her down sometimes, but she wouldn't admit it to Pat. Pat took the hint soon enough, with Jo's nit-picking, bad temper and the way the other women spoke down to her in loud, patronising tones. She left in tears one day to stay with Tina. Though Jo had to admit she was relieved, for a while the bitter smell of betrayal hung in the air.

Oh, well, Jo thought, ruffling the letter, Pat had obviously forgotten, or forgiven. She folded back the letter into the envelope. Even though part of her was jealous, she was glad the twins were settled.

She stretched up and went into the living-room to check on Bobby, peacefully asleep, as if in a great boat, in the voluminous maroon and white pram Eamon's girlfriend Mary had borrowed for her. Bobby had never been in a pram before. The first few months he'd spent in a sling close to her chest: a modern mother she'd been determined to be, mobile, agile, free to be up and off at any opportunity. When he got too big, she planned a backpack and, for walks, a lightweight pushchair. But he'd grown faster than she'd reckoned, and lately had wanted to be carried in her arms most of the time, bringing backaches, leg-aches, headaches. A pram, though practical, seemed so old-fashioned, and brought back the smell of wet nappies and a yellow teddy-bear that dipped and bobbed with movement as she and Eamon were pushed to the shops. The woman who'd lent the pram seemed old-fashioned herself. Six months pregnant, she wore long loose dresses and plaited hair tied in a bun. With three months to go, she had neat piles of nappies ready and waiting. Jo felt scrawny and undersized beside her. Part of her felt that proper mothers had big breasts and wide hips like that woman, and capable hands that flew in all directions tending to things before they got out of control.

Jo sighed, and picked fluff off Bobby's blanket. In her heart she knew all that was rubbish, but she still felt inadequate. She touched her breasts absent-mindedly and felt the warmth rush to them. Bobby would wake soon. Her breasts were shrivelled like fried eggs again after several months of looking buxom, but Bobby didn't care. He still suckled avidly, an addict, even though he was now taking other food and drink. Her hand traced the outline of her breast. Mary had praised her for still feeding him.

'It's marvellous really – I mean most women give up nowadays, but our mothers used to do it, didn't they? Marvellous.' Jo felt ambivalent about the praise. She didn't want to be like 'our mothers': pegs stuck in mouth, curlers on head, a haggard, sunken face from bearing too many kids too soon. And was breast-feeding to her be only skill now? Fine for a few months, gurgling and cooing at the baby, marvelling at the softness of his bottom, fascinated by the consistency of his shit, his vomit, but now . . . now she felt herself stretching out, like a caterpillar turning into a butterfly. She wanted to test her wings and plunge into the real world again, use her brain, her voice. She wanted to speak to other adults.

'You know how your tongue gets tight in your mouth when you haven't had a good conversation for a while . . .?' a friend had said to her once. Jo had laughed at the time, but that was how it felt now; a strange unused muscle lolling around uselessly in her mouth.

Looking after the baby had been nothing like she'd imagined. She'd thought the baby would be more of an idea, less of a solid presence and had envisaged her golden-haired infant rocking in its cradle, while she scribbled a few notes in the corner. Out of the job market, no longer a student, it would be a good time to put her ambitions into practice and dabble at writing a little, or so she thought. There would be sunlight shafts through high French windows, peace and order. What she hadn't reckoned on was a small human being who took up time and space in her head out of all proportion to his size, or her constant tiredness, her body no longer her own, but a fuel pump for his needs. It was a constant tug of war between his needs and her own, a tug of war in which she vacillated between one camp and another. The breast-feeding for instance.

'Is the milkbar still open?' her mother had asked sarcastically on a brief visit down.

'You should have weaned him by now, he's getting too big, he's draining your strength.' Jo had become stubborn and silent in the face of her advice and breast-fed Bobby more than was necessary to spite her. Everyone in the world was willing to give advice, everyone in the world would say where she was going wrong, but nobody ever praised.

She placed the blanket back over Bobby again and sat in a leather, wing-backed armchair. The cool, dark interior contrasted with the heat outside. So dark in this flat you needed artifical light even in the day, with the late-spring sun belting down. She switched the small table-lamp on, and leaned her shoulders back against the chair, trying to relax. In the knowledge that Bobby would wake it was hard to let go.

Jo opened the paper, but her mind darted like a firefly from subject to subject. Home News. International. She took in small items of nourishment, like an insect imbibing nectar, going for the small, human-interest fillers. The main headlines about interest rates, wars, diplomatic missions had become like a foreign language.

She carried the paper back out to the step, to stare with satisfaction at the deepening whiteness of the nappies. Alone, she would have used disposables, in spite of the expense, but Martin had claimed, as if it were a subject that he'd been studying all his life, that babies preferred the softness of real cotton against their skin.

'If you want real cotton, you can bloody well wash them yourself,' she'd said. So he had, every morning. After three months, they'd compromised, with real terries by day, disposables by night. She'd kept to this system, like a computer programmed for action, even when coming away for this weekend.

Jo stretched out her arms above her head, luxuriating in the movement like a cat. Martin was so sensual with Bobby, so confident, she envied his calm. Once, when Bobby was a few weeks old, she'd caught him licking snot from the baby's face, like a monkey with its young.

'God, you'll be eating his shit next,' she'd cried, and he'd laughed, unembarrassed.

So rooted to tangible objects, he found little shame in the body, hypocrisy and bullshit were what annoyed him. She laughed, remembering the first time she'd seen him, Australian knees sticking out of a long pair of shorts, on a hot London day. The middle-class Englishmen she'd met had no chance against his direct brusqueness.

'Actions speak louder than words' seemed to be his philosophy. With him you didn't have to talk, or explain, just touch. It was the first time in her life it had been easy.

The warmth of the sun soaked into her bones, making her limbs feel lazy and heavy. She abandoned all attempt at the paper, and concentrated on the view. In neat intervals, along the side of next door's staircase, tubs filled with red and yellow tulips burst their bright colour, pollen-encrusted stamens offered themselves provocatively to bees. Opposite lay a church, a graveyard and a small, tree-enclosed park. Eamon worked in the plant nursery at the back. On her first afternoon, Jo had strolled over, curious to see him. They hadn't spoken since the previous September, and she'd been surprised to get the invitation. That summer he'd looked awful; stringy-haired, wild-eyed, thin, his clothes shabby and torn. In her first flush of maternity, she'd let him stay on their living-room couch.

'I'll only stay a few days,' he'd promised. But then days had become weeks, and weeks became months, until finally her whole summer was gone, eaten away by his presence, like an apple eaten by a maggot. He'd gone to a cold vermin-ridden hostel in Kilburn. Weeks later, he'd written once.

> There's bugs and fleas, and you can't put a thing
> down without it being robbed. It stinks of piss and
> disinfectant and the walls are full of tobacco stains.

Her guilt sprang up like a giant plant each morning. She couldn't get the image of him out of her mind – flat on his back, in a urine-filled cell. Worse than a cell, at least in a cell you might have privacy. A dormitory, twenty-four to the room, people coughing, retching, crying; bugs, fleas, lice.

Jo stretched out her legs. A faint line of pink had erupted on the right-hand side, and a small line of freckles like flecks of brown sugar. She covered her legs with a towel. All that was over, all that had passed. Eamon seemed stable now, settled. She'd been surprised to get the note, in neat careful handwriting on plain blue paper (not his, she'd guessed).

'Me and Mary would love to see you and the baby.'

'Take him up on his offer soon,' Martin had urged. 'He's never offered you anything before. Go on, take him up.' Martin had been keen for her to go away so that he could get on with all his pet projects. Martin, continually an optimist, had a succession of half-finished projects: a rattan chair with the cane springing out of it like rats' tails, that he planned to re-cover; a leather bag he'd been meaning to sew; a picture frame he intended to make. Recently he'd taken up knitting, and the house was now full of half-finished jumpers and scarfs and strange-looking garments that, if nothing else, would make up squares on a blanket, he promised. Martin loved to mess around, and could be a one-man cottage industry. He looked forward eagerly to any break from his plumbing job. He rushed out to do emergency plumbing for others at Christmas, New Year, Easter, but their own house stayed full of dripping taps, broken washers, an upsurging toilet and a bath with an airlock. Still she loved him for his optimism. He was never happier than with a small, concrete project he could complete.

Cypress trees waved in the graveyard opposite, where, on that first afternoon, Eamon had shown her the badger setts. His fingers seemed as delicate as thread as he picked up shrubs for planting out.

'This is where I saw the fox,' he said, pointing at a tangle of bushes. For a few moments his face was alive and alert, like the young boy who'd once been excited about fishing. But then his face hardened over and a stubborn closed look came over him, a look so like her father she could have cried. He'd mumbled something about 'getting back to work' and left her looking at coke tins in a rubbish bin, and Bobby balling his eyes out.

'He is like your dad,' said Mary when they sat in the large gloomy living-room, drinking tea, later that day. Bobby had slept until four thirty, enabling Jo to read all the newspaper. With Mary just in from work, they were discussing Eamon.

'What do you mean – you never met my dad – how do you know what he was like?' Jo kept her eye on Bobby, who thrust a hand into his bowl of food, scooped some up like a digger truck, and planted a chubby fist in his mouth. In this manner he slowly demolished the contents of the bowl. He still preferred his hands to a spoon.

'There, you wanna do everything yourself, don't you? You've got into textures now, haven't you? Yum, yum, can I have some?'

Mary rolled her eyes and Bobby gurgled with delight, splaying his hands out towards her. They were covered in potato, carrot and beef dinner. Mary wiped his hands expertly, then offered him a drink from his cup. He started to cry, and turned round to Jo. Automatically, without thinking, Jo put him on the breast and wiped his clothes free of potato with her other hand. It was second nature now to do several things at once. Sometimes she felt like an octopus with not enough arms.

'What do you mean?' Jo continued, 'How would you know?' You never knew my father.' Jo stared back at Mary without rancour, waiting for an answer. She felt relaxed with Mary, and had liked her from the start. Now, after a few days, it was as if they'd known each other for years. It was probably Mary who'd prodded Eamon into inviting her, but Jo didn't mind. Mary was calmer, more cheerful and easier to get on with than sullen Eamon. His moods, variable as a weathercock's, were still a mystery to her. He was supposed to be better, but Jo wasn't sure.

'I know because he told me as much himself,' continued Mary. 'He told me all about your family. He says he's scared of becoming bitter and twisted and narky like your dad.'

'And is he?' asked Jo.

Bobby began to bite at her right breast, craning his head backwards to see Mary, a wicked toothy grin playing round his fat little face.

'There you are, you fat pudden,' said Mary, tickling Bobby's chin. She paused, looking round at the heavy furniture, the giant chaise longue that had come with the flat, the two enormous paisley-printed armchairs, the coal fender and implements, as if she were seeing these things for the first time. She sighed, and knitted her brow, as if contemplating something that should be simple, not a mystery.

'He's always so dissatisfied; an eternally dissatisfied person. He'll never be happy, he hasn't got it in him – he changes like the moon. Look at this flat for instance – he's always going on about what a bourgeois area this is, and what a bourgeois flat. But Christ, he's better off being bourgeois now than he was not being so a few months ago. Anyway, we're only renting it, it's not as if we've got a right to it, or could stay here for ever. Everyone needs somewhere decent to live.

'Why does he always wanna show how oppressed he is? Why does he always wanna be right? What's so great about always being the oppressed one, hey?

'He's doing a damn sight better than before. You should have seen him when I first met him.' She paused for breath. Jo had a mental picture of Eamon as he was – scraggy haired, skinny, face pock-marked with old acne scars, a developing widow's peak, a deep line between the eyes.

'I don't think he could have got much lower,' Mary went on. Jo grunted.

'At least he's got a job now, and somewhere to live. It may not be the liveliest place in the world, but it's safe and warm, and he should be bloody well thankful to have it.' Mary sighed as if exhausted by the effort of speaking.

Jo let Bobby down. He began to crawl, awkwardly, like a crab, towards the telephone, then held it up to his ear, chattering like a monkey. He looked down the earpiece as if waiting for an answer.

'You see, the trouble with Eamon,' Mary went on, 'and the trouble, it seemed, with your dad, was a question of too-high expectations of people. People just can't measure up, not to the high standards he expects, he's bound to be disappointed, and he's setting himself up for failure.' Bobby crawled back on to Mary's lap, dragging his toy telephone behind him. He stared earnestly into Mary's eyes.

Jo contemplated Mary's words.

She remembered how her father had changed into a sullen aggressive individual after he had been ostracised by his mates.

'And then he makes himself unhappy,' said Mary, distractedly ruffling Bobby's hair.

'This job for instance – it's the third one he's had in a few months. I hope he sticks at it for a while, OK, it's not the greatest job in the world, not much money, but he was lucky to get anything, and he decided he'd rather be outside for the summer and mess about with plants, than stuck inside in that civil service post they found for him. But what does he do? Instead of treading softly, he falls out with the boss in the first week, tells him he's going to unionise them all and gets branded as a raving Trot. He could have taken it a bit slower, and besides, he probably won't be there for that long, so why waste the energy?

'It's like he goes out of his way to mess things up. Of course they should be in the union, of course they should have better conditions of work, of course they should have a proper tea break instead of standing outside carrying on working in the pouring rain. But these things take time, and one person can't do it all immediately. You've got to bring them with you. And he's not going to get them, not acting like that, not now.' Mary banged her fist on the table. Bobby started for a moment, then began to kick his legs up in the air, gurgling and singing away. He rolled over, discovered his toy drum, and began to bang, loudly.

'Oh, he's great on the big things,' said Mary, emphasising the words as Bobby's drum boomed out – 'strikes, disputes, even the local library closing down – he got all the people going in to sign a petition and it's been reprieved for a while. But where the hell is he when I need some support? What about my job, heh? He doesn't want to know about the stresses of my job. He laughs at me teaching, day in, day out, but it pays the rent when he hands in his notice yet again. Sometimes it just gets to me.' She placed her head in her hands. Bobby banged on her back with his drumstick. She laughed, hysterically.

Jo felt battered with surprise. And she'd thought, like an idiot, that all was sweetness and light, she'd thought that the past had been obliterated for Eamon, like a blackboard wiped clean. She'd thought Eamon was as normal, as sensible as the rest of the world, and that in Mary he'd found a miracle. Part of her had hoped that Mary had discovered a gentle, vulnerable side to his character, a side he never showed to his family, but part of her, green with jealousy, had wanted him to crack up again, wanted Mary to discover how rotten his core was. Why should he get out of life unscarred? Even Mary's patience would give out with the shifts in his moods. Like a magnet shifting polarity, Jo swung between jealousy of Eamon, and friendship with Mary. In spite of the previous summer and all the discord between them, she felt akin to Eamon, she'd shared a childhood with him, a history. But the truth stared her in the face. Mary continued to work, day after day; Mary had no time for hysterics, except at the weekends, her life was too busy for that.

The needle swung to Mary.

'I'm sorry, I'm just overwrought.' Mary was apologetic.

There's no need to be, Jo wanted to say, but her mouth remained resolutely shut. Mary's hands, short, stubby-fingered but oddly graceful, kneaded at a cushion as if it were dough.

'One of the kids had an accident in class and I'm scared they're going to try and do me for negligence. I was actually out of the room for a minute, there was a fight in the corridor. And Eamon hasn't even asked about it – he's so full of the bloody stress of his own life he doesn't even notice the stress in mine.' Angry now, Mary wiped tears away. 'I'll be all right,' she said. 'The union'll support me. I was acting within my duty. If classes have got so big now that one person can't control them all, then that's the education authority's fault and not mine.' It sounded as if she were trying to convince herself. Bobby stopped banging, and looked up puzzled at her tears. She took him on her knee and bounced him up and down. He chuckled with delight.

Soon after, the conversation dried up of its own accord like a river bank deprived of water. They switched on an inane quiz show that soon had them laughing. When Eamon came in a short while later they were both giggling and Bobby grinned contentedly, picking up on the mood. Eamon locked himself away in the kitchen, cooking the curry he'd promised. Jo stayed seated: there was no point offering help; Eamon considered himself king of the kitchen and besides, he always made her so nervous she dropped things and sliced into her fingers.

By the time he brought the curry in, he seemed in a much better mood. Cooking always settled him.

While they laid the table, Eamon took Bobby on his knee for a few minutes. Awkward and shy with her child, he sighed in relief when Bobby was lifted down and strapped to his chair.

After the curry, and two glasses of lager each, they sat round mellow and satisfied, Eamon with his arm round Mary, Bobby lying against Jo, eyelids growing heavy as he looked at a book.

'Those stupid sods,' Eamon broke the silence, spitting the words out as if he'd been savouring them all day. 'They've been spraying that pesticide round in work as if it was air freshener.' Jo nodded, past thinking. His words washed over her like water. Mary slumped sideways down the sofa, Bobby's eyes flickered shut. The coal sagged into the grate, a few sparks hit the guard.

'I nipped down the library at lunchtime,' continued Eamon,

unaware that he was talking to himself, 'and this publication I read reckons it causes sterility, and can affect the whole central nervous system. They're spraying it on all these plants, just near where the kids' playground is. When I mentioned it to the foreman he said "We've been using it for years and our balls haven't dropped off yet".' Eamon inhaled deeply on a cigarette. He'd been trying to give up smoking again and had switched to a new, low tar brand. Jo tried to rouse some interest but the lager had gone to her head, and the room was so warm now.

' "Just because you're worried about your manhood," the foreman said to me, in front of the whole caboodle.' Eamon smoked in quick, nervous movements. Mary opened one eye and stroked his arm sympathetically. He leaned forward as if addressing an audience.

' "It must be all right if they've approved it", one man said.

' "They approved thalidomide and look what happened there", I told him. Stupid bugger. He was standing right over the stuff, breathing it all in as he was spraying. I asked for a mask and they gave me this flimsy gauze thing that wouldn't even keep paint out.' Eamon's hands waved in the air. He stubbed out his cigarette, grinding it into the ashtray as if stubbing it into the foreman's neck.

' "I'll bring it up at the branch meeting", he said, "see if I can get anything done." Anything done, my arse. With hardly any of them in the union, how are we going to do anything? That's what I ask.'

Jo couldn't think of a single thing to say. Eamon was as prickly as a hedgehog sometimes. She was surprised he was so bothered about pesticides; he'd never struck her as environmentally conscious before. His attitude in the past had been to throw rubbish on the pavements. ' 'cos it keeps someone in a job, like'. It made her think she should be sympathetic, but it was hard to be so after the previous summer. He was still her little brother, awkward, bloody-minded, crazy. They had no way of speaking as equals.

Soon it was time to put Bobby to bed. Eamon snapped to from his reverie, made them all coffee, and put on the television.

The opening credits to a forties film were just rolling when the doorbell rang. Mary, curled up on the couch with Eamon, rubbed sleepy eyes. Jo jumped up and glanced at her watch. Ten o'clock.

'Expecting anyone?' she asked, but they shook their heads, eyes focused on the screen, where a door opened in heavy rain and a body was thrown out into a ditch. Jo got up, annoyed at having to miss the beginning of the film. There were so many she'd watched where she'd had to fill in the plots, like trying to decipher half-visible messages in bottles on the beach. Like cold cups of tea, it seemed part of motherhood. When Jo opened the door, a middle-aged man with a red face and a paunch, in a smart grey suit and striped red tie faced her. He looked like an official, seemed flustered, and stammered something she couldn't catch. Jo waited, arms folded. She hated officials of any kind and wasn't going to give anything away.

'Well, actually, is Eamon in?' said the man, more clearly now. 'Is he your brother? You do look like him, I presume he is.'

Jo agreed that he was but added nothing, standing tongue-tied, hands waving vaguely in the air, then, feeling the brush of Eamon's thickset body behind her, she turned as he thrust forward.

'Oh, hello.' His voice was cold.

'He probably knows him,' thought Jo.

'Do you want something?' Eamon continued in the same belligerent tone. He obviously didn't like this man. Who was he? she wondered. A strange time to call, this late at night.

'Well, actually, yes.' The man hesitated. His voice bore a slight trace of West Country but, she suspected, education or effort had eradicated most of it.

'Actually, yes, I wanted to talk to you about nappies.' Eamon looked blank.

'Nappies, yes, nappies,' said the man excitedly, sounding like a bad *Monty Python* sketch.

'Those nappies to be precise.' His hand reached out and grasped the white virginity of a clean nappy, still draped over the railings where Jo had left it that afternoon. She'd forgotten to take them in, and stared at the nappy, well pleased. The sun had clearly bleached it; only a very slight yellow stain was visible down one corner. Automatically, she reached out, took it and began folding it, turning her attention to the man. She gathered he was a neighbour. Was he mad? Strange time to discuss nappies. Maybe his partner was due to have a baby and he wanted to know the relative merits of disposables and terries. Well, she could keep going on that subject for hours, but not at this time of night. Jo yawned, clutching the nappies.

'What about these nappies?' Eamon snatched one up out of Jo's hand. He sounded aggressive.

'Well, actually, what it is, old chap,' the man hesitated, 'it's just, it's just, we don't do that sort of thing round here.'

There was a moment's silence. Jo heard a clock ticking somewhere and then Mary stealing up behind them, quiet in slippers.

'Oh, you don't do that sort of thing round here,' repeated Eamon, very slowly. 'What exactly do you mean?'

'I mean,' said the man, as if he were talking to an idiot, 'we don't hang nappies on the railings like that. It's just not done.'

'Oh, it's not done, is it?' Eamon delivered the words sarcastically as he cocked his head on one side. Jo had a terrible feeling of foreboding. Maybe Eamon might ram the nappies down the man's throat. He did have a temper, and he was being so quiet and controlled it was unnatural. Jo stepped forward.

'Oh, I'm very sorry . . . but . . .' Jo tailed off. Eamon ignored her and faced the man directly.

'What do you do, then, when a baby shits?' He emphasised the word. 'Plaster it all over the walls so you don't clog the plumbing up?' The man's mouth hung open like a fish, he looked at Eamon, then at Jo, then back at Eamon again.

'We, we . . .' He crouched slightly, as if to fend off blows. Eamon took a step forward. They were about a head apart, noses almost touching.

'You see, the problem is,' Eamon began. Jo had the feeling he'd forgotten where he was. She hid behind him like a shadow. 'The problem is, my sister, she's got a child,' Eamon went on. He indicated a baby, rocking with his hands.

'And it shits, like. SHITS.' And when it SHITS,' Eamon paused for effect, the man's face had gone white, 'then she has to wash nappies. And when she washes nappies, she has to hang them somewhere, see? And we've got nowhere out the back to hang them, it's a jungle out there, the landlord doesn't provide drying facilities, so she brought them out here. And these nice little Georgian railings seemed ideal, like. They get the sun, they get the breeze, they get nosy neighbours like you around, when we've never seen you since the first day we moved in.'

'But it lowers the tone of the neighbourhood.' The man's tone was indignant. He appeared not to have listened to a word. A small creature ran swiftly across the road. Was it a cat, or a wild creature ready to begin its night work? Jo wondered. She wanted to escape with that creature deep into the wood, away from the embarrassment and sticky mess of her family.

Undaunted, the man continued, 'My house is worth a lot of money, you know. I don't want prices in the neighbourhood going down because of things like this. It gives an area a reputation, you know. Things get around. And this is such a quiet district.'

Eamon balanced on one foot, speechless. His face was now pale, salmon pink.

The man began to speak again, taking advantage of the silence.

'I know you really want to fit in, get along with us, Eamon, I know you're OK, it's just your sister made a mistake. She didn't realise how we do things round here.'

Jo thought he should have watched the clues on Eamon's face, changing from pink to red to purple so that veins stuck out in his neck, like a vine choking a tree stump.

'Fit in?' Eamon exploded. 'Get along with you lot? You must be joking, mate. I wouldn't want to get along with you lot if you paid me, you smarmy southern bastards. I've hated you all since the day I moved in. And I'm glad of a chance to tell you now. And any of you lot listening,' he shouted to the empty square. Lights came on, windows drew up, heads leaned out into the square. Somewhere opposite a dog began to bark, insistent and deep, followed by the high-pitched wail of a baby. Jo had the impression of bodies, frozen for centuries, cracking open like ice-floes.

'I haven't had much opportunity to meet you in the flesh,' Eamon shouted now, aware of an audience, 'you're so busy creeping round, locking yourselves up in your bloody great houses, with your burglar alarms and your spyholes and your intercom systems. You think you're so bloody great, don't you, with your quiet little square and your quiet little lives? You pretend to be concerned about things. Oh, yes, let's keep the trees in the graveyard, let's turn this square into a pedestrian area. But all you're really concerned about is yourselves and your bloody property. You don't give a damn about working-class people.' He seemed to lose heart and turned to the man in an almost pleading manner. 'Do you know there's a strike going on in the factory down the road? Do you know how much the cleaners there earn for a forty-hour week? Do you know how many solicitors there are in Huyton?'

The man looked blank. ''What's Huyton got to do with this?'

Eamon spoke rapidly, ignoring the question. 'There's one solicitor per 66,000 in Huyton. The national average is 1 to 4,700 and in Bournemouth it's one to 2000. One to 66,000 – if that solicitor goes on holiday, you're dead. You twerps down South don't know what it's like.' Eamon snorted in contempt, as if the man was such an idiot he wasn't worth bothering about.

In the still summer night, the silence became as oppressive as a blanket. Lights were extinguished as people grew tired of the entertainment, the dog stopped barking, the baby grew quiet. And into this silence came the low quiet voice of the man on the doorstep. Like an admission of failure, a long-buried memory too painful to wrench up, they heard his voice.

'I was working-class once.'

For a few seconds they were all stunned. Then Mary shouted from behind in a broad Yorkshire accent:

'O, get t'coals out t'bath', luv.'

'Mak cup'tea, luv. Ee, but 'ere, luv, we can't afford tea, have t'sup water.' They all laughed, breaking the tension.

The man looked confused, turning his head from one to the other like a spectator watching a tennis rally. It seemed as if he didn't know whether to laugh or cry.

Eamon didn't give him a chance to do either, 'You're the worst!' he shouted, banging his hand against the wall for emphasis. 'The aspiring ones, the class traitors.'

He moved forward to shut the door and squeeze the man out. The man put his foot in the way.

'Do you want to come for a drink?' he asked hopefully. His

eyes were pleading like a puppy's and it was almost as if he had a tail wagging. Eamon shut the door.

They collapsed in laughter around the fire, sipped at cold coffee and then watched a closing shoot-out in a deserted house. But as the two film stars fell into each others arms and the room became silent again, a more sober mood descended like a cloud. By the time the cups were washed, hysterics had long passed.

'It's a pity, really,' Mary reflected, putting cushions back into place. 'It's a pity it had to blow up like this. His wife's really nice. She used to rescue our cat when it got stuck on their window-ledge. Maybe she'll just leave it now, or I might have to get it down myself. That'll be awkward.

'Such a smug bastard,' said Eamon. 'See how he was licking up to me in the end. As if I would really go for a drink with him. Who did he think he was?'

'I don't see why not,' said Mary bluntly, turning on Eamon. 'It seems like he's hardly ever spoken to anyone. Maybe he's lonely.'

To Jo's surprise, as if he could see something of the man in himself, Eamon agreed. 'Yeah, I think maybe you're right,' he admitted, 'nobody speaks to anyone in this damned place, the sooner we're out of it the better.'

Bobby began a long, drawn-out howl, wild as a dingo in the bush. When Jo picked him up from the pram, he was soaking and cold. Soon she was caught up in feeding and changing him, and drifted off to sleep with her clothes on. When she woke again it was dark and a horrible sour curry taste filled her mouth. Slow as an old woman, she stumbled to the bathroom, and quickly cleaned her teeth in case Bobby woke again. When she went into the living-room, the large spacious room was empty, full of hidden corners, mysterious, unknowable. The furniture looked clumsy and heavy as if, like the tenants, it was in temporary residence. Jo stared through the open curtains. Houses were dark and enclosed, dustbins lodged neatly on pavements, waiting to be emptied in the morning. A few 'For Sale' signs dotted the square. The area had reached the point when it had become popular again, and houses were being restored to their former grandeur. Canny buyers like the man on the doorstep would later reap fortunes from timely sales. Old houses, tumbling and decrepit, with impoverished elderly gentlewomen desperate to hang on, were giving way to flats, newly converted for young childless couples planning on a future. No wonder Eamon didn't fit in here – he'd never be happy just working to pay the rent and, locked in his past, he couldn't see the future. The damage went in so far, it was like a rotten tooth where, no matter how deep you dug, you could never scrape away all the badness. There'd always be something wrong. Mary was right. 'An eternally dissatisfied person.' Like herself, she supposed, like herself. She sighed as she quietly shut the door and went up to bed. From now on, she thought, as she carried Bobby into the bed beside her, and finally gave in to sleep, from now on, like a snail advancing two inches and falling back one, it was a question of trying to go forward, like her sisters, not back.

Hospital. Central Liverpool. Early evening. November 19 1982.

'You're all the bloody same, you women.' It was as if Eamon was talking to himself. The bag dripped steadily, pumping out its life-giving liquor. A small piece of paper caught in the draught from the window fluttered like a moth's wing.

'You're all the bloody same, you think you can control it all, you think you know what's going on. Like when my dad died – Mrs Jones fussing round making cups of tea, as if cups of tea would make any difference.'

Jo, silent, let Eamon speak. He didn't need an audience. They'd already been arguing most of the evening. Pat had been by the bedside when Jo arrived back but Tina was nowhere about. As Eamon ranted on, Tina slipped back in, looking excited, patting her belly, the neat round lump that would bring forth new life, new hope, a mushroom rising from the dungheap of their family.

'She wouldn't have my baby, she wouldn't have my baby.' Eamon's mouth opened wide, as if he was about to scream. Pat shifted in her chair.

'Oh, are you still upset about the abortion?' Pat's words rang out, clear as a bell. Mary had written a few months before, telling them of her abortion. Jo remembered the letter.

'We've split up since then,' she'd said. 'As he jacked in his job and sat round all day doing nothing, I had no choice, he was a millstone round my neck, I couldn't support him any longer. He'll probably turn up on you again.'

'Upset?' Eamon's eyes were large and filled with tears. In one pupil was a fleck of orange, the result of a childhood accident. It made him look odd, slightly deranged, like a rabid animal. What do you sodden think? Wouldn't you be upset if your baby had been murdered?' His face was wild. Jo envisaged a bloody blob in a dish somewhere, a primeval hump, a tail, a yolk, a small dot for its heart. A baby – no, how could it be?

'You go on about a woman's right to choose. What about a man's right to choose, hey? What about it?' Eamon fingered the drip as if testing his strength. Jo had no words.

'I would have brought it up,' he said. Pat coughed, and held her hands over her mouth. Jo suppressed a laugh.

'I could have looked after it while she went to work. Children don't have to just belong to their mothers, you know.' His eyes were misty with tears. 'I would have looked after it, she could have trusted me. She could have carried on teaching. I can look after things. I had a rabbit once.' Pat guffawed, and the corners of Tina's mouth turned up. Jo smiled to herself. Once, she remembered, she'd shown him pictures of Bobby's third birthday party. She thought he might be interested in his nephew, but no, his eyes grew watery and glazed with boredom. He'd never been interested in her child, never.

Eamon sobbed. His shoulders heaved up and down and loud snorts came from his flabby white body. 'She wouldn't have my baby, she wouldn't have my baby.'

'Shut up,' Jo cried. 'Shut up, shut up.' She couldn't listen to his words, and pummelled at his body, like a small child furious with its parent, willing him to stop. She felt his stomach tense like a wall against her blows but the sniffling ceased.

'Shut up.' She slapped his back, hollow as a drum. 'Who the hell do you think you are?' He offered no resistance. Her breath came short and sharp. Bang, slap. 'Look at flamin' Tina – see her sitting there, she's knackered. I'm worn out, Pat's worn out, we're all worn out, my mother might be bloody dying.' Slap, thud.

'Ssh,' said Pat,' she might be able to hear.'

'And all you can bloody do,' Jo pushed him away, 'is go on about an abortion that happened months ago.' She twisted her body away from him, as if avoiding a particularly nasty insect, and sat down heavily. Her body trembled, she wanted to cry.

'If you're quite finished.' It was Tina's turn to take control, 'if you're quite finished, I'm going back up to see Sheila. She had the baby a little while ago, while you were out Jo, it was all a bit of a shock, it happened dead quick, just after we'd been to the canteen. It must have been the curry. The midwife said she must have been in labour for a while and we didn't realise. Anyway I'd like to get back up and see her – I said I'd take her some Lucozade. Do you wanna come?' The remark was made to them all. Tina looked round.

'Go on, you go up and see her,' Pat turned to Jo. 'I'll come up later, send her my love.' Pat seated herself next to Eamon.

Tina turned to Eamon. 'Do you wanna come as well?'

He sat, hair ruffled, shoulders hunched. 'No,' he spoke slowly, clearly.

'No, I'm not interested in babies. I don't know anything about them.' The two women got up to leave. The cold air from an open window rushed in, making them shiver in the tropical heat. As they left the ward, Eamon twisted a lock of hair round and round in his fingers.

Tina, Summer 1982.

Tina was vomiting in the sink when the invitation for Eileen Loughlin's hysterectomy party came through the door. Jamie was still asleep, so she took a cup of black tea, a plain Ryvita and the 'phone back to bed and read over the card.

> You are invited to celebrate Eileen Loughlin's first
> and only hysterectomy. Dress appropriate. Bring
> something hysterical.

There was a crude drawing of a woman's insides, with an arrow pointing to the womb, a dotted line labelled 'Cut', then two cartoon faces, one grimacing, one smiling, and a sign saying 'Before and After'.

Tina chuckled over the invitation. Trust Eileen to do something like that. Most people would hide away and try and ignore such an event, see it as a tragedy, but Eileen no, not her. She was always one for celebrating, any excuse. Every fortnight they went down the Dome for a dance and a laugh, every other Saturday they stayed up till three, getting a taxi back, drinking, talking, smoking dope. Eileen had been her friend for about two years now – ever since Tina had moved into her own flat in the street, away from Pat. Eileen had lived next door. At the time Eileen had been working as a prostitute and her kids had just been taken into care for reasons that were never fully explained. The pain was raw then, with her visiting them twice a week, and crying all the time, hoping for them back. But 'I'm a lousy mother', she'd decided after a while, after endless months of arguing in court, and put them up for adoption. Now it was a case of birthday and Christmas cards, and visits once a month.

'I don't wanna disrupt their lives, they're getting on so well – settled now. They're getting everything I could never give them.' The irony was that Eileen had gone all respectable now, working as a barmaid and a part-time stripper in a pub.

'Not much different to being on the game,' she claimed, 'except you get less money.'

Tina felt she couldn't even begin to discuss her situation with Eileen at the minute. Eileen would think her mad for getting pregnant, Eileen would warn her she better watch out or she'd end up like she had, unable to manage on the pittance you get on social security. Eileen would tell her to book in for the abortion. Tina absent-mindedly touched her breasts. Her breasts and belly seemed to have softened and swollen up almost straight-away, and she was starving all the time. If she didn't have the operation soon, she'd need a bigger bra. Surely Eileen must suspect something. Surely she'd ask her why she hadn't gone out the previous week, why she'd become so quiet lately?

When Tina 'phoned to check on the party, Eileen was as bubbly as ever, not like a woman about to lose a large part of her insides three days later. She instructed Tina to wear 'something short and tight and sexy.'

'It's not a miserable type of party you know. No black armband numbers. I won't be in mourning.'

'Do you think they'll let me keep it?'

'What?' Tina had no idea what Eileen was thinking. Sometimes she found her hard to keep up with.

'My womb, divvy.'

'I doubt it. What do you want it for?'

'Well, you know the way people keep gallstones in jars?'

'Yeah.'

'Well, I reckon my womb's a lot more important than any old gallstone. I'd like to see it, know that it's still there, like. Do you reckon they'll let me keep it? If I ask nicely, like.'

'I don't think so,' Tina tried to be gentle. 'I think they keep it for medical research or something. Maybe they make soap.'

'Aren't you thinking of a foetus, like after an abortion, or is it the placenta?'

'I dunno, maybe.'

'Anyway, I don't fancy my womb getting rubbed all over some fella's balls as he gets a bath. It's my womb, I think I deserve better than that.'

'Yeah.'

The conversation petered out, with promises to see each other at the party. Tina put the 'phone down.

Yes, of course, she was thinking of foetuses. She thought of little else lately, pretending not to read books about pregnancy, gazing at pictures of tadpole creatures in their little plastic bubbles, noting the stages of development as bumps formed for the brain and heart, as faces became more recognisable, as hands and feet evolved. It was the photo showing a tiny hand with the fingernails perfectly formed which always got her in the pit of the stomach.

Tina fell asleep dreaming of wombs wrapped up in brown paper parcels, tied up in string, arranged on a shelf.

She was wakened by Jamie sitting on her head with a letter in his hand. She'd missed it on first rising, but it was the appointment, early the next week, for the abortion counselling. Tina put the letter under her pillow.

In work that week she couldn't stop thinking about pregnancy, and babies. Everyone would think she was mad, everyone would think she was crazy. The most sensible thing was obviously an abortion. Jamie was only two, there was plenty of time for another one, she was only young, and, after living on social security for the past couple of years, she'd be crazy to give up this chance of work now. She was a volunteer in a CAB bureau, and they'd offered to train her up and find her a permanent position at the end of six months. She was into her fourth month. It wouldn't be brilliant money, but it was a step out of poverty, enough to give her just a bit more each week, and be independent. She wanted this chance.

Tina spent the morning dealing with a succession of credit card debts. HP renegements and social security problems. She felt like a hypocrite 'advising' people, when she had to juggle her own debts each week, paying off one, missing a week on another, so that there was enough money for food in their belly. Still, on a Friday night they often ended up eating chips in front of the TV and had nothing else in the house. But Jamie never saw it as hardship, being allowed to stay up such nights, and sleeping in her bed. Tina felt she could cope with the everyday things – the week's meals planned out in advance, with left-overs for lunch most days, a ten pence 'mix' for Jamie as pocket money on Saturdays, walking to work, sandwiches brought from home eaten while claiming expenses for a café lunch, cheap haircuts once a month from a woman up the road – all this she could cope with. But it was Jamie needing new shoes that did her in, or the time her purse was stolen from the supermarket, or the time her bra fell to bits – those were the times it was difficult, with no spare money to do anything. Then it was not eating for several nights on the run, cocoa with water, not milk each night, then it was hard. Those were the times she despaired, advising CAB clients how to 'manage' on pitifully small sums of money. Lol, the co-ordinator, was encouraging, though, whenever Tina felt down.

'At least you know where it's at girl, you've been there. Not like some of these do-gooders up from the Wirral for the afternoon, they haven't got the faintest. You hang on in there, you'll be a bloody good advice worker one of these days.'

Sometimes Tina felt she had no identity at all. The proper workers had a badge with their name on it, the volunteers had a sticker, saying 'voluntary worker'. But still, if she kept it up, she'd get something out of it, and the playgroup for Jamie was handy and cheap.

After lunch of a tuna curry roll and feeding the ducks in the park with Jamie, Tina had a whole afternoon with no clients. She spent the time staring at the wall, nibbling at rich tea biscuits, trying to keep nausea at bay. There was no getting away from the fact that it would be crazy to have another baby at this particular time, it would be throwing away her chances, throwing away her future. The man didn't even figure – he'd gone back home to his family, after being up north on a sandwich placement for six months. Their brief affair had been a pleasure, and convenient for them both. She'd lied to him and said she was on the pill and, like most men, he hadn't checked. After the grand passion with Jamie's father, she'd never felt much like getting involved again. Still she didn't know what had possessed her, going to bed with that man with no contraception. He was sweet and kind, and, for a few short weeks, she even had fantasies that they could work it out together, and set up home. But she dismissed the fantasies soon enough. She was used to being on her own and, besides, he had some really annoying habits, not least waking up full of beans and ready to talk. She had enough of that already, with Jamie.

By the end of the day Tina had confirmed the appointment for the following Wednesday. She only hoped they could fit her in quickly at the clinic. She was nearly eleven weeks, still early enough for the operation to be simple, still early enough for people not to notice. Afterwards, she'd go back the doctor and get fitted with a coil and everything would be simple again, sensible, and she'd have the goal of a proper job to aim for. She'd have to tell Pat, and ask her to pick Jamie up from playgroup. She'd just tell work she had a hospital appointment, it was none of their business, they weren't paying her yet. But she'd have to swear Pat to secrecy, make sure she didn't tell Jo. Jo would slag her off for getting pregnant, Jo wouldn't mince words, she'd say she was in danger of ruining her life again, giving vent to emotions. She didn't want Jo to know. No way.

The room was dark and lit by candles. Down one side of a table,

Eileen had arranged crisps, nuts and a few ritz crackers with twirls of processed cheese spread. Food was never Eileen's speciality, drink was more in her line. On the other side of the table she had put out vodka, bacardi, bottles of wine, cans of lager, coke, orange. The music was loud, reggae, the beat insistent. The room was full of black and white faces, bright colours, the air thick with smoke. Eileen, dressed in bright red with black stockings and black high heels, was covered with an assortment of gold chains and had a kind of black mantilla on her head. She looked as if she were part of a Spanish fiesta. Tina had put on a black shift, loose. Her breasts hurt. Eileen was slightly drunk already, becoming cross-eyed, like an angry lion. She stretched out her arms in greeting, effervescent as ever.

'Hiya Tina, come on in. Grab a drink and some food, have a dance. What have you brought to add to my collection. Have you seen it?'

Tina opened her bag and produced a packet of Hedex. She was led by the arm to the 'collection'. Others had obviously had the same idea. There, on a shelf, like in her dream, were a packet of sanitary towels, a box of tampons, some vitamin B6 tablets, evening primrose oil, a baby's nappy, a bottle of gin, a sanitary belt, a packet of valium, a picture of a screaming baby, a photo of a crying woman, a book of jokes. 'Hysterically funny', said the cover. In the corner, almost hidden away, so small it tugged at Tina's heartstrings, was a first size baby's flannelette nightie, soft cotton with a pattern of ducks. Someone had written 'Goodbye to all that' on a piece of paper at the side of the collection. Tina added her Hedex.

Tina sipped at an orange drink and scraped the cheese off a Ritz cracker. She got a sudden craving for salt, and piled a paper plate with crisps.

'What time's your operation tomorrow?'

'Three-thirty.'

'Should you be drinking?'

'I don't know. I don't care particularly. They said not to eat in the morning, and they'll give me a pre-med when I go in. If necessary, they can always pump out my stomach.'

'And how do you feel about it all?' Tina was having difficulty keeping the crisps down, she wished she hadn't eaten so many.

'Oh, kind of relieved, you know. I mean I've had these bad periods for so long, I've forgotten what it's like to be without pain. But it'll feel strange screwing without the chance of getting pregnant.

'Mmmm.'

'Not that I ever wanted to become pregnant again, not after the kids were taken away.'

'No.'

'It's just – it's just, the thought that it won't be possible anymore.'

'I know,' said Tina, burping at the fizz in her orange.

'You never forget their births you know, my mother always said that but I didn't believe her then. You never forget when they were born.' Eileen looked misty-eyed. She took another swig of vodka. A dark-haired young man tried to entice her on to the floor. She pushed him away like a fly.

'I remember when our Terence was born, it was freezing cold – November – it was so foggy everywhere, and the pipes had all frozen at home, and there I was sweating on the tenth floor of that bleeding hospital. I remember all you could see were fog lights all over the city, and I thought I'd pass out with the heat.'

Tina sat down, she didn't feel as sick that way. She took tiny sips and nibbled at another Ritz. Her tongue tasted salty.

'Then with Leila it was dead different – the height of summer – I was wandering round the woods near our house, picking flowers, I didn't even know I was in labour, and when they got me in she popped out twenty minutes later. You never forget, do you?'

'No.'

'Worrabout with you? Remember the day Jamie was born and you were up all night cleaning the house like a maniac?'

'Yeah.' Scrubbing and cleaning, the windows, the walls. Tina laughed. Jamie had been October; sun glinting through gaps in the trees, a mild autumn day, red, orange, yellow leaves, squirrels in the park. Jamie awkward, taking hours, getting stuck, eventually coming with his head and his shoulder at the same time – 'multiple presentation', they called it. Jamie crying for two hours, feeding constantly that first night, Jamie not settling until she got him home. No, you never forget.

'Come on, let's dance,' said Tina, breaking the mood. It was no time to be miserable. She shook her head like she had as a teenager and in the dark, shyly touched her already ripening belly. When the baby came it would be January: cold, bare trees, the ground covered in frost, the heating turned up full. The baby would have to wear bootees and a hat, the baby would have to be wrapped up warm at night, but, by the time spring came, it would be alert and awake and she and Jamie would push it to the park in a big old pram, sit amongst the trees, hold it in their arms. Her arms would be full of child again. Her fingers wound round the clinic card in her bag. She ripped it up without memorising the number.

At three in the morning, when the room was almost empty, she caught Eileen fingering the tiny flannelette nightie, holding it close to her nose, as if trying to imprint the smell on her brain.

'Eileen,' said Tina.

'Eileen . . . I . . .' She'd have to tell her. She should tell her now. Eileen looked up with large, sad eyes, wiping away a tear.

'Yeah, what is it?' She put the nightie down carefully. Tina sighed. 'Oh nothing – it's just – just – I'll come and see you straight after the op. OK?'

'Thanks, Tina, thanks,' said Eileen. 'You're a mate.'

'It's all right,' said Tina, knowing the moment would never be right for her to tell Eileen about her pregnancy.

8

November, 1981.

The pub was smoky and crowded with Sunday afternoon customers. Round laminated tables were filled with half-drunk beer bottles, liquid spread outwards from already sodden beer-mats, people lounged sideways against each other. Jo stood at the bar, waiting to be served. The barmaid, all hair and bangles, arms full of glasses, glanced over at her.

'I'll be with you in a minute, love,' she said. Jo nodded, unworried. There was no hurry any more. Now that Sam was dead, they had to think of their mother, Rosy.

'All right there girl.' A hand tapped her on the shoulder. Jo turned to see the grinning face of a dark-haired man of about fifty.

'Oh, I'm sorry girl, I thought it was our Lizzie – you look like her from the back.'

'Never mind. Busy here, isn't it?' Jo agreed. The bar was certainly fuller than she'd ever seen it.

They waited side-by-side for the barmaid.

'He's a good singer, isn't he?' Jo grinned back inanely. On the small dais a white-haired man belted out a Frank Sinatra song. He side-stepped and tilted his hat onto the back of his head. A middle-aged woman with blond hair shouted 'More, more,' and clapped her hands enthusiastically.

'At least he's got one fan,' said Jo's neighbour.

'Gerroff,' shouted someone else. 'Put a record on.' The strains of *Viva España* erupted in Jo's ear and the group of elderly women opposite began swaying from side to side.

'You've got to admit he's energetic for sixty-two,' insisted her companion.

'Aye, he's certainly energetic,' agreed Jo, and then the barmaid saved her from having to think of any more adjectives. Jo ordered a double brandy and a bottle of stout for her mother; three halves of lager for herself and her sisters.

'I'll have to open another keg,' said the barmaid, and disappeared round the back.

'I'm off,' said the man. 'It always takes ages when they get a new keg on. I'll go the other bar.'

Jo nodded goodbye and looked around as she waited. Although faces seemed half familiar, she didn't recognise anybody. They'd be mostly parents of people she'd been at school with, grandparents like her own mother.

'The young ones go to a different pub now – a posher one up in the town centre,' she'd heard her mother say to Tina, who was interested, as always, in knowing where the action was. Having a child hadn't stopped Tina from dressing fashionably, or from getting out on the town with her mates. But the 'young ones,' Jo reflected, they wouldn't be her mates, not now. The young ones would be seventeen and dancing away to disco music. Her contemporaries would be stuck at home with kids, maybe ungracefully fading into an early middle age, or those with a bit of liveliness down at the clubs in town. When she was seventeen, her crowd had been going into pubs for over a year, tarting themselves up to look older so they could drink. Nineteen seemed past it then.

'And I definitely, definitely don't wanna get past twenty-two,' she'd whispered to one boyfriend as they'd stood in a backstreet in Liverpool, bodies pressed against each other. A freezing cold wind had come up from the Pier Head and the fountain behind them kept running and running, so all she could think of that time was pissing, not romance. Later that summer, she'd admired a girl who was nineteen, not married, not engaged, and who still 'made an effort' to be attractive and flirted with boys two years her junior.

Well here she was herself now, nearly thirty, still upright and not drawing her pension yet.

'Won't be long, girl,' shouted the barmaid, looking flustered. Jo heard banging and watched pale-yellow liquid seep into a glass. She glanced through the open doorway to the lounge bar. In there, the wallpaper was flocked, deep-piled red stripes with the border coming off, like an Indian restaurant that had seen better days. Her mother had told her the staff wore uniforms.

'Like in the army?' Jo had asked, incredulous.

'No, you daft bugger you,' said her mother, 'to look smart.' Jo could see a man with a black waistcoat and a dicky bow, serving up a green cocktail with a red cherry in it. Her eyes switched back to the public bar. The only uniforms here were on a couple of bus drivers having a quick pint after their shift. This bar was more basic, with sweating walls stained brown with nicotine, and tasselled sidelights that cast a yellow tint to lined, hard faces. It didn't seem to have changed much from when she was a kid, running past on her way to the shops. She'd always got a heady waft of urine as the men 'caught out' relieved themselves in the doorway. They frightened her then; some would grab and touch her as she tried to speed past, and sing sentimental, out-of-tune songs in her ear. Now most looked grey-faced and harmless, with teeth missing and either red blotchy skin or pale complexions that rarely saw daylight. There were few under forty and she rose a head taller than many.

'All right there, love? Sorry to keep you waiting, but it's quite a rush on today.' The barmaid pumped out the lager and started to pour the stout. She glanced across to where Jo had been sitting as she went to get the brandy.

'Oh, are you Rosy's girl then?' Jo nodded. The woman was about forty-five, with frizzy hair, large black earrings and an armful of gold.

'Give her my sympathy, love, it was hard losing him like that. I'll maybe call up later to see if she's all right. And she'd been up the hospital every day, you know, when he'd been in for the treatment.'

'I know.' Jo didn't know. She didn't know anything about how Sam had died, or what had happened in the last few weeks, but she let the woman carry on talking. She'd hardly been in touch with her mother over the past few years, and prickles of guilt pinched like gnat bites. The woman deftly carried over three half-pint glasses and paused. 'You don't live up this way then, girl? I haven't seen you around.'

'No, I live in London.'

'Well, that's where the work is now, isn't it, girl? You should stay for a while, though, look after your old mum. We'll get a whip round going for a wreath tonight.' She leaned forward confidentially. 'Her and Sam were two of my best customers. Regular as clockwork, never any trouble, especially near the end. He couldn't drink any more, you see, so he used to sit and have an orange juice, just to keep her company.' The barmaid straightened up. 'I better get back to the lads before they start complaining. We're short-staffed today – there's only two of us on. He was all right, Sam, you know. I think your mam really cared for him.'

She added up the price of the drinks and pressed coins back into Jo's hands.

'No, your mam's drink's on me,' she said. 'She needs a drink at a time like this, it's the least I can do.'

Jo balanced the glasses and walked back to the table, oddly touched. People were so nosy and friendly after the cool anonymity of London she felt self-conscious, as if they could all see through her and knew that she wasn't a dutiful daughter after all. She put the glasses down carefully and went off to the toilet. They'd had one round already, it had gone straight through her. The toilet door didn't lock and she pushed in on Pat, trying to flush the unyielding chain. After Jo relieved herself, she was surprised to see Pat still standing by the mirror, cracked, and the soap dispenser that had never dispensed. She thought Pat would have hurried back to their mother. Through the open window, a stale fishy smell drifted in from the men's toilet. Pat drew herself up to her full height and looked Jo in the eye.

'What are we going to do with my mother?' she asked. 'She's in a real state; I don't know if she's capable of looking after herself for very long.'

'I don't know,' answered Jo, annoyed. 'I've got to be back by tomorrow morning. I've got to go to work and I've got a meeting in the evening.'

'Oh, you with your bloody meetings, you're always so busy, aren't you?' Pat spat out the words. 'I've got to get back to work as well, you know. I've used up all this year's holiday time, this time's coming out of next year's. And Tina's got an interview lined up for tomorrow. Jobs are like gold dust round our way now, you know, she's desperate. If she gets a job they'll take Jamie in at the nursery full-time. And, by the way, her mate can only have him for a couple of days, she can't hang round here for ever.'

'I know,' said Jo. Tina's child was two years younger than Bobby but, somehow, right from the start, Tina had always managed to get other people to look after him and keep up some life of her own. Jo felt her own life consisted of work and looking after Bobby. She had to admit she was jealous. She breathed hard and faced Pat.

'Just 'cos Sam's died doesn't mean everything's changed, you know. I always hated him.'

'What do you mean? I'm not saying everything's changed. I'm just saying we've got to do something about her. We've got to get her sorted out. There's no-one here who can look after her.' Pat looked exasperated.

'She can bloody well look after herself, I had to.' Jo whispered under her breath.

'Well, why did you come up then, Miss Hoity-Toity?'

' 'Cos I thought she might need something doing,' Jo snapped. She'd half hoped that with Sam gone, everything would be right between her and her mother, words would flow between them, released like toy soldiers from a box.

'Well, she does need something doing, she needs a bit of help to get the funeral sorted out and get herself together,' said Pat. Jo saw the days peeling off, tending to others. She felt the old resentment building up.

'I've got a child too,' she hissed.

'Don't I know that?' said Pat angrily. 'From the way you go on, you'd think no-one had ever had a child before. Jamie is younger than Bobby, remember, it's even harder for Tina, especially on her own.' Seeing Jo's crumpled face, she softened her voice and touched Jo awkwardly on the arm.

'Look, we've all got things to do. Don't take it out my mother. She was with him for a long time remember, and she is upset. Did you think she would change now that Sam's dead?'

'No.' Tears welled up in Jo's throat. Stubborn, she pushed them down. Her thoughts were of revenge. 'Let her suffer, let her stew in her suffering. She left me when I needed her, and gave all her love to him. Now I want her to know what it feels like to be left.'

'You can't keep on blaming her all of your life, you know.' Pat interrupted, touching her on the shoulders, surprisingly gently.

'Blaming who?' blurted Jo, twisting away. No use hiding – she knew that Pat could read her thoughts. Pat, always put out feelers to other people's emotions, honing in on their weaknesses, while, like a crab, she deflected prying eyes from herself. Ever since coming out as a second, unexpected baby from the womb, all those long years ago, she'd watched and kept quiet, always knowing more than she'd let on, so that Jo had often feared her criticism.

'I was the afterbirth,' Pat had joked for years, pre-empting criticism. She had made fun of herself before she could be attacked. But she'd changed. When Jo looked at her through angry, tear-stained eyes she saw how Pat now held herself erect and confident, her hair shiny and wavy around her face, no longer the old straggly grease-pile Jo associated her with. Jo saw in a flash that Pat was now a young woman reaching her prime.

'She left me as well, you know. You can't spend the rest of your life blaming other people.' Pat spoke low, with dignity, and held the door open for them both. Jo felt hot tears envelope her eyes as they went back to the table. She wiped them away. Her mother had known what she was doing all those years before, she'd made the decision to leave and to be on Sam's side. Now he was gone, were they all supposed to be supportive, and forget the past? She sipped her drink and banged it down. Lager splashed on the table. Pat caught her eye and moved a beer mat over to soak up the liquid. Jo seethed with resentment and anger. Pat was right, she shouldn't have bothered coming if she felt like this. Shifting uncomfortably in her chair, she noticed how old her mother looked; bent and hunched, with dark circles under her eyes, cracks through pancake unevenly smudged on her face. Dark red lipstick overshot her mouth, like on the face of a crazy woman. Her grey hair was frizzy-dry and unbrushed, a blue scarf slipped down off her head. Her mother lit a cigarette, took a sip of brandy and leaned forward. 'See them chairs, Josephine?' She ignored Tina, beside her. 'See them chairs?'

Jo looked across to two maroon, studded, leatherbound chairs, placed at an angle to the gas fire. The chairs had narrow brown legs like the kind in doctors' waiting-rooms before they turned over to cheap foam settees. There seemed to be nothing unusual about them. Was her mother going mad at last?

'They're our chairs, mine and Sam's, we always sat there. Every day, same time, dinner time and evening. Joan from the bar used to bring our drinks over. Nobody else would sit there, they wouldn't let them.'

They all stared at the chairs, as if in respect, then Rosy began to cry. Tears flowed out with no resistance. A weave of smoke from her mother's cigarette caught at Jo's throat and she began to cough. She coughed on and on, almost retching. The only thought she was conscious of as she tried to control the spasm, was the knowledge that the whole place, the pub, the town, stank. It felt like she might choke but then breath came back. Tina's voice, clear as a flute, rose through the smoke.

'Come on, Mum.' With one hand, she moved the stout out of the way. 'Come on, we'd better get you home now, I think you've had enough.'

'I don't wanna go, I don't wanna go, I wanna stay here, I don't know what to do without him.' They looked away, silent and embarrassed, while she sobbed. People ignored them, averting their eyes. One man came over. Ginger-haired, hesitant, he pressed a sympathy card into Jo's hand, then scuttled off as if he too might be tainted by death. Eventually they hauled Rosy out of the pub, Tina and Pat supporting her arms. They were taller than her; Jo was surprised, she always thought of them as small. It was mid-afternoon, a cold November day. Bright sun illuminated empty boarded-up houses, graffitied garages. One of the few shops open on a Sunday had a wire grille over the front, like in Belfast. Jo expected to see a forman peeping out, checking the bags.

They passed a few houses which looked more substantial than she remembered. Extra porches had been built on, dimpled glass doors, a wooden cartwheel or two.

'They're private,' said Pat, as if in answer to her thoughts. 'The council sold them off.'

The block of maisonettes, almost empty for as long as she remembered, had nearly gone. Jo was astonished. It had seemed like a permanent monument to bad housing, suffering from blocked drains, a caved-in roof, condensation, ill-fitting window frames, vandals, graffiti – the lot. Everything that could have gone wrong there had. But the few remaining tenants had held on stubbornly amidst boarded-up windows and padlocked doors. Now even they were gone. The block was half down, with hoardings round it, and mounds of rubble, a wall still standing.

'What happened to that block?' she asked.

'Demolished,' said Tina in a matter-of-fact voice. 'They've got rid of a load of them. They said no-one wants to live in maisonettes anymore, people want houses with gardens.'

'So much for a housing shortage,' commented Jo.

'Flats like that would be sold for a bomb in London. They'd say they had character, were interesting period pieces.'

'They had character all right, a bloody bad character,' said her mother, livening up suddenly, waving her hand in the air, 'in common with people who lived in them.'

'Bloody con merchants, the lot of them. You should have seen them on the telly, when the council was talking about demolishing the maisonettes, crying all over the place in front of the cameras, saying they were losing their homes. Losing their homes my eye – they were all given brand-new houses with gardens up near the town centre, they just wanted people to feel sorry for them. Nobody wanted to live there anyway, they were all glad to get out. Bloody con merchants.'

When her mother stopped talking, her jaw seemed to sink back into her neck, as if the effort of speaking had exhausted her. Her face assumed its skull-like appearance, skin stretched thin and tight over the protruding bones. She hunched her arms down into her coat and stuck her head into the wind.

When they got her back to the house, Tina made tea while they unwrapped themselves. There was a terrible damp smell everywhere, like the smell of woollens drying in cold winter bathrooms. Water had seeped into the living-room carpet, so that it squelched under foot. The floor was covered in clothes protruding from upturned drawers.

'One of the pipes burst while she was at the hospital, there was a flood and someone broke in,' explained Pat, rolling her eyes at the mess.

The house was dark and barer than Jo remembered. The burglar had rifled the sideboard; the contents were scattered over the floor – papers, balls of wool, old pens, envelopes. Photos were dispersed randomly, the water soaking into their fading prints.

Jo squatted down and picked up a large picture of herself as a toddler. The photo was wrinkled like corrugated iron, buckling up at the edges. Aged about two, she wore a sun-hat and bloomers; her hair was curly, her eyes unnaturally blue. When she stared closer she noticed the photo had been tinted. Cheeks were rouged in, eyelashes painted on. She felt a sudden stab of disappointment. Had she really been so ugly they'd had to touch up her photos? She sighed, throwing it down, and picked up a wedding photo of her parents. Jo stared at them; they were stern-faced and serious with flowers in their buttonholes, trying hard to smile into the camera. They wore suits; her father's crowned with a trilby, her mother's a pillbox, her skinny legs sticking out from the tight, pencil skirt. Her mother had dark good looks, her father was still handsome in a stiff, hard way. Inside her mother's slightly protruding belly and ever-widening hips, Jo knew that she, herself, lay. 'And was that the beginning of the end?' she silently asked the photograph, 'Did my birth mark the end of your freedom, the end of your youth? And you thought you might be stuck with him for ever?'

'Can I have these?' Jo asked of no-one in particular, as she gathered up a pile of photos. Her mother grunted.

'They're all ruined, everything's ruined, even my marriage lines.' She moved her arms vaguely, like a stiff, out-of-condition windmill.

'We'll have to get rid of them, throw them out. We'll have to tidy up.'

'Yeah,' Jo answered, putting them surreptitiously into a plastic bag. She wasn't throwing anything out. This was her history, she might not have a chance to view it again.

Pat began to pick up papers from the floor, putting them into small neat piles beside the sideboard. Rosy stared into space. Tina brought the tea, Rosy jumped up quickly, as if awakening from a dream.

'It's dark here,' she murmured and went to turn on the light. There was a flash and she jumped back startled, to land on the sodden wet carpet.

'She's had a shock! She's had a shock!' screamed Tina, putting the tray down and rushing over. Rosy, white-faced and dazed, allowed herself to be helped up from the floor.

'I'm all right, I'm all right,' she croaked, as if to reassure herself. Tina sat her down on the hard wooden chair and thrust a cup of tea into her hand.

'It was only a little one, I'm OK now, I'm OK.' Rosy sipped her tea, gratefully.

'Look, this is ridiculous.' Pat's voice seemed strong and assertive in the gloom. 'The electrics aren't safe. I'm 'phoning the council, as soon as I've finished my tea, to see about getting you somewhere else to stay while they fix this place up. You can't stay here, you'll end up electrocuting yourself. It's partly their responsibility to help you get cleared up after the flood anyway.'

'But I don't wanna go anywhere else,' said Rosy, looking frightened. 'I don't wanna leave here, this is where we lived.'

'It's dangerous,' said Pat, as if there was to be no more argument. 'Look at the state of this place, we couldn't fix it up even if we worked all day and all night. The carpets are soaked and the wiring must be completely buggered. It's too big for you on your own, anyway.' Rosy sat cowed like an obedient child. Pat put her coat on to go out. 'We've got to talk to the undertaker as well, I'll come with you tomorrow morning.' Her tone brooked no argument. Rosy mumbled agreement and Pat banged out, her actions shaking the house.

The afternoon wore on, dark and cloudy, threatening rain. Tina busied herself mopping up water. Her white blouse acquired small specks of dirt. It was cold but they didn't dare turn on the electric fire, so Tina made up a small coalfire and lit two candles.

Jo felt as if she was locked in a time capsule. An early memory surfaced, a picture show on the shadows of her mind. She was two; they'd only just moved into the house, there was plaster dust and bare wood everywhere, no gas or electricity connected. They'd sat round in candlelight to eat burnt black sausages cooked on the fire by her father.

'Do you remember?' she started to say, but stopped. There was no point. Her mother looked as far away as the moon. Grief stamped her face; she had no room for such memories now.

Pat returned, to say she'd be back on to the council the next morning. They continued to wipe down surfaces, squeeze up water, but made little headway. Rosy dozed and Jo sifted through the photos she'd rescued. She concluded her mother was right. Most were ruined; they'd probably have to be thrown away. She ended with a small pile of salvage, and a plastic bag full of grey soggy paper pieces like toilet paper. Tina served up eggs, beans and toast. Tina and her mother both pecked at the meal like birds, while Pat shovelled the food in, as if fuelling herself for a race. Jo played around with the contents of her plate. She couldn't eat. Her food touched a photo of her mother and she picked it up, curious. It showed her mother, Sam, and Josie, his daughter by his first marriage, outside a pub: sunshine, tables shaded by umbrellas, Sam haggard, thin as a reed. Rosy's eyes lit up as she too spied the photo. Her fork clattered to the floor as she pounced for the photo, fondling it as you would a baby.

'That was in September, one of the last pictures we took of him. See, he still had some spirit left, even then, yeah he did.' Her eyes misted over as her hands tightened their grasp. She stared into the distance and repeated the story to herself.

'Josie wrote to say she was coming to take us for a meal. I mean, she hadn't been near him for years and she suddenly gets it into her head he needs feeding. He was only eating mashed vegetables by that time anyway, like a baby, but I didn't have the heart to tell her. He thought the world of her. But when she turned up and saw the state of him she had the sense to realise, so we all just went for a quiet drink anyway, out in the country near St Helen's.' Rosy brushed away hair from her face. Tina moved her plate. Jo leaned closer. This was important. She shouldn't miss a word. Her sisters continued eating, but their faces were turned towards Rosy. Rosy ignored them and seemed intent on telling the story to her, Jo.

176

'It was lovely that pub, the people were really nice to us, they could see Sam was ill, they even gave him a straw for his orange juice, and he never complained, not once, not even when I knew he was in pain. He could hardly swallow his juice, while we were all sitting there drinking, but he never spoilt anyone else's pleasure, not once, never let on how bad it was.' Rosy's eyes shone as she recounted the incident.

'He held on to me like a kid, and he gave me ten pence to play one of our old songs on the jukebox. He was still romantic, you know,' she said defiantly.

A coal fell into the grate, a sudden shower of sparks went up the chimney. Jo poked the fire. The warm glow bounced heat around the room.

'When that man came round taking pictures, we had to have one, it seemed like fate.' Rosy, oblivious of everyone else, seemed determined to finish her story. 'Look at him there, he reminds me of when he was young and he used to play in the band and march all over the streets.' Her mother clutched the photo tightly. Jo could see Sam's white gaunt face, puffy pig eyes and the remains of his pale ginger hair. What her mother had seen in him, she didn't know. But then again, maybe Sam had been the first to call her mother beautiful when she surfaced from the straightjacket of marriage. Who could tell?

'Worrabout when he died, hey?' Words cut in, jolting Jo's thoughts.

'Who?' Jo blinked.

'Sam, of course,' said Rosy, in surprise. 'He was dead grateful to the twins you know.'

'Aye.' Jo looked blank. She had no idea what her mother was talking about. Death did affect people in strange ways, they'd have to watch her for a while.

'For the presents, I mean – for the Christmas presents.'

'Oh, yeah,' said Jo, the sense becoming clearer.

'The twins have always been thoughtful,' her mother added, gazing into the distance.

'Unlike me,' thought Jo, 'unlike me.'

'Always sending a card and a little thing for birthdays and Christmas. They're good girls,' she continued. Jo ground her teeth together. It was Pat, with her little book of names and addresses and family birthdays neatly marked in, who always prodded Tina into it. Pat never forgot a date.

'Even though it was only November,' her mother remembered, 'they sent everything early,' Jo imagined the card in Pat's careful hand, the parcel neatly wrapped. Why couldn't she be more like her sisters?

'I took Sam's present up to him, I thought it best to open it, in case something happened. And he was made up with it – this small pen with his initials engraved on it – SG, in fancy gold lettering. He kept fingering it, like a little kid. And then he gave me a kiss and said he was tired, so I came down here. And do you know, I never once told him he was dying. I never did. Only one time did he question me, just before they said it was no point him having any more treatment. He was puzzled and said he couldn't understand why he wasn't feeling any better after all the treatment he'd been having. But I didn't have the heart to tell him, he was always scared of pain, you see. I had to protect him.'

Jo nodded, and held herself stiff.

'We held hands for a few minutes that morning, then he said he was tired and wanted to sleep.'

Tina and Pat melted towards the fire. Her mother, as if in a trance, talked in a monotone. How precious this time felt, this time after death. Never again would words flow so easily, never again would hearts be so open.

'When I came up an hour later,' her mother's voice faltered and a tear dropped down her cheek, 'I tried to wake him, I did, to give him some of the stew I'd made. I'd mashed it especially – it seemed such a waste to leave it. But it was too late, I knew it was too late. Old James the doctor had said it would probably happen in his sleep.' Pat stroked Rosy's hair. Tina rubbed her back rhythmically, as if she was were comforting a child. Jo's hands stayed by her side. She couldn't touch her mother. After all this time, she still couldn't act naturally. She thought of Martin. He always said you couldn't fool the body.

'I ran like the clappers over the road to 'phone the ambulance and tell Ellen Mack. Then I ran straight back up the stairs to wait for them. I didn't want to leave him alone, you know.' Her eyes appealed to them.

Tina nodded, 'It's all right, it's all right.'

'And then the ambulance came – great big burly men they were, like when your dad died. They stuck him on the stretcher and I sat in the ambulance. I looked at him the whole time and held his hand, tight, but it was getting cold already. When they asked me what was wrong with him, I just said "He's unconscious", in case he could hear. They say the hearing goes the last, you know. I didn't want him to know he was dying, he would have been too scared.'

Tina rolled up a blanket under the door, to cut the draught. Rosy dragged deeply on a cigarette, eyes bright.

'Then they got us to casualty. We had all the sirens blaring you know, all the way to town. The ambulance pushed the other cars out of the way. They rushed him in quick, like, but I'd hardly sat down when the sister came out. "I'm afraid your husband's gone, Mrs Greenby," was all she said, hard as nails, no niceties, no comfort. I collapsed, I tell you, they had to bring me round later. It was only then they brought me a cup of tea and some tablets, I suppose they have to then – procedures or something. But they were awful hard, not a bit nice about it, you know.' She stubbed out one cigarette, lit another. 'I can't believe that was only Tuesday, I tell you, it seems like ages ago.'

It did. The time capsule enclosed them, quiet, wafting over them, lulling them into inaction. Suddenly, snapping the spell, like in a ballet, they all leaped into action. Rosy carried plates to the kitchen. Pat went to make the beds, Tina washed up by candlelight. Rosy hunched herself in the armchair and drifted off into dreams of her own. Shadows shifted out from the kitchen. After helping, Jo joined her mother by the fire, soaking up the memory-filled silence. Her mother's large eyes were stung with grief. Maybe now Sam was gone they would talk, become proper mother and daughter at last. Their conversations had been stilted, staccato, over the years. Jo recalled those first frightened years away, with many a 'phone call from Belfast.

'Mum, I don't know what I'm doing here,' Jo would begin. Her mother never listened.

'Do you know, Ellen's done up her kitchen, she's got a kitchenette and a dining-room now. And old Frank Collins has died, and Mary Jones had another baby.' All the news of the street, as if it was the centre of the universe. No questions, no curiosity. Later, in London, after Jo had Bobby, she'd thought they would grow closer. But her mother had only been interested in telling stories of her own birth experiences, as if the past was more real than the present. Jo stoked the fire. A piece of silver paper sent a flurry of green and blue flames up the chimney. No, they wouldn't start talking now, it was obvious. You didn't change the habits of a lifetime just because someone had died.

'Come on, what are we sitting in this miserable old place for. Let's go out.' Her mother leaned forward.

'Again?' Jo was shocked. Why did her mother always want to go out?

'Come on then, let's go out for a bit, I don't want to stay here, let's bugger off,' her mother insisted, jumping up out of the chair like a much younger woman.

Pancake in front of the mirror, lipstick replenished, scarf pulled on; she performed these actions quickly. Jo felt as if she'd been watching this routine all of her life. A slight adjustment to the mac, blue, always blue, a backward glance into the mirror.

'Do I look all right?'

'Yes,' they all murmured, well trained at agreeing.

Back to the pub, more crowded now, desperation in her mother's voice as she ordered a round she insisted on paying for, Jo forced words out.

'I've got to get the train back, Mum, I've got to get back.'

'Yeah, I know, you've got to get back to the baby. I'll be all right, the twins are staying, you go on, don't make yourself late.'

'He's not a baby, he's four.'

'But he's only young isn't he? He'll be missing you.'

'It's not just that, I've got to go to work.'

'Aye, all right love, are you having this drink before you go?'

'Why are you letting me go?' Jo thought bitterly. She whispered 'Why don't you want me to stay?' The words were drowned out in the general mêlée.

In the toilets again, after another drink, she encountered Tina. Tina, emboldened by alcohol, grabbed her arm.

'Why did you never come and see her when Sam was alive? You hardly ever bothered.'

'I couldn't stand him.' Jo felt guilt rise in her belly.

'Well, neither could I but she loved him, you've got to admit that.' Tina held a black court shoe in her hand, and extracted a drawing pin from the heel. Her feet were tiny, everything about her a scaled-down version of a woman. There was an awkward silence between them, then Tina giggled.

'You should have seen him in the hospital, though, when they kept him in that time for the treatment. We came down for the weekend and when we went to visit him, he got all sentimental and soppy. I remember he leaned up to give me a kiss and all I could think of was him slobbering all over that dog – he was in love with that dog, remember?' Jo retained, momentarily, a clear image of the yellow-toothed, mangy mongrel that Sam fed at the table.

They giggled self-consciously. Then Tina sobered up, looking at Jo with grave eyes.

'But you've got to stop blaming her, you know, and be a bit nicer. She's in a state, she needs some help.'

'Maybe,' Jo admitted as they walked back to the table, 'maybe.' Half an hour later, after downing another drink, Jo left.

'You're always going to meetings,' Pat protested, all innocence, as Jo struggled into her coat.

'Your dad was a one for meetings,' said Rosy conversationally. With three brandies inside her, she seemed to have forgotten her grief. Pat shot Jo a withering glance. Jo felt like a leaf blasted by heat. Meetings, meetings, always bloody meetings, she could imagine them thinking. They said Eamon was 'just like his dad'. Was she the same, she wondered – always running away from feelings to lose herself in actions, lose herself in words?

'But you've got to get back to the baby, he'll be missing you,' said her mother tolerantly.

'He's not a baby,' Jo wanted to yell. 'He's not a baby. I just don't want to stay, not with you, here, ever.' But she didn't, and left quietly, like a dutiful mother with demands on her time, making promises to write and send up photos of Bobby.

'Look after yourself,' she yelled to her mother, and got out before they could reach the stage of kisses and hugs.

The instant she was on the train, Jo regretted leaving. She imagined the meeting she'd attend the following night. It would be a smoky great hall, packed; street cleaners, bus workers, community workers all with a common purpose of fighting the cuts. She imagined men like her father on the stage. Yes, they would call for united action. Yes, it was all necessary, yes it was all part of her life. But so was staying up with her mother, facing small details. Brave in the battle, a coward with feelings, she'd left it all to her sisters, stopping short as usual.

Jo jumped up and grabbed the door handle of the train, but the station moved away as the train gathered speed. Too late. She'd lost her chance again.

Pat's words came back to her as she finally settled in the seat to watch concrete give way to green fields and a bridge that carried her away, back down to her life.

'She left us too,' Pat had said. 'But you've got to forgive.'

Would she get another chance ever?

Hospital. Central Liverpool, November 18 1982. Evening.

Tina's face grew bright with excitement as they approached the maternity ward, which was light and airy with a smell of milk and sweet talcum powder, and tired, happy women resting on their beds, and babies, oh so many babies. They did not speak of the incident with Eamon for, as they drew near, they saw a tiny, dark-haired creature lying in the crib beside Sheila. Sheila and Tina hugged without speaking, and Jo watched, mesmerised, as the nurse unwrapped the baby's shawl to change its nappy. She stared as it pawed the air, pink face pulsating with life. A bowl clattered to the floor and its whole body started in alarm. Its mouth opened and it began to yell, high-pitched, urgent.

'There, there.' The nurse gripped its tiny curled fingers.

'It's all right, it's all right.' It sucked urgently at the nurse's fingers, closing its eyes. Its hands flew in all directions, its legs kicked the air. Jo, enchanted with the clean whole newness of it, had forgotten such perfection. The nurse gently withdrew her finger, swabbed at its red swollen vagina and wound the nappy up deftly. The baby began screaming again, then rooting, found its own hand and sucked.

'There, that's finished. Do you wanna hold her?' The nurse presented the baby as if it were her own.

'Go on, have a hold, have a hold,' urged Sheila. Tina got in first, cradling the baby close to her. A longing crept over her face, as if she'd like to speed up her remaining weeks of waiting. A craving for this tiny pig creature stirred in Jo. It had been so long since she'd held a baby, so long.

She was not prepared for what happened. When Tina handed the baby over, Jo clutched it tightly and wrapped her arms round its own strong softness. The baby's opaque eyes stared past her, through her. Jo touched the soft downy hair, felt the child's strong legs kick the shawl away. Her breasts stung suddenly and hardened, like when Bobby was small, and then the tears flowed out, and streaked her face with wetness. Her shoulders heaved.

'What are you crying for?' asked Sheila. 'They're supposed to make you happy. Do you want to put her in the cot?'

'No.' Jo tightened her arms fiercely round the baby, and drew it close to smell its sweet baby smell.

'No,' she sobbed. She felt the baby's toes spread out, and relax, she felt the give of its body, the smoothness of its skin. These little pig creatures held the key to the future. They knew nothing of the world, yet promised everything.

She cried for her mother, she cried for her father, she cried for Eamon.

'I'm sorry,' she said, 'I'm sorry.'

The child's fingers opened and reached out towards the sides of the cot. A knowing worldly smile spread over its face, as if it knew what she meant.

Jo turned, and went back to her mother.

It was dark in the night when her mother grew cold. Her nose was filled with mucus, and Pat had remained by her side, faithfully wiping it away. Jo placed herself on the side of the bed further away from her mother. She was disgusted by the rotting, foetid smell. In another part of the ward an old woman lay with a bandage over her head, moaning through the night. She'd been beaten up on her estate, Tina said. Another elderly woman connected to an oxygen cannister, sat up reading a book.

'In the morning she'll disconnect herself and go off for a ciggie,' said Pat. All was quiet, save for the noise of the air conditioning turning on and off, save for snores and wheezing.

It was two in the morning when Jo noticed a change, a cooling of the atmosphere, as her mother's life-blood seeped away. Jo leaned over the bed. She hadn't touched her mother in years. Her sisters had made the leap long ago, with kisses and hugs and hands on backs, and strokes.

'You were the only one I had to lie with – you were the only one – everyone else used to go to sleep by themselves,' her mother had said.

'You were nearly born in a graveyard – I was just walking through when I felt the pains beginning. It was a Wednesday, I remember.'

Wednesday's child is full of woe.

'Josephine, Josephine, I know it's not fair, but that's the way it is.'

'Josephine, your dad and I have come to an agreement.'

'You're big enough and bloody soft enough to look after yourself.'

'I hate you.'

'She's had a shock. She's had a shock.'

Pat was almost asleep when Jo leaned over and took the handkerchief. Jo edged closer to her mother, unsure, halting. She bundled the handkerchief up into her fist, then began the time-honoured ritual. Her mother's cheeks now felt as smooth as a child's as the handkerchief slipped over them. Jo stroked her bristly grey hair and touched her forehead, then wiped away the drips from the end of her nose. It was as if, between her fingers, were all the words she'd never been able to say. And so, with the deep, deep wisdom of the body, she used her hands, and forgave and hoped that somewhere, deep beneath her fingers, her mother knew.

Pat's eyes caught hers as shadows shifted round the room. Together, they waited for the morning.